Sleep And a slap

Birth of a psychopath

VIVEK H. WAGH

Invincible Publishers

First published in India in 2016 by Invincible Publishers

Copyright Vivek H. Wagh 2016
ISBN: 978-93-86148-13-1

Vivek H. wagh asserts the moral right to be
Identified as the author of this work.

The views and opinions expressed in this book are the author's own and the facts are as reported by him, and the publishers are not in any way liable for the same.

All rights reserved. No part of this publication may be reproduced. Stored in a retrieval system, or transmitted, in any form or by any means, electronic, mechanical, photocopying, recording or otherwise, without the prior permission of the publishers.

Invincible Publishers
F-55, Sushant Lok II, Hong Kong Bazar Lane Sector 57,
Gurgaon-122003

Opposite Kasturba Ashram, Radaur Distt Yamuna Nagar,
Haryana- 135133

Dedicate to my parents.
And the person because of whom this book is not just a dream anymore,
"My Best Friend".

Acknowledgement

* * *

It has been more than three years since I had started to write this book. I had stopped writing so many times and had almost lost all hopes of publishing this book before my graduation. Writing this book was a big dream and completing this remaining story is an aim. So first of all I would like to thank my publishers to give me a platform not only for fulfilling my dream, but also to give a chance to express my feelings for the important people I am grateful for.

I would like to thank my family to tolerate me and to pamper me all the times in spite of my every perversity. My parents Sujata and Haribhau Wagh, my aunt and uncle, Dwarka and Janardan Wagh, my siblings Nandini, Chaitanya, Jyoti and Santosh Wagh.

Countless apologies and thanks to my father for placing laptop on my bed for those nights of year drops when I used to forget to take it for writing. Thank you for supporting and helping me for completing my every little and big desires. And thank you for always giving me my *last chances*. And Aai, if I said '*thank you*' for your efforts to convert Papa's mind always in my favor then I am afraid it might be insult of a mother as only '*thank you*' cannot compete the motherhood. Your efforts for my book are way more than mine.

The biggest help and support I got for this book was from my friends Aniket Gatkhane and Samyak Alte and Nikhil Rane. I would not actually say thanks to Aniket for reading all the drafts and suggest more options. Not even for the sleepless nights to listen my boring lectures about my dreams and empty stomach days to work on my poems to convert them into songs. Because 'thanks' cannot fulfill the support and your company I had when I needed it most. Instead of that I would demand more of it in future whenever I need. And yes I am still trying to figure out the difference between a 'living room' and a 'leaving room'.

And Samyak, the '*aal izz well'* person, you put that smile on my face when I was depressed about this book. You even don't know but you rebuilt my confidence to complete and publish this story. I would even suggest to the guys out there to meet you whenever they are sad or depressed instead of going for boozing or to a psychiatrist.

A big thank you for the person who gave me the source of happiness, Mr. Ganesh Sonwalkar sir, who formed the best group in the world in all aspects, 'Sizzlers'. (Ganesh sir, I hope your wife doesn't read this line.) And a big thanks to all the Sizzlers for being part of my life and for all the memories which we had and still counting.

My HD gang from Sizzlers, Abhijeet Tambe, Abhishek Shastri, Aniket Gatkhane, Kushal Mashalkar, Mohit Duggad, Nikhil Rane, Rishi Demda, Sagar Pawar, Saheel Moon, Sumit Sonwalkar, Vaibhav Harale, Yash Soni.

Rushikesh Jaju, Harshit Modani, Samyak, Atharva Shukla, Abhishek More, Harshada Borse, Aditi Rathi, Kalyani Kulkarni, Mayur Somani, Pawan Dhaktode, Surbhi Sanghai, Rutuja Jadhav, Sneha Rajan, Tanvi Khandelwal, Vaishnavi Apastamb, Pratik Mandlecha, Malasha Chordiya, Maethili Gagrani and Aarti, and all the members of my

Sizzlers family.

And the one special thanks to my little 'Angel', whose one word calling me, 'Bhai' cheers me up even from the death, Anjali Bangar.

The particular vote of thanks to following people who knowingly-unknowingly became my inspiration, sometimes my mentor, my supporters and even sometimes acted as my parents while I was away from my home. Akshay Deshmukh I can't put in words what I have to say about you, Anil Sathe, Bhagwat Ghule, Dnyanu da, Ganesh Sakunde, Manjeet Wagh, Mukram Bhai, Pradeep Aput, Sachin Rathod, Sambhaji Jagtap, Sandip Ghuge, Sharad Wagh, Umesh Darade, Vijay Wagh, Vishal Takle, Rahul Patil, Akash Lote, K. Mule.

My professors, Prof. Dr. M. S. Kadam sir, the most supportive and prudent professor I've ever seen. Prof. Dr. A. B. Kulkarni sir, who paid attention on my discipline, my sincerity and my tests more than me and my parents. Prof. Dr. A. Chel sir. Prof. S. B. Pawar sir, the coolest professor who always pushed the students to chase their dreams with studies too, who pushed me too while I had almost left writing this story. Also I thank honorable Ghute Sir who always supported and motivated me.

And thanks to my publishers, Invincible Publishers and my publishing team. Thanks for your help and support, Mr. Ajay Setia, Ms. Swati Malhotra, my editor Mr. Abhijeet Singh and his team, Sneha Agarwal and the team of Invincible publishers.

1. Prologue

* * *

'*The number you have dialed is on another call. Please call after... The number you have dialed is busy...*' It was the 53rd time in one and a half hour of that evening when Karan had heard that operator's voice. Nevertheless, he was dialing her number unstoppably as if he had gone crazy.

He dialed again, '*The number you have dialed is on another call. Please call after... the number you have dialed is busy...*'

His breathing had increased due to frustration. His eyes were red like blood. Cheeks were wet due to tears and sweat. He was continuously calling her but, she was not only cutting his call but even kept him on waiting to torture him even more.

Karan could not believe that the girl who was torturing him, leading him to craziness, or even death, was the same girl who was once ready to do anything for him, once who used to go crazy even if she did not hear his voice in a day.

'*The number you have dialed is on another call. Please call after...*' He went crazy after hearing that sentence again.

'I HATE YOU JANVI...' He shouted and started punching to the wall after throwing his phone, which broke into pieces.

'Why are you doing this to me?' He started crying again horribly, running his hand through his hair and grabbing them, stretching them in helplessness.

'NO. I don't hate you, I love you so much. Please, please talk to me.' He was crying, he was talking to himself while whimpering, sobbing.

He saw at the small statue of Lord Ganesha, kept on the table beside his bed. 'Why are you doing this to me?' He asked and ran to gather the parts of his phone again. He assembled his phone with trembling hands and switched it on. 'Please, please, please talk to me. I LOVE YOU YAAR.' He yelled while dialing her number again. He was going crazy to talk to her.

'The number you have dialed is on another call. Please call after...'

'NO, NO, NO...' He shouted and started crying again. He saw the statue of Ganesha with dejected eyes. He was so helpless. Nothing worst could have happened in his life. He wished if he was dead. He knew that this type of condition comes in every one's love story. But he was having the worst time of his life. He was not only losing his girlfriend, he was losing his everything. She was not only his girlfriend; she was his best friend too. He had considered no one that important in his life apart, from her. In last two years, he had hurt to all his relatives, all his friends just to be with her. And now, she was gone.

'ERGGGHHHG... YAAAAAA...' He shouted and wished to throw that statue too, but he couldn't. Not because he was having any fear of god to fall any wrath as nothing worst could have happened because that statue was a symbol of their love. That statue was a big part of their love story.

'Do I really deserve this?' He asked looking at that statue with very poor face and trembling voice. He felt his body had become warmer due to fever. His head had started splitting and shooting with pain like his brain was trying to hop out of his skull.

'Please talk to me.' He said once again closing his eyes slowly in weakness. He started thinking. 'I am so alone. I need to talk to you Janvi. Please Chiku, talk to me.' He dialed her number with his almost dead hand again.

'The number you have dialed is on another call. Please call after...'

'BLOODY SLUT. I HATE YOU, I hate you...' he started crying again, 'I hate you... I love you.'

While crying he was remembering all the memories with Janvi, just leading to more tears falling from his eyes. He was thirsty to hear her one word she would speak with good mood. He remembered the time when he was everything for her. But, now his one mistake had led to his seclusion.

His loneliness was not the only issue for him. The thing, which was squeezing his heart, was his position in her life had lost. He used to be everything for her and now she was talking with someone else who would try to poison their relationship.

'God, please help me. Bring my Janvi back to me.' He started crying again. He was thinking about the possibilities. Now that he was alone, and she was talking with other guy, she will complain to him about Karan. That some other guy would console her and convince her to break up with Karan. She would think that he is right. Then she would think that Karan was bad and her new friend is so sweet to understand her. And the worst part, she will replace Karan in her life with that guy. Not only as boyfriend but also as best friend. Moreover, Karan would be then nothing but a known stranger in her life.

Karan could not do anything except crying alone and abusing that guy. She was not even giving him a single chance to talk with her. He had become like a beggar who is hungry for months. The glow on his face had faded. His eyes had red stream like blood due to ceaseless crying.

He had never cried like this in his entire life. He looked at the guitar and started playing some sad song. He was bonded to universe's unwritten rule to play sad song at such instants. He started playing the song '*tum bin, kya hai jina. Kya hai jina… tum bin kya hai jina…. Tum bin jiya jaye kaise…. Kaise jiya jaye tum bin……*'

****

'Karan…, Karan? Wake up.' Vijay, his friend came to his room and tried to wake him up while removing his guitar from his almost dead body.

'What happened to you?' This one question was enough to make him cry again.

A couple of tears fell down from Karan's eyes, which he tried to hide.

'Oh, so you know already.' Vijay said.

'What?'

'About results?'

'What? Results are out?' Karan said with his weak voice.

'You don't know? Then why were you crying?'

'Vijay, tell me my result.'

'Err… I thought you knew it, that's why you were crying.'

'Vijay tell me don't make it worse.' He tried to shout but couldn't because of weakness due to crying for few hours continuously.

'Err… you… you failed in third year too.'

****

Karan was alone again standing in front of the statue of Ganesha with nothing to utter. He had tried calling Janvi so many times but she seemed to have added his number to blocklist of her phone.

'What did I do? Why are you doing this to me?' only these questions were running through his mind. And the longer he stared at the statue the more he was going crazy.

He looked into the mirror. He felt so pity for himself. He could not even remember the last time he had smiled was. He could not recognize himself in that weird and poor face.

Mana ki hai maine galti, Jo chhod gayi tu.
Chhodna hi tha bichme toh Saath thi aayi kyu?
Saath tera paake maine mere dilko tha sambhala.
Tu gayi toh chayi raate, kal yaha tha jo ujala.
Tere jaane ka asar ye dil pe mere hai hua yun
Saans meri chhin ke, jinda mujhko chhod diya kyun?...

'What did I do? Why is this happening to me?' he asked himself.

'Is this a misfortune?'

'No, it's just payback of your bad deeds.' He got answer from his soul, 'The bad deeds you did and you are responsible for them.'

This one sentence led him to the truth. Within a flash, his mind ran into past few years. His hands ran towards phone after realizing his mistake. He dialed Purvi's number. But his fate was not with him at all. Purvi had also added his number to rejected list. He dialed again but it was of no use.

He was totally lost. He had nothing to do with his life now. Not a single good reason to live. He headed towards the balcony. He went straight to the end and climbed on the grills. With every step he took, he reminded what he deserved and what Janvi had done to him. And for other people to think, he had failed in third year too was good enough reason for suicide. He didn't look down.

There was dark outside. He closed his eyes. This time his legs were shivering, but not due to the fear of death. He was completely helpless. To check whether fate is on his side or not, he took out his phone and dialed Janvi's number once again. '*The number you have dialed is switched off...*' she had cut that call but switched off her phone so that Karan would not irritate her anymore. He got angrier. He could not bear the rejection. He threw his phone away and took a deep breath. Making his fist tight, he got ready to jump. His hands, his legs, his body, everything was shivering. His heart was pouncing.

'That's it! This is the end of my life.' He thought and closed his eyes, 'I... h... I...' he wanted to say 'I hate you Janvi' but he just could not as the person near to death never lies.

'KARAN.... WHAT ARE YOU DOING?' His friend Pradeep shouted as soon as he saw him.

With his shouting Karan got startled and lost his balance. His leg slipped from the grill and he could not get anything to take support of and headed straight towards the ground.

He fell on his right arm and leg. For a couple of seconds he moaned out of pain but, was relived as he had fallen on the balcony side and not on the other side to ground.

'Vijay, come here fast.' Pradeep shouted as soon as Karan fell down. He picked him up and took him away from the balcony. Karan tried to push him away but Pradeep was stronger than he was. Karan struggled to get rid of Pradeep's arms but he was so weak, even to push him. After a long struggle, he stood still with wet eyes and crying face, resting on Pradeep.

Pradeep saw Karan's phone ringing, he picked it up.

'Why the hell you called me now?' Purvi spoke from other side. Pradeep had no answer except to tell her what had happened to Karan. He gave phone to Karan.

'Purvi....' Karan started crying as soon as he heard Purvi's voice.

'What happened? Are you crying?' Though she was not with him now but she still could not bear Karan's sulky voice.

'You were right Purvi.' Karan said followed by sobbing.

'What are you talking about?'

'Tit for tat.' He said and Purvi recalled about their last call they had made about 2 years ago.

'What happened, Karan? Tell me, but please don't cry.' She said while feeling pity for him.

Karan felt shame that the girl who was caring for him was the one to whom he had tortured and had given fraud as reward. She was the girl to whom he had ignored all the time, made her suffer all the time. And for whom? For the girl who was making him suffer now. The same girl who was ignoring him now, forgetting their love, relationship and the bond of friendship.

'Purvi.... I... I am really very sorry.' He said with the bottom of his heart and with immense guilt.

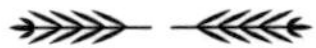

2. How we used to be?

* * *

August 2011

'Karan… Karan… Karan... Karann….'

Everyone started cheering as that beautiful girl anchoring at my college's annual function asked if any guesses who would get first prize for singing.

All the girls had dressed up like a dreamland and all of them were like 9 on 10 or 8 on 10- and few boys- who had to steal the time from staring those girls to listen my song- were cheering for me while others were only getting jealous. Not jealousy only because I got the prize they were willing for, but also because of the fan club I got in my college.

However, the worst part of their jealousy was obviously the best part of my night. Which was the only beautiful girl looking pretty like 10 on 10 with her open and shiny hair was standing with me, her hand wrapped around my arm. She was looking sexier with that shiny and plain red sleeveless dress with that handbag or a purse in her *'whiter than milk'* hands. I don't know which dress was it, or what kind of dress was it. Because I never get whether which one is salvar or which is kurta, what skirt is or what is one piece, three-piece. It just confuses me more with different kinds of names. I just knew sari and Punjabi. However, I must say they are very much clever to *make their work done* with those dresses, which makes them look more beautiful.

Anyways, I had to go on stage to collect my prize for singing, which I had written for that girl and sang. So, I left her hand and started making my way towards the stage through the cheering *fans.* Everyone was congratulating me, shaking my hand and congratulating me again. I went on the stage took the trophy and that beautiful anchor gave me the mic to speak. As I got the mic every one shouted and then stood silent to listen my speech.

'Sahich naaaa...! Itni shiddat se maine tumhe paane ki koshish ki he, ke har jarre ne mujhe tumse milane ki sazish ki he.' I spoke my very own dialogue while looking at the trophy and continued, 'Friends, thank you so much for all your support…' claps and whistles came from crowd. 'I mean, I know I deserve this more than anybody else, because I've worked so hard to reach here, which is not so easy for everyone.' I said and ran my eyes from one point to another in audience, reminding myself something to say,

'Ab hai raat toh savera kal he,
water ko hindi me kehte jal he.
Asaan nahi tha competition jitna,
par yeh toh meri mehnat ka fal he.
Aur teri hi yaado me duba har pal he.'

As soon as I finished my poem, they just could not help themselves from clapping. 'Thank you, thank you. Thank you so much. At the end, I'd really like to thank a girl, to my doll, to the most beautiful girl I've ever seen, and the girl who was always been there for me. To support me, to hug me when I was sad, and to yell at me whenever necessary….' As I was praising her, I could see her getting flattered and shy with those pink cheeks. I continued, '…I'd really like to thank her so much whose name is …. Whose name is…?' I just stared at her and tried so hard to recall her name, but couldn't. Oh god, what is her name? 'Whose name is…' I just stared at her and she spoke, 'Oh come on Karan.' She spoke in male voice, 'Wake up. Wake up u lazy boy'

WHAT?

All of a sudden, the crowd was gone; there were no beautiful girls or cheering of my name, or any kind of jealous guys. Not even my hot pinkish girl with red sexy dress wrapped on her fair body. There was just a crazy, stupid guy who was trying to wake me up from my sweet dream's sleep, just because I had told him to do so, last night. All of a sudden the glamour of my prize winning ceremony had turned into the spider's web hanging at a corner of ceiling and dust all over, in which I was sleeping with that *'tip…. tup… tupuk, tip… tup.. tupuk…'* sound of leaking tap of bathroom.

All of a sudden, it was like, I fell from, 'aaj *mai upar, aasma niche, aaj mai aage... zamaana hai pichhe...*' to '*yeh.... Kya hua?*

Kaise hua? Kab hua? Kyun hua?....'

'Oh c'mon, wake up, and bring your tiny little ass out of the bed.' Mahi, that crazy guy I was talking about, shouted again. Actually, it is Mahesh, my roommate cum cousin brother. 'So, I guess you want to be late on your very first day of college life.' He again tried to wake me up while applying gel to his wet curly hair and with those greasy hands applied some powder on his *idli* like face. I always wondered if *idli* is fluffier or Mahi's cheeks. He is a funny guy, always having some *aade-tede* taunts for everyone and mostly for my poems. I don't know what the matter with him is. I mean, I write good poems, they are not that bad! If I get time further, I will definitely show some of my poems. But while Mahi was yelling at me, I was kind of trying to get up and still I couldn't recall what her name was. Anyways, doesn't matter! I will ask her tomorrow again. She meets me every day since I broke up. All I have to do is just sing, '*Jaan-e-jahan, dhundata fir raha, hu tumhe raat din, mai yaha se waha....*' And then there she comes.

Since I had broken up with Purvi, I always used to have dreams like this. And I used to win any competition; sometimes I became a singer, sometimes dancer, and most of the times a rockstar with an electric guitar in my hand. Many of the girls shout my name, cheer for me just to get my one look. Everyday, everything remains the same. Just the award name and song I sing to call her changes. Huh, but all those things remain just a dream.

****

Well, after Mahi left the room, I woke up yawning and rubbing my face and eyes, in sleepy mood. I went to bathroom to get fresh. I got ready after 15 minutes of bath and 45 minutes of struggle with that tap to close it well. I turned it, turned it again, and turned it again and again. But, it was of no use.

'Life is so great.' I mumbled with a sigh, 'Just that tap has to close WELL in a SECOND.' I shouted in my head.

Because of that bloody tap, I was late for college. So, I started running to get into lecture at least before it finishes. Thank god, my college was just about five minutes from my place. I reached the main gate. 'Javaharlal Neharu Engineering College, Aurangabad' I read the name and got feeling of, *'Papa kehte hai bada naam karega....'* But I was thinking kind of, *'Bachna... ae hasino... lo mai aa gaya.'*

For the sake of moment, I had to put my filmy feelings aside and run again to get into the class. I ran again and stopped right in front of the door of my class, GF15.

Some professor almost about 45 year old age and with half white hair, well tucked shirt and hands white due to chalk stood up in front of me on the dias. I dared to look into his eyes and he gave me that look explaining like he was checking whether I had lost all my shame or still I am carrying some. I looked down and tried to stop chuckling as I heard few of students' taunts. I didn't get permission to get into the class. Or rather, I had been scolded and thrown out of the class. Who does that on the first day?

Well, not first day actually. It was college's third day but mine first. Pretty bad start though, huh!

So, '*papa kehate hai....*' Was finished for today, so I thought to focus on *hasinas*. I thought and started sight seeing.

J.N.E.C. was the college where I felt like my dream coming true. There were students sitting beside the fountain. All were my seniors who I guess were thrown out, just like me.

In that white shirt and blue jeans with an ID card hanged around my neck, I was feeling so proud. I didn't know the reason, but it was just the feeling of satisfaction that at least I'd reached somewhere to make my parents proud. I overlooked the campus again.

I saw some beautiful girls; I mean the 'OUT OF REACH' material. But I won't give up. I kept looking but no one was in my reach. *'Yaha apni daal nai...'* I was thinking and heard the 'sheela ki javani...' ringtone in a very loud tone.

'Must be some idiot guy who kept that ringtone.' Someone might have said this. But it was me who had that china phone with 'sheela ki jawani...' ringtone. I saw the screen, it was Purvi's call. I just looked at the screen and my mind and heart started debating about picking up and cutting that call. I just thought for a while and cut that call. I did it for seven times. I mean, it was for our own good. I should have stayed away from her happily instead of talking with her and fighting daily. But she was still calling, and I was cutting her calls like… a… like a…

Ah, I have no words for me.

I left that place to avoid the awkward situation due to my '*sheela ki jawani'incident* and went to parking, and stood nearby a car. I saw myself in glasses of car's window. 'Just look at you, you dumb ass.' I thought to myself, 'Sometimes I wonder, how you could think higher than your reach even after watching your face in mirror daily, like 100 times.' I started humiliating myself as usual.

'Kaha raja bhoj aur kaha gangu teli ke dhobi ka chaprasi.' I thought after watching my face with curly hair, fat nose, tiny pothole like eyes with a big plane forehead resting on them overwhelmingly. That big forehead face resting on a thin 5 ft 7 inch body was looking like a perfect caricature. I looked at myself and thought that I should be happy in my dreams only. At least there, I get my girl always. However, in reality, I could feel the rejection even if I see a girl from backside. Her flying hair tells me to not to even think about it, no need to look into my eyes.

****

'I hate u' said Janvi's message while I was waiting for my next lecture. My lips got curved into a smile for that message. . Janvi, an evil girl with an average hight and short nose on her fairly bright face.

'What happened now?' I replied.

She: I m getting bored in this bakwas city & bakwas hostel.

Me: What can I do?

She: U dnt do anything. U just go to hell and enjoy in ur college. I m stuck here alone…

I smiled on her reply. She had just moved to her new hostel of her college in Beed.

Me: *bass kya…?*

She: shut up, u *chhapri*.

I couldn't stop myself from calling her. I dialed her number.

'I miss you so much… I want to go home.' She said like a puppy as soon as she picked up my call.

'But you just moved there.'

'Don't tell me things which I already know.' She shouted at me.

'What happened now?' I said while giggling on her mood.

'This college and hostel are situated outside of the city. I don't like this hostel.' She said like a K.G. kid.

'Hmm, have fun! Enjoy yourself. All the best for your next few years while I will suffer here in Aurangabad in a nice college, awesome campus, tasty food, theatres and all the enjoyment. You are so lucky that you don't have it and you can concentrate on your studies only.' I said with some lodded sarcasm.

'BITTU…!' She shouted, 'Stop teasing me, I'll kill you.'

'Ok, ok. Are you alone there? I mean don't you have any roommate?'

'I have one. She is in college.'

'What is her name? Is she pretty? Is she single?'

'Her name is Bhumi and way out of your league. And you mind your own business with your Purvi.'

'Come on, Chiku. You know I don't speak with her anymore.'

'But you still love her.'

'What are you doing at hostel at this time? Don't you have lectures?' I asked her to avoid the topic of Purvi.

'Well, same to you.' She said while mouth full of something like she was eating.

'Err…I was kind of scolded and thrown out of the class, very *respectfully.*' I said and she started laughing there like a ghost. 'Shut up! At least I have nice view here. You are stuck there in desert.' I said and she tried to control her laugh.

'I know that.' She said while controlling her last stroke of laugh, 'That's why I called you.' She said and I chuckled.

'For your information you didn't call, I did. Do you remember when had you called me the last time you Ms. *missed call*?'

'Shut up… I want to go home. I am bored here. How am I supposed to survive here?' she started whining again, 'You are coming to meet me!' She ordered.

'What? But we just met last week.'

'I told you to not to tell me things which I already know. You are enjoying there and I am stuck here. How could you leave me alone?' She started blabbering.

'Well, I didn't suggest you to choose biology. Not even medical, and in addition to that the college like that! It was your discussion so *ab bhugto.*'

'I hate you! You are world's most mean best friend.'

I chuckled and continued, 'Chiku, we will meet soon. It's just a matter of few weeks now. We will meet in Alandi for Diwali. Ok?'

'NO. It's not ok. You know Bittu…?'

'No I don't know.' I inturrepted.

'Listen na!' She scolded and continued, 'My mother's dosage has increased now. I am worried about her too. She had just come back from her treatment a day before of my departure.' She said and started crying.

'Come on, Janvi. Don't cry. She will be fine.' I tried to console her, 'How is her health now?'

'I don't know. Papa told me that sooner or later she might need an operation.' She said while sobbing silently.

'Hmm, don't worry. Everything will be fine.' I didn't know what to say. I heard the bell while we were talking.

'Chiku, I got to go for the next lecture.' I said and waited for her reply. She acknowledged by sobbing from other side.

'Ok, I promise you, we will meet soon.' I said and she cut that call while sobbing.

****

Well, my college days were just passing. Just passing, in learning new things, new concepts like defaulters, common offs, mass bunks, and sometimes if by mistake we even concentrated in class then we used to learn new concepts of study also.

Hey, remember I told you I write good poems. Now it is time to show you one. The one about my, or rather our college life.

Days were just passing,
enjoying college life.
I learnt how to proxy,
and learnt how to bribe.

New friends and new subjects,
new topics, new stuff.

Learnt sharing & caring,

3 shares of 1 puff.

Practical, attendance,
birthdays and class test.
Whoever helps you copying,
is the buddy your best.

Common off, defaulters,
tea-poha, canteen.
We were just growing up
enjoying our nineteen.

Nice na? I knew you'd like it. I don't know what is the matter with Mahi is to laugh at my poems.

Anyways, I had evolved some new dreams also. Lectures were my favorite place to dream about something. I don't know how many times I have become rockstar, dancer, singer, or a hero who saved so many people and my dream girl, from terrorist attacks, earthquakes, fire, or even tiger attacks.

And the professors! If I used to get scolded by any professor, then he used to be so dead by falling of a ceiling fan on his head by earthquake, in which I used to save everyone as a hero but him.

And somehow I told myself that I am not 'Rancho'. Yes, I had to tell myself that, after I short-circuited my hostels all electricity doing some stupid experiment on multi-charger while showing Mahi that I have a creative brain.

And being an engineering student, 'AAL IZZ WELL' had become the motto for every situation. Class test, hard paper, 'aal izz well' stress released but result failed. Retest, 'aal izz well', no study, result... you know!

So, after so many days, so many mornings where Mahi struggled so many times to interrupt in my sweet dream to wake me up, and after so many dreams, Diwali was the only thing I was waiting for. And it was the time for Diwali now.

****

Yup, diwali! Not the diwali with crackers only, not with fireworks and sweets only. The diwali, which was the occasion leading me to go to meet my parents. The diwali, which was the reason for bringing all the old friends together and create some new memories after laughing on old ones. Diwali, which was inviting me to play cricket, watch movies and sleep untill sun comes right above your head. Diwali, which was leading me to go and meet my evil best friend, Janvi.

Unlike last few Diwalis, this time I had no reason to fight with Purvi for not giving time to her, or not meeting her. This time I was totally free. On the other hand, may be alone.

So after a long wait for Diwali, I was going to Alandi, my *Mama's* village, excited about meeting my cousins and friends. Janvi's cousins were my good friends. My grand parents and her grand parents were neighbors; our mothers were close friends since there childhood and so are we. I always think that we are best friends, better than 'Ritesh and Genilia' from '*Tuze meri kasam*' and 'Imran and Genilia' of '*Jaane tu ya jane na*'. And I could compare her with Genilia, but I was far far away from being compared with Ritesh or Imran.

I was so excited to meet her. She was a bit angry because I had refused to meet her in Aurangabad. So, to chill her down I had written a poem.

I saw Janvi, coming out of her grandpa's house. It was a big *Haveli,* like an old Hindi movie, where our grandparents used to live like brothers since their marriage.

Overall there were seven rooms at ground floor and two halls were there situated in a C section of the open space. There was a well, right at the corner of the open space where we all children used to play since our childhood. At the other corner, there was a veranda for sitting, and a set of four hearths on the right corner where all the cooking of both the family used to take place. On the first floor there were three rooms and a big hall again, and a big open terrace where we all children used to sleep in a bunch while romping. Whenever I go there, I feel like I am still a kid.

I saw Janvi and gave her a big ear-to-ear smile. And she gave me her sweet famous angry look where she used to make her both big eyes so tiny, that close enough to just a pin can fix in it. She even used to fold her lips inside due to teeth rubbing on each other, and sneering her short nose and making it a bit more little.

She was standing in front of me, with her both hands on her

waist in her angry look. With that short nose she tried to sneer as much as she could and stood there looking up to my face.

To calm her down I went to her and was about to hug her, but I saw her father and just stood there.

Her father was not that strict, but strict enough to tell his daughter that avoid even friendship with a lower cast guy. That's me. But this different cast stuff never mattered to us.

'*Bass kya*…? Sorry na!' I tried to convince her and she sneered again and turned away. 'Come on, Chiku. I couldn't come to meet you due to my college. My attendance is very low.' I tried explaining, but she just was not in a mood to listen.

'See, to calm you down I have written a poem for you.' I said while taking out a page and she sneered again looking at that page with a peek.

So, after saying sorry to her it was time for my poem. I gave the letter in her hand. She just looked at me in her sweet anger and opened that letter.

I am sorry, I'm so so sorry.
Manne maaf bhi karde chhori.

Sharmana chhod dal, raz dil ka fuk daal.
Aaju baju dekh ke, gussa tu thuk daal.

Chal ganpat ab hawa aanede ,
Bhav mat kha ab gussa jane de.

Don't ask me why, what and how.
Ab bass bhi kar jyada bhav nako khau.

Tu mera god, karu me tera bolbala,
Tuzko laga dala toh life zingalala

I didn't show this one to Mahi, as he'd have laughed like hell on it. However, Janvi did the same thing. She laughed and laughed and then said, 'So sweet, Bittu. I guess I am never going to be angry with you now.' She said and started laughing again.

'Really? I knew my poem would work definitely.' I was flattered.

'Obviously! I mean what the hell is this!' She said controlling her laugh, 'If I have to suffer from reading your poem when I am angry, then why would I be angry on you?' She said and started laughing again. But, never mind, she is allowed to laugh.

'Anyways, so now you are not angry, right?' I asked, and she acknowledged, 'Ok. By the way where are other people, I am dying to meet everyone.'

'Not everyone has come yet.' She said with a little disappointment.

'Why? What happened?' I asked.

'Sanjay and his family are not here yet.' She said. Sanjay, her cousin, I always used to doubt that he likes her. But never mentioned it in front of her.

'Oh, so that's why you are so disappointed.' I tried to tease her.

'Shut up!' She said while trying to hide that blush, and ran away punching me after I started chuckling.

****

Well, we did all the things, which we used to do since childhood. We enjoyed the holidays, we teased each other, we wandered in our uncle's farm, we went to the temple on the hilltop with both families, and recalled our childhood era and did romping until we got tired and fell asleep.

After all these days of happy period, the time was to pack things up and get ready to go back to college. It was our last night of that Diwali at Alandi. If it were my childhood days, I would have stayed there for more days bunking my school. But it was not going to happen this time as we were going to be fined, per lecture we would bunk.

I was sleeping in veranda. It was just the time where I was falling asleep with my evergreen sweet dreams, and I was just designing the dress of my dream girl where I felt a slap on my forehead.

'Chikkkuuuuuuu…..' I shouted.

'Oh, I am sorry! Were you sleeping?' She spoke with that sarcasm, and tried to wake me up.

'Let him sleep Janvi, poor guy is missing someone.' Manav, her brother teased me.

'Oh, stop it. Now let me sleep. I have to go to college tomorrow.' I spoke in a sleepy tone, as I was thinking about that per lecture due, which would be fined to me if I did not attend it.

'Wake up, Bittuuuu. One should not sleep facing that side.' Here comes her well organized behaviour, 'Wake up, you lazy boy. I have news for you.' She said by pulling my hand to wake me up.

'What? Let me sleep you short nosed girl.' I said with that sleepy tone again. But she was like deaf to me, and continued talking while moving my legs to another side where my face was. Because she thinks that, it is not good to face north side while sleeping. Sometimes, I just am so fedup of her nature.

Well, she kept talking, and this time I was deaf. But after every full stop or coma in her sentence she used to wake me up by shaking my head and I had to acknowledge her sentences replying, 'Hmmm,…. Ummhmmm…. Hmmmm….'

She talked with me, rather alone for like an hour as much as I know. And then she woke me up again slapping on my forehead.

'WHAT?' I shouted angrily, and she startled.

'Chidu nakos na…' She said with that innocence on her face and puppy voice while putting her forefinger in between her teeth, 'And now it is time for news and the news is that your sister's marriage is fixed.'

'What?' I got surprised, 'How did you know that?'

'I just heard your mother telling my mom, and the marriage is in February.' She said with a typical excitement of a girl, 'I just got Sanjay's call and that's why other families didn't come, so that they could make it to marriage.' She explained everything.

'Wow that's great! But why did my mother hide it from me when everyone knows?'

'Ooops! Right, that's what she just told me to not to tell you about this.' She mumbled to herself stupidly, and continued, 'But I think she doesn't want you to be disturbed in studies. She'll tell you in a week before marriage.' She was right and she knew my mother very well.

When we were talking, my phone rang. Janvi gave me my phone. I saw the number,it was Purvi. I didn't even think of anything and cut the call.

I got back to finish the discussion with Janvi as soon as

possible, and as usual, Purvi called me again and again. I did the same thing again, cut her call on the first ring. I had not saved her number in my mobile. But as I was continuously cutting her call, Janvi guessed the situation, and was waiting for next call. As phone rang again, she grabbed phone from my hand and picked it up.

'Hello? Who the hell is calling up so late?' She started in anger.

She knew that it was Purvi's call. Purvi spoke something from other side and then Chiku continued, 'Yes, I am Janvi. And do not call Bittu at late night.' She said and cut the call.

'Why did you speak like that?' I was shocked.

'If you feel sorry for her, then call her back and speak with her.' Janvi said so normally looking at her nails.

'No. I...... I...... I mean I didn't feel anything, but this isn't good manners.' I didn't know what to speak.

'Oh really? And cutting someone's call without any reason is good manners?' She tried to make her point, 'Bittu, if you like her then speak with her. You have to leave your ego.'

'I don't have any ego.' I tried to defend myself, 'I just.... It just... it is complicated. I don't want to talk her. Leave it.'

'Come on, Bittu...'

'Anyways, leave it. I am getting a headache and I have to go early tomorrow.' I interrupted her and she turned towards me and started rubbing my forehead.

'You are going so early. And even not spoke to me well.' She spoke with that puppy voice and those puppy eyes.

'Sorry. And don't worry we will meet soon.' I said and made myself comfortable putting my head on her lap.

'I want to tell you something.' She said in serious tone.

'What is it?' I asked with my eyes closed and feeling the relief from my headache.

'Nothing, leave it.' She spoke while looking at her brother who was sleeping beside me.

'Anyways. What did Sanjay say?'

'Nothing much. Just that we will meet at your sister's marriage, so they didn't come this time. And a little bit of this, little bit of that....' She said and ignored Sanjay's topic.

'Hmm, anyways. Can I sleep now? I have to go early in the morning.' I said

'Just get lost. Don't come back.' She said with fake anger.

'Come on, Chiku. Now don't act like a kid.'

'You don't understand, Bittu. You will go to your college and I have to suffer there in Beed. I really miss our days of Aurangabad.' She said followed with a fake cry.

'Please, don't start again.' I said closing my ears with my palms. As soon as I said that, she pushed my head from her lap and stopped rubbimg it.

'Ok, ok, sorry. You can start it again. But please keep rubbing my head. It feels so good.'

'You know what, Bittu….' She was saying.

'No, I don't know.' And I interrupted as usual.

'Listen na! Why don't you do me a favor and just go to hell?' She said with a loud annoyed voice and I chuckled.

She smiled and settled down there. She gave a kiss on my forehead and slept before me. Such a lazy girl!

I stared at her for few more moments and closed my eyes, collecting all the memories of the Diwali. And slowly slowly I fell asleep.

****

I felt something biting me on my chest, due to which I got awake in the morning, suddenly. I woke up and saw, it was not a bite, it was Janvi's earring. I just slowly got her head off my chest and put a pillow under her head. And thought, 'Look at her! Such a sweet beast! Cute ghost, Small monster or puppy like evil. How? I mean how can I let her sleep so silently?' I kneeled down, got close to her, flicked her on her forehead, and pinched her short nose.

'Aaaaaa…… mommyiiiiii…… umhaaa unnmmhaaaa….' She started crying like a baby. And while I was going towards door laughing, she threw a pillow, but missed.

After few more minutes – that's me- and few hours – that's her- we were ready to leave for our places. Janvi and one of her cousins had come to drop me at the bus stop. When the bus came, Janvi held my hand and said, 'Let this bus go. I want to talk to you.'

'We can speak on the phone; let me go I'll be late for my workshop.'

'No, you will not listen to anything on phone.' She insisted.

'Ok, tell me what is it?'

'Do you still love Purvi?' she asked the familiar question I was expecting from her.

'I knew you'll ask me this only. But trust me I really don't know the answer.'

'What do you mean Bittu? Don't lie to me.'

'Oh come on Chikee, I never lie to you and you know that. But I really don't know it. I mean.... I mean.... Oh god.... I mean I wait for her to call me and ..... When she calls me I don't know what happens to me, and I can't pick up her call. Something stops me and, I... I.....'

'And you cut the call, right? Like you did last night?' She completed my sentence.

'Yes. And I want to call her back, but I dial her number and before it rings I cut it too.' I was so confused.

'Bittu.... You really love her so much but you are loosing it in ego. Don't do this to her and yourself.'

'Chiku, you were just opposing me for her previously and now all this stuff, why?'

'Because... coz.... Bittu she loves you so much. When I picked her call yesterday, she was just crying. She said that she wanted to hear your voice just once.' She told me this while holding my hand so tightly, as if she was feeling Purvi's pain.

I didn't say anything and boarded the next bus towards Aurangabad, thinking about Purvi and whatever Janvi told me.

Next thing, which I did, was a call to Purvi, as I could not attend my college in thinking about her. She picked up my call but didn't speak anything. I struggled with words, 'Hel... hello?' after this, I could just hear sobs from the next side.

I tried to console her, 'Hey, Purvi look, please stop crying.

Please don't do this to yourself. We can't..... Err.... We can't become..... We can't get..... You know what I mean. I am just sorry.' I didn't know what to say.

'I am so sorry Jaanu..... I need you.' She said while sobbing. She was crying so much. I wanted to say those three magical words but I was unable to say, I don't know why. It was on my tongue but I couldn't say it. As I was going to say it, my mind told me to cut the call and my heart was speechless. So I heard what my mind said.

Of course, she called me back so many times, messaged so many times.

As she was feeling more for me, I was getting much attitude. But I reminded what Janvi said and messaged Purvi back.

'I am so sorry☹,

Jaan☺'

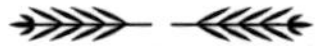

3 Back to home for marriage

❄ ❄ ❄

Days after days and weeks after weeks were just passing and there was nothing exciting in life. Sun used to rise daily without fail but I still don't remember watching it coming up even once. Life was going just well. I had experienced a new thing called 'defaulter'. For which I had to pay fine in my college. It was hundred rupees per lecture. And as much as I remember my attendance was less than 70%. So somehow, by not getting much screwed up I managed to pay that due and eventually attended the semester exam.

Since Janvi had told me about didi's marriage, I was unable to concentrate in studies.

Actually, it is just an excuse; I was anyhow not concentrating in studies well. Well, I was waiting for February to get back to home. I mean I had gone there after semester exams also, but this was more exciting.

Janvi was excited about something. She was continuously saying that she wanted to tell me something but not on phone. Anyhow, she used to ask whether I spoke with Purvi or not. And, insisted me so many times to do so.

My parents were too much anxious about my studies and college. Moreover, they had told me to not to get excited about my sisters marriage and concentrate on my studies and attend every lecture in college. My mother even ordered me to not to come a day before marriage to home. That was so sick. However, I managed to conquer it and it was the day of my departure for my sister's marriage ceremony.

A day before leaving for home, I was at internet café, checking my fb account. Android and whatsapp were yet to be discovered in India. I saw Janvi had uploaded her roommate Bumi's photo to show me her long hair. She sent me message that she'll be in Ambad – my hometown, a small town in Jalna district- next day with Bhumi. Wow! I got more excited.

Mahi saw Bhumi's photo and said, '*Munna, yeh toh thari bhabi se.*'

I just gave him a look and said, '*Beta*, I saw her first. She is friend of my best friend. *Wo thari bhabi se*… I mean *chhe*, whatever it is.' Both of us didn't know Gujarati, though we were trying to speak as Bhumi was Gujarati.

'You saw her first! So what? She is not a bus seat to reserve by putting your handkerchief on it. Let's see who approaches her first.' He gave me challenge.

'Done!' I accepted.

We left the cafe and went to our room, to get the packing started.

Huh, Mahi gave me a challenge. Anyhow, I am going to win it. I am allowed to. I don't have any girlfriend now. Though he is elder than me, I am the one with some experience in this field. So what, if he has a better personality, or is more funny; I will not let him lead to her.

****

After few hours of our departure, as we reached Jalna, I got message from Janvi, 'I've reached home. Where are you? Come soon. I wanna tell u something.'

I replied, 'what do u mean by I've? R u alone?' I was worried about my challenge.

'no. Bhumi is with me, why?'

'nthing. Cuming in an hr.'

I started planning how to flirt with Bhumi and calculating points 'plus one, plus one, minus one….' comparing with Mahi.

Within an hour, we were right in front of my home. There is no happiness like coming back to home, no matter whether in a day or a year.

I opened the gate loudly so that everyone in house would know that the youngest devil of house has arrived. Who cares about the world? I was always the evil in my home. Evil from my siblings' view and prince from my parents'.

Well, I entered the living room and threw my bag in a corner.

The whole living room was full of flowers and some wedding stuff. My brothers Rohit dada – a healthy guy with 5.7 ft high, silky hair with an conflicting attitude towards me in his pajamas – and Rahul – same height, gym junkie with perfect body and fit personality – were doing some work with some stuff in a corner of the hall. They didn't bother themselves to welcome me as they were already tired with their work.

I ran straight to my didi's room, she wasn't there. I ran to other rooms to search for Janvi and Bhumi. But all I could find was some different mess in each rooms concerning the wedding. My house had become a typical bridal house, as it would be in Maharashtra. I asked Rahul whether where everyone was. He told me that everyone has gone for either shopping or to the beauty parlor.

Mahi reminded me about the challenge by his eyes and been sited there with Rohit and Rahul. I went to get fresh in the washroom.

While I was getting fresh, someone came from behind and closed my eyes with her palms, 'Guess who?'

'Come on, it's obviously you Chiku.' I answered with over confidence.

'No stupid it's Bhumi.' Janvi replied and they both started laughing.

Wow! Bhumi touched me! I mean, my eyes. Yes! *Plus one.*

She removed her hand and as I turned back, I saw her. Her sky blue coloured 'dress' which was Punjabi for sure, was looking great on her well shaped figure. Her long beautiful hair had rested on her shoulder from front side till knees, were looking like a black poisonous Cobra rolling on her body. Her big black eyes were becoming tiny while laughing.

When I saw her, just one thought came into my mind, 'Dude, back off. Janvi must have uploaded a photo taken from digital camera, not from HD one. She is out of your league. It's better to leave instead to loose.'

But nooo! Here comes my heart, the great enemy of my mind, 'Bro, don't worry. We never change our goals due to hard path. So what, if she is out of your reach……'

'Far, far away of reach.' Mind interrupted.

'Whatever. Just go for it. It's better to loose after trying instead leaving. At least you will fight for your goal.' And I had to listen to my heart, because I knew I didn't have that sharp of a brain. So I decided to go for it.

'HI, BHUMI. KEM CHHO?' I started with Gujarati. Rather I shouted in Gujrati.

'*Majama, an tame Bittu*?' she said and I just heard my name.

'Yeah, aame Bittu, urf Karan.' I said waving my hand stupidly.

She laughed on my reply and said, 'No no. I meant how you are, Bittu?'

'Oh! Fine, fine! Fit and fine.' I struggled with my voice because of my stupid behaviour. 'Wow, such beautiful long hair.' I tried to make some positive conversation.

'Thanks. I get that compliment often.' She said, showing that I should try some thing new other than these common things.

'You look prettier actually, than in photographs.' This must be new.

'Bittu, if you have done here, can we go to bedroom? I am waiting to tell you something.' Janvi, the little devil I had forgotten about, spoke in between, disturbing us. And I knew, though I didn't ask her, she is going to tell me anyhow.

So we headed towards bedroom and Bhumi went to watch T.V.

'Tell me what is it?' I asked her to get back to Bhumi as early as possible. But she stopped as she heard someone coming.

It was my elder brother, Rohit dada. 'What's going on? And why do you both always speak secretly? Let us also know your secret.' He came inside and spoke while looking around for something. And before I could say something Janvi chipped in, 'Dada, its nothing. I was just scolding Bittu. He was trying to flirt with Bhumi.'

'What? Bittu, have you lost your mind? Will you never change? She is our guest, and you better behave nicely with her. Got it?' He scolded me with his big voice and big eyes.

'Yeah, that's what I was telling him.' Janvi said very innocently. Bloody liar! And before I could explain anything, dada left room giving me a livid look.

Doesn't matter! At least this time he scolded me for a reason. Otherwise, he never needs a reason to scold me and screw me up.

But I looked fumingly to Janvi. And she just started laughing, and to avoid that chuckle when I was angry, she put her forefinger in between her teeth and started biting so that she'll cry instead of laughing, but it didn't work. This was her trick, which she always used, biting her forefinger in between teeth and smiling foolishly with eyes wild opened. These stupid, childish things always make me forgive her.

'Any way, what were you up to tell me?' I asked.

'Listen...' She started so excitedly, '...you know?'

'No I don't know.'

'Listen na! Someone proposed me. And I want to ask you what should I do? You know who is he?' She asked so cheerfully.

'Again, I don't know. But I can say looking at your excitement, you should go for him, unless...'

'Unless what?' She got tensed.

'I meant, you know your father. If that guy is not of your cast then you should not even think about him.'

'I was going to tell you this in Alandi but then I thought let this take some more time.'

'Hmmm. So you will be committed now.' I said softly, 'And I am still SINGLE.' I said loud enough so Bhumi could hear it.

'What? Then, what about Purvi?' Janvi asked.

'I didn't make it up with her.'

'What? Why Bittu? Why didn't you tell me that? I would have never been committed when you are single.' She said.

'And Why is that?'

'I mean how I can live in a relationship when my best friend is single. I meant you'll need me to cry to forget her or to console yourself.' She said and started chuckling.

'Ha ha. Very funny! Now let it be and do whatever you want to do.' I tried to finish conversation as Bhumi was sitting in the next room where Mahi was also there. Therefore, he might have been in more plus points.

'Hey, Bittu you know...?' Rahul came in with annoyed face.

'No, I don't know.' That's my regular habit.

'I just scolded dada.' He completed.

'Why, what happened?' I asked him.

'He was flirting and trying to hit on Bhumi. How could he do this...?'

'Yes, you are right. I mean she is our guest. Bloody dada, so it was just drama to scold me.' I said and thought now I have one more competitor, 'Very good Rahul. And thanks for it.'

'Yeah, I mean how could he hit on her when I saw her first!' He explained. And I just thought, SERIOUSLY?? *WHAT IS WRONG WITH MY FAMILY?*

Hey, man there is no more vacancy for competitors now.

****

A day after wedding. 13th Feb.

We all were so tired by all the stuff of the wedding. We spent the whole day sleeping. After dinner, every one else was doing some work, and was getting ready to sleep. We kids were sitting in the bedroom while playing *antakshari*. Rahul dada, Mahi and I were not leaving a single chance to flirt with Bhumi. While I was trying for Bhumi, Janvi used to interrupt. She did not let me lead to her. I gave her an angry look so many times but she just would not back off.

After midnight, everyone fell asleep. Dada went to sleep in other room, Bhumi was sleeping on bed and Janvi and I were talking. Therefore, to make place for Janvi to sit, Rahul went on her place with Bhumi on bed. We both were settled on mattresses on the ground. All the elder family members were sleeping in hall, so most of our talk was just whispering.

'Why the hell you were interrupting? Don't you have your boyfriend to talk with? Just go to hell with him and let me flirt with her.' I said while pinching her and torturing her as usual.

She laughed and said, 'Bittu, first of all don't call it flirting. You know…?'

'No, I don't know.' I interrupted habitually.

'Listen na! You know you suck…' She insulted me and laughed again, '…and second of all, I don't have any boyfriend now. And she is not good for you. You can't handle Bhumi.'

'What? But you told me yesterday that you had a bf. What happened? Who was that guy? Did you guys fight?'

'Nope, we broke up. And if you want to know his name NOW, then it was Sanjay.' She said while taking my hand as pillow.

'Your cousin? And why did you break up? He is a nice guy. I

bet you would have done something wrong.' I got shocked.

'Wow Bittu, you know me very well. But to let you know I didn't. You did.'

'What did I do?' I asked getting surprised.

'You broke up with Purvi. So you were single. And how could I be committed when my best friend is single?'

'Oh come on Chiku! Don't be a kid. I was committed when you were single. It doesn't matter.' I tried to convince her.

'It matters to me, Bittu. I know how alone I was when you were committed. You didn't used to pick my calls. I used to wait for you. And you! You were with your girlfriend. I don't want you to suffer like me. I don't want you to wait for my one call. You may have so many friends. But I have only one best friend, and I don't want to loose him coz of someone else's love. And even I know how Purvi might be feeling, because, I have gone through the same situation, when you were with her. That's why I used to hate her.' She was becoming emotional.

I was so speechless. I was not aware of this situation.

'I am so sorry. I had no idea. But you should not break up with him.' I said and unknowingly I kissed on her forehead, and she closed her eyes as if she wanted to feel that kiss deeply.

'Did you break up during the marriage?' I asked.

'Yes. And he had called me at 12 o'clock to wish happy Valentines Day, but I cut it and sent him a message of good bye.'

'Why?' I shouted while whispering.

'*Arre*? You also cut her call. So did I.' She clarified, and continued, 'And Bhumi is not of your type, so don't flirt with her.' She said like a baby.

'Hmm. I will not. I promise.' I said and made a place to sleep, 'Good night.'

'Hey, don't sleep until I get asleep.' She said.

'Aren't you going up there to sleep?' I asked pointing towards Rahul sleeping on bed.

'No. I want to sleep here. Tomorrow I am going back to that prision in dessert. I will miss you so much.'

'But, Bhumi is with Rahul.'

'So what?'

'Nothing, I was just wondering that he'll get more advantage towards her, and I will… not…' I said and she looked at me with her famous angry look, 'I will miss you too.' I added instantly.

'Bittuu!' she said with normal anger. I just pinched her nose and said, 'Just kidding, Good night, you sleep.' She closed her eyes while looking at me for few seconds silently.

****

I also fell asleep while patting her head like a baby. My one hand was stuck under her head as pillow for her. She had put her right hand on her head towards my hand and touched her palm to my palm, rubbed it and after few seconds, she grabbed my hand through fingers so tightly, as if she had a bad dream. She didn't open her eyes.

I got up. And I saw, my best friend rested beside me so silently. After reminding what she told me, a sympathy smile came on my face. I was just staring at her. I didn't know what I was looking for or why I was staring. But, it was something new. First time I realized that how fair she is when her face looked bright in light of zero bulbs. A bunch of hair was flying on her cheek disturbing her sleep and it was great to see. I tried to place the hair behind her ear with my forefinger. As soon as I did it, she came closer, hugged me for a moment, and after taking a deep breath suddenly stepped backward saying sorry in sleep.

I just stood still as her hug resulted in goose bumps on my whole body. Suddenly everything went silent in my head, and slowly, slowly violins started playing. After a few seconds she held my hand so tightly again but her eyes were still closed. I was still staring. I could not help to stop it. I don't know what I was looking in her. So I responded her by holding back her hand. The music in my mind had changed its mood and it was feeling like now someone is just running his fingers on a piano, one by one so softly. Then she came closer again and wrapped her one hand around me and this time she didn't say sorry. I was confused. I didn't know what was happening but I hugged her too, may be the music in my mind made me to do so.

My eyes were just rolling on her fair beautiful face, from her well shaped chin to her *always kissable* and perfect lips, from the curve of her lips to the… to her short nose, 'A buffalo must have trampled on it.' We used to tease her. From that short nose to her soft cheek, which was inviting me to run my fingers on it. From that cheek to her ear which was looking more beautiful with that earring, which used to spike me every time when she rested her head on my chest or shoulder.

My eyes rolled towards her big fishy eyes and from those eyes to her forehead, which usually I'd have slapped on. But I leaned forward and applied my lips on her forehead, and she responded uplifting her neck and took a deep breath. I could smell the fragrance of her hair. It was feeling like I am in an ocean and cold breeze was flying through my warm body making me feel like heaven. It was different. When you were a kid, you used to get attracted to the earth after smelling its natural odor of first rain. That smell, when you go to wander outside at evening and a light breeze with the fragrance of nature runs through your body and you wish to integrate it into you by opening your arms. This was way beyond that feeling. Then I realized why in movies they take slow motion scene while heroine passes in front of the hero and her hair flies on his face and he feels it closing his eyes and smelling the beauty of a woman.

She made her hug tight and came closer. We were now so close, close enough that our noses crossed and we were breathing same air. I ran my finger on her cheek again to keep that hair back. She felt it good and took a deep breath while moaning and grabbing my t-shirt in her fist due to which her neck was lifted up and our lips touched each other.

With this sudden change in position she didn't even left her breath back, neither did I. She opened her eyes so softly. We stood still like a statue there with our lips touching each other. We stopped there in that awkward position as much as we could stop our breath. I was the one who left the breath first so softly and slowly with those shocked eyes. Then her one hand ran into my hair grabbing my hair so tightly while other hand was on my neck itching it unnecessarily. Then opening her lips, she locked it with mine. I didn't know what to do; both, my heart and the brain went on a strike or holiday. There was no sound in my head or no debate of brain. So I just responded her putting my lips deep into hers, and experiencing a grab by her fingers on my neck. God! Those long nails! They look great in those fingers only, and not on my neck! This is what I am thinking now, but at that moment, I was not having any sense, or any hurting. Those long nails were also feeling pleasant to my neck. Our breathings increased. I could feel our heartbeats going faster.

I tried enough to make a *good kisser* impression on her. I followed everything which I saw in Hollywood movies or our *Hashmi* does or whatever Purvi had taught me. With every moment and every feel, I used to grab her close to me, running my hands on her waist and on her neck copying her; just the difference was that I was not having long nails to take revenge of.

After few seconds I realize that we were not alone in room, so I stopped and after kissing on her forehead I leaned backward, and tried to sleep. I felt my heartbeats going faster and body had become warmer. (Kareena Kapoor was right. *Sachme, Naak bichme nahi aati.*)

While I was trying to sleep, suddenly my mind and heart came back from their strike. 'Dude, what did you just do? Not good! Soooo not good.' I don't know who it was whether mind or heart but other one was silent. I woke up and went to drink water in kitchen, and thought that whatever it will be I'll handle it and went back to sleep.

I don't have to behave awkwardly like they do in movies. She is my best friend. And it's not like, that I did it alone! She took advantage of me first, right?

While I was thinking this, Janvi came closer and hugged me again from backside. She hugged me tightly and my eyes- which I was trying to close- popped up wildly in shock.

Man! What the hell she had in dinner! I thought.

'Bittu, I … I love you so much.' She whispered and a sudden silent spread everywhere.

4. The awkward morning

* * *

I didn't realize when I fell asleep or even I slept or not. What the hell did she just say? Did she really mean it? Does she really love me? Or it was just a casual friendship type 'love you'. I don't know, but her hug didn't lead it to the casualness.

At the morning of 14th Feb. we were just speechless. Like, we had any type of '*maun vrut*' or something. As I woke up, I saw her resting her cheek on my chest and her earring kissing my shoulder through the T-shirt I had worn. My hand was wrapped around her, and her arm taking a grip of my neck.

It was hurting but I didn't focus on it. I was just staring at her, waiting for her, to wake up. I saw her lips and was reminded of the kiss. Oh man! I just lost in the night again for couple of moments.

Suddenly realizing that we were in my house sleeping in an odd position, I took my brain back to the morning from last night.

I tried to wake up but stopped still as soon as she opened her eyes. She removed her hand from me quickly and tried to wake up but got stuck in my arms as her earring was still hooked up with my shirt. She moaned as her ear got hurt. I didn't say anything but tried to unhook it as fast as I could. I was just struggling with it. So she removed it from her ear and left without saying a word. Her earring was on my shirt now.

She took her toothbrush and sat on stairs which were near bathroom inside house. I went to take my brush and there Janvi just spread her hand opening her palm in front of me while looking towards her feet, avoiding eye contact. I gave her earring in her hand and started walking to other side. After few seconds, I felt a flap on my shoulder. I got startled. Was it a flap or a slap? Is she angry on me for taking MY advantage?

I turned back and gave her a gaze. She shook her head and showed me her hand.

She was flapping her hair from my shoulder. As I turned to her, she pointed towards my chest. Few of her hair were still there. I flapped it all well and then saw at her, if any of my hair found on her dress. But she went off.

OH MAN! May be she thought I was staring at her breasts. Then I was really feeling like we had a *maun vrut.*

'Bhumi, wake up. We have to catch the bus. Wake up fast.' Hush, she broke her *maun vrut* at last, and it was so nice to hear her voice.

****

Well, we all got ready and left for bus stop. I should mention here that I never left for Aurangabad without listening to my father's lecture. I know it is obvious.

Rahul had come to drop us. I was going to Aurangabad and Janvi and Bhumi to Beed. We reached to platform. Janvi was still avoiding me. And I was trying to make conversation now, because the silence was killing me.

Rahul came to me and muttered, 'Bittu, there is still half an hour for the bus to arrive, so why don't you and Janvi take a walk to that temple there. You know, what I mean.' He said hinting towards Bhumi. Obviously, he wanted to be alone with her for flirting. Yeah, whatever! I am out of the race now. Do whatever you want to do. Now it's just you, Bhumi and Manav. I thought.

Janvi and I just saw each other and started walking silently. As we came a bit far from them, I thought about last night and wished to say sorry to her. However, I had no idea what to say and how. My soul started inspiring me, 'Come on, boy. You can talk to her; she is your best friend. Go and...'

'I am going to tell Sanjay about yesterday.' She interrupted between my soul and me. Whatever, at least she started the conversation. But wait! What did she say?

'Come on Chiku. I am sorry. It... it was a mistake.' I tried to convince her.

'I don't think it was a mistake Bittu. And you please don't say sorry. It wasn't your fault at all.' Her voice a bit loud, but was she speaking sarcastically?

'Whatever it is, but do not tell Sanjay. It will split your relationship. Rather it will destroy it. He is a nice guy.' I tried my hard to console her.

'That's what I want.'

'What?'

'I know he is a nice guy, but didn't you hear me last night. I will tell him about us and it will be easy for him to forget me.'

' Listen, it just can't happen.'

'You know Bittu? Since childhood, I used to like you. My mother, my brothers they always used to tease me after you. But you were just acting as a friend.'

'Try to understand, it can't happen.' I tried to convince her.

'Why, Bittu? You know I have been waiting for you since 7 years of my life. When the first time you showed me Purvi's love letter, I almost died. But then I saw how excited you were about her and you were so happy, hence I never let you know about my feelings.' She was crying and I did not know what to do, we were in public place.

'Janvi, please calm down. I know you are sick. Don't cry.' I tried to calm her down.

'I am not sick.'

'By sick, I meant… I know it's one of those five days of the month.' Why did I say that! I am such a brainless!

'Bittuu…' she said with surprised and shocked eyes. Obviously, she got embarrassed after hearing that from a boy. But I said it habitually, like I say anything to my best friend.

'I am… sorry. Last night, by mistake I felt …'

'I DIDN'T ASK, STOP IT!' She said in displeasure.

There was a silence for couple of minutes because of my stupidity. I tried to look at her after those awkward moments. I could see her wet eyes.

'Come on, Ciku.' I tried to console her.

'Bittu, you don't understand. You are everything for me…'

'Oh really? Then why do I come to know about Sanjay when you broke up with him? And not when you were together? If you were waiting for me then why were you with him? And even didn't tell me. For me, to be in a relationship, loyalty and transparency are the most important.'

'Bittu, I was so alone. And he loved me so much. I saw you with her and hence I decided to go with him.' She was crying.

'Ok! But it can't happen. Let us be straight. We are middle class people. I don't want to make fun of our families. Those inter caste marriages and modern society all those things are just made for movies and rich families. In real life people just make you suffer, and to your family too.' I wanted to say the real reason but I was just fooling around, 'And you know your father, so I think there is nothing much to explain. To be honest, you are the one who belongs to the upper caste. So if some one saw you even wandering with me then your father will be the first to suffer from people's taunts and torture. Even our parents will not allow it neither the society. I want to be in relationship with a girl with whom I am allowed to marry.' I said in anger and she started sobbing. I got irritated as we were in public place. Somehow, I tried to console her and said that we'll talk on phone.

I don't know what I was doing. I could not have been in a relationship with Janvi. She was my best friend. Moreover I was still having feelings for Purvi, but there also I was being a moron and ignoring her due to my ego. I was damn confused. I had no idea what to do. Whatever I had just said to Janvi to just fool around was also true.

Somehow, I managed to tell her that we will talk about it later on phone and we headed towards our buses. While going towards bus, she was sobbing silently and wiping her eyes. Bhumi and Rahul were happy from their long chat. Before boarding the bus, she held my hand for long time, which resulted tears in my eyes too, and reminded me the last meet with Purvi at the same place. She was going to Baramati and I had come to drop her. After which I never met Purvi, and fought on phone only.

We boarded our buses and left for our destinies.

Our buses went to opposite directions.

Janvi went to south and I went north.

5. Flashback

* * *

OCTOBER 2007

A kid with big loose shirt and cargo jeans was wandering in search of a coin box or a telephone booth with some money collected from his piggy bank. He was trying to set his small curly hair repeatedly while walking on the road. The combination of his dressing was a bit funny for his 4.5 ft thin personality. Overall, in his personality, his fair face and clever brain was the only advantage for him. These advantages had led him to get a girlfriend at 16.

His name was Karan. Right! That's me. It was my school days, and I was in 10th class. I was searching for a booth where nobody would be standing so that I could speak alone with Purvi.

Finally, I found a coin box and dialed her number. As it was my school period, at this early stage I didn't have any cell phone. I used to collect money from my piggy bank. And when other boys of my age were interested in eating *ice-gola, pani-puri, ragada, bhel, chaat*, I was using my piggy bank for coin boxes and STD booths. People say, I was always a step ahead since childhood.

Anyways, I dialed her number. Phone rang and my heartbeat increased like a railway engine. What if her father picks up the call? What if he finds out and tells my father? What would I speak if she didn't pick up the phone? All thoughts were just making me upset and afraid.

'Hello?' someone picked up phone, but I couldn't recognize whether it was Purvi or her mother.

'Hello? Can I speak to Pritesh?' I spoke while changing my voice and shivering hands.

'Yes, I am Pritesh speaking. Speak my friend.' Purvi said and started laughing as she caught me while changing voice. Whatever, I just got relieved that she'd picked up my call.

'Purvi, I want to meet you to tell you something.' I said with confused tone.

'What happened? Tell me.'

'No, no. Not on the phone. Because I don't know when we will meet again.' I said, as if I was going on a war and will die there and never come back again.

'Umm, ok then. Come to my home in 15 minutes. My parents are not home. You can come.' She offered me a lonely meeting.

I quickly put receiver down saying ok, and started walking towards her home, gathering all my courage to enter in her house and planning an 'escape plan' if her parents or anyone came suddenly. I still remember, the best plan I could come up with was either hide under bed, or cover my whole face with my hands and run for my life as fast as I could at the very moment her parents would enter.

Purvi and I used to be in same school. Our school was great but badluck was that they were having separate divisions for girls and boys. We were in same tuitions though. Once we had fought in tuitions in childhood. It wasn't a small fight, she had hit me with her writing pad and my finger got cut and started bleeding. Since then each of my friend started to tease me after her, which led me to fall for her. Then after following her everywhere, I gave her hint that I liked her.

I don't know whether my school's attendance was even close to 75%, but I can definitely say that I was 100% present in tuitions. It never mattered whether I was sick or it was raining or it was very early in morning. I used to go to tuition anyway, just to see her, and to spend time in watching her face, her laugh, her gaze that she used to give me from corner of her eye. I must say, it was the best time of my life.

Well, after few minutes I was just in front of her house. I didn't enter directly as I was afraid. Because I lived in a small town where if a girl and boy seem even talking to each other, all other people would complain to their parents that their son or daughter has some bad habits. And in such town I was going to enter in a girl's house where she was all alone. Oh man! I wish, now I should get such chance.

I firstly made two rounds around her house making sure that no one is watching me and then entered in looking around. Hush!

Half the battle was over. The door was completely opened for me. I didn't think of anything and got into the house as my heart-beat was about to kill me. I entered and looked around, and I heard door unlock. Daunting my heart I saw backwards, Purvi was waiting for me standing behind the door and locked it as soon as I entered. She came uptill my shoulder at that time with fair face, fluffy cheeks, healthy personality and with the hair till shoulder, covering the neck only as it was some fashion trend of those days in my school.

Well, she stared at me and gave a lovely naughty smile. She went to get water for me offering me a seat. I sat on the bed instead of sofa and looked around. There was a photo frame of her father hanging on the wall; it looked like as if he was staring right at me angrily. On the left side there was a showcase carrying her family pictures and her several certificates of different competitions. Purvi came with a glass of water.

Oh my god! I am a boy of 10th class and I finally have a GF with whom I am in a lonely house, totally alone. I was damn scared. To increase my fear, one of her friends, Pallavi came out of the kitchen.

'Hi, Karan bhaiya.' She said with a smile.

Ok! So we were not all alone. She was same of my age, but in my town, we had to use suffixes like 'bhaiya and didi' to let other people know that we are only friends and nothing else. It was like an unwritten rule.

'Tell me, Karan. What's the matter?' Purvi got my focus on point.

I saw her and started, 'Purvi, I am going to my uncle's village for some days.' As soon as I said, she gave me that old Hindi movie look like a lightening had struck with a sound of thunder starting in background.

'Why?' She asked in murky tone.

'Purvi, its Diwali now. I am going there for holidays.' I answered and stopped as Purvi turned around with a sulky face.

'Purvi…' I tried to convince her and her face made me think of that *pipani*, trumpet and *sitar* had started playing sad music automatically from the same Hindi movie. She came close hugged me tightly, 'Please, don't go Karan. Please.' I got shocked as soon as she hugged me. This was my first hug. I got goose bumps all over my body. And I will not lie to you but as this was the first touch, I got some erection too. With this hug, Pallavi went to the kitchen again.

Oh My God! Again! I was so confused. I had no idea that she'll get this much emotional. I had never come up with situation where, you need to handle a girl who is crying on your chest. I was just a novice. It was like ragging to me. She was hugging me and I was trying to take my below waist portion away from her. You know what I mean.

'Purvi, stop crying.' I tried to console her while taking her away from me. Because I don't know about her but, I was feeling kind of awkward, because if she would have hugged me for few more seconds, then…

'Karan, we don't have holidays. Our extra classes will start for S.S.C.' She made a point to stop me.

'I know Purvi, but I have to go. I had not gone there in summer vacation, so now I have to go.'

'Why? Is it so important for you to go there that you are ready to bunk classes? You are ready to live away from me?' She said while crying. As she was crying more and more, the sound of sad music of trumpet was becoming louder in my mind.

I had to sit down and put my one leg around another. So, I sat and said, 'Purvi, I want to meet somebody, I want to tell them about you, about us.'

'Who?' She asked wiping her tears.

'Janvi, and my cousins.' I answered.

'Oh, so you are going there for other girls.' She walked away in anger and again I could hear the sound of lightning.

So now, it was my turn to hug her. I started preparing myself, *'Jay Bajarangbali, Jay Bajarangbali…'* Not that I was a gentleman or something, to pray to God there, but I had to, to *calm myself* down.

It was not like I was so trained in love and hugs, but I was just copying Purvi. I went to her; I turned her face to me. She was avoiding eye contact due to her little anger which used to be always on the tip of her nose. I lifted her face while putting my palms on her cheeks, and I was about to hug her. But she was Purvi, all trained and ready for these kind of stuff. Before I could hug her, she hugged me again.

She was so trained. She must have seen lots of romantic movies in this small age.

I clutched her close to me, and she looked up in happiness and tried to kiss me. I didn't answer her kiss as I was wearing jeans and they were so tight, and were making me extremely uncomfortable. I just hugged her and let her sit on bed and I sat on chair in front of her. I started to explain,

'Purvi... don't you trust me?' I asked. She shook her head and I smiled, 'Come on, *yaar*. Janvi is my best friend. I want to meet her. I want to tell her about you, about us.' I put my hand in my pocket and got a letter out from it.

'See Purvi, this is your first love letter to me, and I want to show her this.'

'Why? Is it so necessary to show her?'

'Purvi, I had not gone there in summer vacation also, so she is really angry with me. She is so mad at me. I have to convince her. She is my best friend.'

'And what about me then? I am nobody, right?' She said with her memorable sulky tone.

'No. You are my love, sweetheart.' I said while taking her face in my palms. She looked at me, smiled and taking my hands in her hand, she kissed them.

After a long speech, I convinced her, and after 3 hours of meeting, I was ready to go back to my home. Our hands were so wet due to sweat. Obviously! If you put your hand in somebody's hands for like 3 hours non-stop, it would definitely start sweating.

When I said I had to leave, she started staring in my eyes a bit emotionally and romantically. And at the age of 16 it was quite normal. (?)

'Come on, Purvi I have to go now...' As soon as I said this, she jumped towards me and hugged me again. As now I was sitting, she was able to kiss me and so she did.

It was unbelievable for me. All I used to fantasize about and wonder how it would be to feel was happening with me in real. I didn't care about my erection and I hugged her so tightly so that she could also feel the thing. I felt like I was not a boy any more, I had become a man. It was my first kiss ever, which lasted for 4 to

5 minutes. We were kissing each other, sucking our tongues and licking lips as long as possible. I switched my place and sat on bed taking her on my lap. She ran her hand through my hair and took them into her grip. With other hand she cluthed my collar pulling me towards her more and more. I felt my body getting warmer. Our breathing increased, which was driving us more crazy. After a long kiss, I removed my lips slowly and started kissing her neck. She grabbed my hair, clutched it so hard, and started breathing faster. Oh Boy! That was unbelievable!

I realized that I should leave before some one comes. So, I stopped it and gently putting her down I took a deep breath. There was a weird smile on my face, a big ear to ear smile with teeth popping out foolishly. I was laughing inside very imprudently with eyes opened wide in the achievement of something. She was avoiding my gaze in shyness. She just looked down and came closer. While hiding in my arms she said, 'Idiot! Now I will miss you even more. I love you so much.' She said and punched me gently on my chest.

I smiled and said, 'I love you too dear.'

'Please come back soon, and please don't forget me.'

'No, I will never.' I said and pecked her, and left.

As I was in the doorway putting on my sleepers, she came from back and hugged me. God! I really wanted to stay there forever. Why did I kiss her, now I don't want to go!

I turned back and kissed her on her forehead. I had to go before someone arrives. I had to control my heart from being rash. I headed towards the gate with heavy steps.

I left her home same way as I had entered. Just like a thief or a spy. Once I was out of gate, I got relieved. Purvi was standing in the gate watching me until I got out of her eye's reach. I was also watching behind at her after every 4-5 steps.

Once I was out of her colony. I got a weird naughty smile on my face. It was like; I had done some great job, or won a war. Like, I had discovered a new world. I was happy. At last, I had my first kiss. I was like on top of the world. I was so eager to tell about what happened at Purvi's house to Pritesh, my school friend.

And suddenly, my happiness turned into fear within a second because of a thought.

Suddenly I felt like I would faint. One thought came in my mind and I lost my smile of great achievement.

I thought, 'I kissed her, I leaned on her, put my tongue deep into her mouth. But.... but... now... what if.... what if she got pregnant because of my kiss?' After all, I was just a kid having no knowledge about these things.

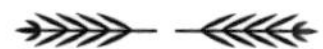

6. In new relationship

* * *

It had been almost 5 hours since I was in bus, thinking about Janvi, my family, my heart, my mind, my soul, her father, our different castes, society, and my real love.

'I love Janvi. No, no. I mean I like her. She knows me well. We could be good together. We can be a great couple, rather best ever.' My soul started suggesting me.

'Oh please!' My mind interrupted, 'Stop being a fool. Purvi used to love you so much, yet you guys broke up. And now do not even talk to each other. What if Janvi and you both end up the same way?' I got goose bumps with that thought. 'And Janvi's father has a lot of ego, mostly because of their upper caste. Even if it happened, all the relatives will be ashamed of you. We are middle class people.'

As my mind was winning, my bus stopped at its stop. I took my bag and got out of the bus. I took an auto rickshaw and left for my destination. Switching on my phone I dialed Janvi's number.

'Bittu, where are you? I want to meet you right now. I want to see you.' Janvi said while sobbing.

'Ok, Chiku, calm down. I am coming, don't cry please. I'll be there in 5 minutes.' I said her while asking rickshaw driver to drive fast.

Yup! I was in Beed, I had changed my bus in Jalna as I could not go further in thoughts of Janvi. While I was on way of Beed my mind was being king and recalling Purvi's memories.

'What! Are you serious?' She got excited, couldn't believe that she asked for something and it was really happening.

'Yes, Janvi I am in front of Adinath dental college. But I don't know where your hostel is.' I said as rickshaw stopped in front of her college.

I must say, these people definitely fraud students. I had

searched about this college on internet. And saw their prospectus. They had shown a big building with attractive look and garden and all that stuff in prospectus. However, there I could see only a building with no plaster on walls. Bricks were naked, no parking and not even a single watchman or security guard. Obviously, there was no guard as there was no gate too. I could realize Janvi's pain about living in this desert.

I saw Janvi coming out from the second building, which must be girl's hostel, and it had naked bricks as well. She saw me and started running towards me, which reminded me the scene of any old Hindi movie where girl runs in slow motion towards her boy and 'la la la, lala…' music joins them to create the scene more funny and less romantic.

Janvi came closer and hugged me. But I took a step back as we were in a college campus.

Yeah! Though it was looking like a desert there, I have to call its college campus.

Anyway, Janvi came to me. She was smiling; she was crying and behaving like a kid who gets chocolate after so many requests. It had been just a few hours to us getting apart from each other, but it was feeling like a year.

'I love you so much Bittu.' She said while holding my hand.

'Chiku… Janvi… I … I love you too.'

****

By the time, I was not only in love with her, but also gone mad for her that I could not go to Aurangabad and reached Beed.

She was just smiling, holding my hand tightly and she wanted to speak so many things, which her eyes told me.

We headed towards Kankaleshwar temple, the well-known temple of lord Mahadeva in Beed. While going there in auto rickshaw, Janvi had seized my hand and rested on my shoulder.

'Bittu, thank you so much for coming back. I love you so much. You can't imagine how my condition was after boarding that bus.' She was really happy.

'Hmm, after all you are my best friend. How can I let you cry?' As soon as I said this she saw me in a sarcastic way, and I got her point, 'Ok, ok. I know I have made you cry so many times, but it was different and this is different, totally different.' I admitted and she smiled.

We reached the temple. There were number of senior citizens and number of couples sitting. It was Valentine's Day. We got place to sit near the small stone bridge there which was joining the two temples in that place. We sat after praying to lord Mahadeva.

'Chiku, I am damn confused.' I started.

'Don't be confused Bittu, just accept that you love me too.' She said and looked into my eyes.

'I do, but...'

'There it is! I just hate this type of 'but's.' She said interrupting me.

'You know our families; our parents would never accept it.'

'I waited for you like 7 years and now it's my chance to make you completely mine. I don't care who will accept or not.' She started and looked at me, 'I love you since childhood, and today I got you. I will not let you go away. I will leave everything, everyone for you. I want only you Bittu. If my parents don't allow me to marry you, I will leave them.'

'No, you are not getting it.'

'Bittu, I mean it. Anyhow, I will have to leave them no matter whomever I marry. I want only you. Previously I was controlling myself, but now when you know it, I just can't stop myself. I don't know any thing; I can't live without you now.' She was deeply in the feeling of love. Her eyes were making me fall for her deeply. Each word from her mouth was only hailing me. I was feeling the importance of me in her life.

'I love you Janvi.' I wished to hug her but could not, as we were in the temple's yard, and people were staring at us.

Till yesterday I was single again, I was only having my best friend. And today, I am in relationship with my best friend. But I had loved Purvi so much, and though we could not end up well. Hence, I just wanted to clear few things up between Janvi and me.

'Listen, Janvi. In future, whatever may happen, promise me that we will always be best friends first.' I took her hand near me and said while looking into her eyes.

'I promise, I will always be there for you, till the last breath of my life.'

I just smiled at her answer and continued, 'No, I meant, now we are changing our relation so if we fight for any reason, then I don't want that to be the reason to break our friendship.' I clarified myself.

'Bittu…' She said while putting and running her palm on my cheek, 'I know that. I will take care of it.'

She told me how much I meant to her, she would never go anywhere else leaving me alone. She promised me so many things.

I was feeling so girly, because she was saying and doing the stuff, which I should have said and done. However, I was just listening to her and enjoying the focus on me. I was feeling great. Whatever! I was the luckiest one to have a best friend like her, and now she was my girlfriend.

We sat there for a while and enjoyed our day. The day of valentines', the day of lovebirds', the day of stupid's like us. We even forgot our hunger, our food.

She told me every thing in past about me, where she used to think about me, when she cried for me. How many times I had ignored her and how many times she had forgiven me for all reasons. How special I was for her, and how much she wanted me.

Well, we sat there for few hours and decided so many things about future and laughed on past. We both were lost in the time. We never wanted that time to pass. But it just didn't happen in that way. We had to leave as it was getting late for her to enter in the hostel. We reached back there in auto rickshaw.

We reached to her college. Bhumi was with some of her friends standing there. As we reached there, she caught the smile and happiness on Janvi's face, and winked at me. I felt shy there.

Janvi introduced me with her friends, Pradnya, Sunil and Vinit.

'You must be Bittu.' Vinit said while offering me handshake. A guy with tiny eyes, fluffy cheeks and healthy personality with the same height as mine. His eyes were almost disappearing when he used to laugh or smile.

I nodded and said, 'Err, actually it's Karan.' I corrected him, as I don't like any stranger calling me that.

'Hmm, Janvi always tells us about you. And now look at her, how happy she is.' He pulled her cheek while saying that. I got a little possessive. He continued, 'Even she had forgotten us. Not a single call in these four days, ha? You deserve a punishment Janvi.' He said and tried to hit on her butt and my heart skipped a bit. However, she dodged and he missed. Thank god! Everyone laughed on it. I also had to make a fake laugh, but inside I was burning like hell. Who the hell is he? And even Janvi is not defending herself.

'How are you feeling now Janvi?' Bhumi enquired her.

'Perfect.' She answered while smiling and looking at me.

'Are you her boyfriend, Karan?' Vinit asked me.

'Err...'

'No! We are bestest friends.' Janvi interrupted before I could say anything. Why didn't she tell him truth?

'Oh, bestest? We know that already. But I just wanted to confirm it from him. And there is no such word like 'bestest'. It's just best.' He seeped his knowledge and headed to pinch her nose, and the fire reached to its top most level in my head. Enough! I am gonna kick some ass now...

Before I could do or say anything, his phone rang and he excused himself from us. I gave Janvi a wicked look. She didn't get it, she behaved like nothing had happened.

'What the hell was that?' I asked her whispering.

'He is so funny, isn't he?' She said.

'Funny? Don't you get angry when he slaps you, pinches you?'

'Why? You also do that.' She replied casually.

'What? Are you comparing me with him? And by the way I don't pinch you in public, and what about slap on the butt?' Normally I would not have reacted this much, but now we were talking about my new girlfriend's body parts.

'Bittu, he is my friend.' After this answer, I didn't even feel to stand there with her. I left the place on very moment saying bye to Bhumi.

I was angry on that guy, but moreover I was angry with Janvi. How could she allow him to do so? As I left, Janvi ran behind me.

'Hey, what happened?' She asked.

'Nothing, I was just not aware that you have other best friends too. Anyway, bye.' I said while walking faster in anger.

We reached near rickshaw and she held my hand. 'Leave me Janvi. I gotta go.' I said while avoiding her.

'No. I am coming too.'

'Your hostel will get closed. You stay here and...' I stopped myself completing my sentence.

'And...?' She asked like she didn't know I was angry.

'Nothing, bye.' I sat in the auto rickshaw and asked driver to move, avoiding Janvi intentionally.

On the way to bus stop, I could not stop thinking about that bloody guy pinching my Janvi. I thought Janvi would call me but, it had been 20 minutes and she hadn't called me. (I meant not even a miss call.)

I reached to bus stop and before boarding bus, I called her.

'Hey, Bittu I just entered in hostel and was about to call you.'

'Just entered? I left you in front of the gate 25 minutes before and you just entered? Why? Didn't you get time from pinching and slapping?' The possessiveness was clearly expressing through my voice and anger.

'What is the matter with you, Bittu? He is my friend. It's not a big deal.' Her sentences were just making me crazy. May be I was getting much possessive. Maybe it was because; I never had friendship with any girl except Janvi and Purvi. May be that was the reason I thought it was a big deal. Maybe it was the effect of my town where I lived which made me think so.

But I always thought, rather she always made me think that I have all rights on her as her only best friend. I thought I was the only close one to her. Before an hour, I was so happy, and now, I was just burning inside and the girl who made me so special just then, was telling me that it was not a big deal. Maybe it would be the world's smallest love story. That's it!

After that so casual answer of her, I could not talk to her more. I just switched off my phone and boarded my bus. But, I was unable to control my emotions.

In the bus, I was just unable to forget it. I had just started to imagine about her and that Vinit, playing with each other. I thought why did she take too long to call me? Was he doing something with her? I could not help it, but I was just thinking the silliest things. I was not this possessive before. I didn't know what had happened to me. Suddenly I realized that I was totally acting like Purvi. Yes, she used to act like this. This possessiveness was the reflection of her behavior. This was the reason I had got away from her.

'Oh my god! No, I am not like this. I was never like this. What happened to me? Yeah, that thing about slapping on butt was odd but, she had dodged it, right?' I started thinking about it. Why did I get this angry?

I reached Aurangabad and switched my phone on. While heading towards my room where I used to live as paying guest in a private hostel, I got plenty of messages; few of them were from Janvi and few of them from missed call alerts saying that she had called me 15 times.

Each of Janvi's messages was saying…

'Sorry na, bittu. I love you yar.'

'plz cl me when u switched on ur fn.'

'havn't reachd yet?'

'bituuuuuuuuuuu……'

'where r u?'

'I miss u already.'

'still angry?'

'stop killing me now yar.'

And the last one, which made me to call her back, was,

'hi, bittu. My boyfriend karan fought with me and is so angry. I'm so sad. I need my best friend to talk.'

I had to call her. I was so angry but, I had promised that whatever may happen, we will be best friends first.

I called her; she picked it up on the very first ring, 'Idiot, how many times I have called you. *Kaha mar gaya tha?*'

'Why? Don't you have your other friends to talk?' I said sarcastically.

'Yeah, but they are busy now.' She teased me back.

'Oh, so they don't have time for you, and hence you are calling me.'

'Bass kya…?' She took my *chhapri* quote.

'Shut up!' I said in anger but controlling my smile.

'*Haayee*….! I love the way you say it.' She tried to flatter me by her naughty voice, but I yelled at her. 'Come on, Bittu. What happened to you? You know, you are my only best friend. I am sorry. I love you na!'

'No Chiku, I can't handle it. I called you just because you said you need your best friend. But let me tell you first, I never had any friend as close as you. I can't tolerate anybody else touching you, pinching you, and slapping you on your...' I could not finish my sentence.

'Come on Bittu. I am sorry na! Ok, I promise you, I'll never talk to him again, Fine?'

'No, I don't want you to leave people because of me.'

'That's right. They are people. And I don't care about them. I want you. I can leave anybody for you but please you don't go away from me. What more I should do to calm you? I wish I could write poem, but I don't know how to write like you do...' Well, she said and I was flattered, and thought that she doesn't need to write any poem, she said it, that's enough for me. I know it's not easy for everyone. She continued, '... I mean you suck too. But at least you rhyme, and I can't even write as bad as you do.'

'Hey, hey, I thought you were trying to calm me down. Is this the same thing?' I said quickly before she could insult me more.

'Oops! Sorry, sorry. But, *chhod na yar*. I promised that I will never talk to him now, and no one will pinch me again, that's your right only. Okay?' She acknowledged.

'Oh, so they can slap you?'

'Come on! Anyone will neither pinch me nor slap me anywhere. Even if you want, no one will ever touch me again. Happy?'

'It's ok. Enough now, I am not that much... a... I don't know, I don't have word for me.' I said playing with my empty pocket aimlessly like a reclusive kid.

Anyhow, I was so much angry. I couldn't resist it.

I was standing outside in the balcony. She was trying to convince me, flatter me. She was saying so many things, trying to say good things but somewhere the 'best friend material' used to come in and then her 'to be good sentence' used to turn in to taunt me.

I was getting flattered though, while talking I was moving my leg, and rubbing the tile with my toe for no reason, tilting my neck while smiling and getting a spark in my eyes. She convinced me so lovely and my anger turned into, 'I love you too.' Then after 5 minutes of 'bye, bye' drama, I cut her call. After cutting her call, there was a pleasant smile on my face. I looked at the screen, I smiled and patted my phone on my forehead twice while smiling and kissed the screen, I don't know why.

But the guy who was looking at me for long time, - I don't know how much - gave me a weird look, like, 'dude, should I give you a lipstick now? Or do you want some bangles to wear?'

His look was so weird that made me think how girly I was behaving while on phone, and how my behavior was turning so girlish. 'I am not a girl, I am a boy. I am a man!' I told myself. This was the first time when she had convinced me in such a way. I was so happy to have my best friend as my girlfriend.

****

Days kept passing and our bond became stronger. My friends noticed the change in behaviour. They noticed my girly behaviour.

Though it was so girly and childish, I loved that starting phase of love. Her missed calls which usually used to give me just a smile or some time anger that, 'how *kanjus* she was', was now giving me tremendous happiness and spark. The regular teasing to each other was changing to care for each other.

'How is your short nose?' or 'You are so *chhapri*' had changed to 'khana khaya?' and 'you are so sweet.'

'I love you' had become like a full stop, which comes at the end of every sentence.

Daily timetable also had changed its routine. Previously it was simple: Wake up by snoozing alarm, brush and bath, do breakfast, go to college, take lunch, college, call to Janvi, go to classes, have dinner, call home, do some stuff and good night.

Now it had changed to: Wake up on her miss calls. Call her back, talk to her. Tell her what her shona, baby, prince is doing. Listen her chitchat while doing brush, take bath, and call her back 'again'. Speak while changing; do some breakfast while talking with her. Go to college 'if lecture is more important or interesting than her'. Take lunch, while texting her about menu in the mess. Recharge your phone, recharge her phone so that she could chat with you in next lectures through texts, (listen some scolding and babbling about 'why did you recharge my phone?'). Chat with her in lectures. Call her as soon as last lecture's bell rings. Go back to hostel while talking with her. Speak until you got enter in classes. If you can, then concentrate in classes. Call her back as soon as class finishes. Talk to her, talk to her, and talk to her more. Have dinner if that's more important than talking with her. Call to your parents to let them also have that happiness by talking with you, which you enjoy while talking with her, then call her back again and talk until you or she fall asleep.

Contact number of her had changed from, '*chapti, nakti*' (girl with short nose) to sweety, chiku, love, jaan… and so on.

I don't know exactly what we used to a talk or on which topic we used to spend this much time, but each call used to be a commentary or update of what we did between two calls. She used to tell me about everything, and ask me what she should do. She had also told me that Bhumi is enjoying the tough competition between Rahul and Manav, and it seemed like Rahul is overtaking Manav. In addition, Bhumi tells everything to them about us. So I got alerts, because here Mahi had also some doubt on me about my new girlfriend. And had Bhumi or Mahi come to know about our relationship then they would have shared it with Rahul or Rohit dada. And it would have created problem for us. So we decided on some rules.

1) If Bhumi or Mahi picks our call then we will not talk.

2) While chatting, other people should not see our messages, so, for that we would not start chat without answering code word or number.

3) And in chat or while talking if they are around us, then we can't say 'love you'. But if we could not control, then simply text or say '..' these two dots meant 'I love you' for us. So that other would think, it's a blank message but we would get our feelings transferred.

In between this, my behaviour changed a bit, but my dreams didn't change. Just, that pretty dream girl was having face of Janvi now. And also my phone was full of romantic songs now. If by mistakenly any sad song used to play on radio, then my hands used to run towards my phone to change the channel.

I was also listening the songs with full of feelings and with the imagination where I used to imagine myself at position of hero in song and her as the heroine. We had also started dedicating songs to each other. But she loved my poems more than those songs, as some times poems made her cry too (not because it used to be bad, but due to the efforts I took to write something about her and for her).

My poems had become more romantic too. Love, relation and Janvi were only topic to write about. Lectures had become place to write poems, and think about her.

This one is a Marathi poem, written when I was thinking about the night of 14 Feb.:

Hee hawa…
Athavan janu tichya sahavasachi
Hee nasha…
Veglich ek tichya shwasachi.

Bedhuuund kari…
Oth te tiche gulabi sharabi
Tu maazi pari
Sparsh tuza hava havasa malahi.

Gaal tiche… kamalache,
Pakalich janu kase laale laal.
Tapore te… dole tiche,
Paahatach mann hoi kshanat halal.

Shabd tiche… aikatach,
Waate janu amrutachi god vani.
Jaadu tichi… ashi chale,
Jaadu jashi kari ek pari rani.

Kes tiche… kale kale,
Chaal jashi kalya kalya naginichi.
Yauwan te… baharnare,
Ruup janu jagatachya swaminiche.

Hee hawa…
Athavan janu tichya sahavasachi
Hee nasha…
Veglich ek tichya shwasachi.

It says:
This breeze is giving me memory of her company.
Her breath is giving me a different hangover.
Her pink and soft lips are driving me crazy.
You are none other than my angel, and I am willing to have your touch.
Her cheeks are red like petal of lotus.
Her eyes are big and when I see them, it kills my heart in a fraction of second.
Her words are like sweet treat of nectar to ear.
She brings her magic on, like a queen of angels spreads her magic.
Her dark black hairs are like a walk of black poisonous snake.
And her blooming adolescence makes me feel like she is having the beauty like she is the queen of this world.

7. The First Meet

❄ ❄ ❄

It had been 2 weeks to our relationship, and we both were so dying to meet each other. I was helpless to go to Beed and meet her, as I had already bunked my college for marriage and my attendance was not even close to 75%. But she was not listening. She said they were having some holiday for two days, Saturday and Sunday. So she wanted to come to Aurangabad to meet me. I agreed on Sunday.

As much as I remember, that was the first Sunday of my whole life when I woke up so early. Or I can say that I didn't even sleep whole night in excitement of seeing her. After my school days, may be the first time I saw that big yellow thing popping up slowly to spread light in all over the world. It was more beautiful to see. After so many years, I had seen the sunrise.

I called her, she was getting ready. She told me that she would be in Aurangabad in next three and half hour. In addition, she told me that Bhumi was coming with her as she had told her that she was going to Aurangabad for buying their medical instruments, hence Bhumi insisted to come and she could not resist her.

Whatever, I was getting ready for Janvi. It was feeling like so many things were happening for the first time in life. First time I woke up early on Sunday, first time I was so excited to meet Janvi that I was dying to see her, and first time I was wondering how would I look in front of her, hence first time I was getting ready for her. I had completely forgotten that she was my best friend, she knows me very well, I didn't need to do something more to impress her. But *dil to bachha hai ji... dil hai ke manata nai...*

I set the clock and went to take bath. I took bath and washed my face like hundred times. I didn't care about closing that tap well, as I didn't want to be late. I took Mahi's gel to apply on my hair, but then rejected, as it felt too greasy. And because of that I had to wash my hair again. Then I tried so hard to set my hair with comb, without comb, with fingers and palm but, didn't work. God! I hate my curly hair!

I aaplied some powder on my face followed by some men's fairness cream, I applied powder 'again'. Then I searched for my deo. I found my deodorant bottle was empty. HOLY SHIT! I felt like I was going to my final exam and I'd lost my pen and hall-ticket together. It was Sunday morning. All the stores were closed to buy new pen, I mean hall ticket. Oh sorry, I meant deo! I ran to next room, which was Mahi's classmate's room. 'Prashant bhaiya, do you have a deodorant? I want it urgently.' I asked him.

'*Pagal hai kya, tu*? I do not share my deo with anyone.' He said in his regular arrogance. I took out 100-rupee note and threw it towards him and said, 'I am taking your bottle of deo.' He didn't oppose then, as he got 100 rupees for an almost empty bottle.

I worked that deo out full to *paisa vasul*. Each and every cell of my body was washed in that deo. Even my nails, my hair, my legs and my…

Never mind!

I took out my newest dress to wear, took out shoes, but the socks were so stinky. I sprayed deo inside my shoes too. But stinky socks! I remembered Mahi had washed his socks last night as he was going to watch movie. I took his socks and wore my shoes.

We were having a small mirror in our room. Almost like a 7 inch screen. I saw my each and every angle of in that mirror, my shirting, my face, my hair, and my shoes. And finally I was ready, an hour before of her arrival.

****

I was already at the Cidco bus stop. The powder, cream and powder, which I had applied on my face, was starting to wash off due to the hot sun and sweat. In addition to that the '*chanewale, pani bottle wale*' had irritated me more there. The crowd at bus stop was not going to decrease and those small kids would not take a breath from their crying. The crying was not enough for my frustration level, hence the announcer was yelling after every minute in that speaker announcing the bus numbers. I know, that is his job, but why the hell is he not announcing that my Janvi's bus has arrived?

There were so many buses arriving and many left. But Janvi's bus had not arrived yet. I was waiting for her eagerly. I was dying to see her.

And finally, I saw a bus from Beed. As soon as that bus stopped at platform, my excitement reached to its top level, my heartbeats raised in happiness. I felt like there was fountain spraying hot water inside my body. I took a deep breath.

That's it! It was the time when I was going to see Janvi. Not my best friend Janvi. Now she was my love Janvi, my girlfriend Janvi.

Bus stopped and as usual, all the passengers gathered to increase the crowd and catch their seats, by putting and throwing their handkerchiefs and *Gandhi topis* on seats. I saw Bhumi making her way through the crowd. She gave me a smile and I waved to say hi, but I was searching for Janvi. And finally, she appeared.

After seeing her, I felt like the entire world stood still. I had come to receive her so many times and I swear to god, I never felt like this before. I could see her walking towards me like time was running in slow motion. Her hair was clipped by one single clip taking bunch of hair from front to back and few of them were left free to fall on her face. Her face shined in the shiny sun of morning, and her earrings were moving back and forth with her every step. Those long earrings made her look more beautiful. She had worn a simple golden chain. I don't know again, which dress she was wearing but, it was white coloured with some very girly design on it. After looking her, all I felt was…

(Marathi poem)

Aaj janu pahilyandach pahile mi tila,
Jagachahi visar padla, mazya ya budhhila.

Mazyakade baghun jevha teene dili god smile,
Kaljat mazya premachi, upload zali file.

Udnare kes tiche, janu pahatach rahave,
Chhatitun nighun mann, tichya magech dhave.

Gulabachya paklyach janu, oth tiche gulabi,
Dolyanmadhe ahe veglich, nasha ek sharabi.

Masolichya akarache dole tiche tapore,
Tanhulya balasarkhe, gaal gore gore.

Tanhya bala pekshahi hasane tiche god,
Hasatach rahave teene, ashi mannala odh.

Kokilepekshahi ahe god ticha avaj,
Saundaryacha tichya, ek vegalach ahe saaj.

Chuka kadhnya sarkhe tichyat kahich navhte waait,
Tila pahun punha zala mala, love at first sight.

When I saw her, I felt like I was seeing her for the first time today. She gave me a lovely cheerful smile and I lost my all senses. One would love to just watch her hair flying with the air, like waves of sea. Her lips were pink and so soft like lotus. Her eyes were giving me a strong hangover with that big fishy shape. Her cheeks were fair like a newborn baby's. And her smile was so killer, and sweeter than a small baby. There was nothing wrong in her to point out. I felt like I was falling in love with her again and again, it was feeling like love at first sight.

****

Well, making her way from crowd, she came to me, and said, 'Hi, *mujhe bohat bhuk lagi he*, but first of all lets go to Gulmandi, this is the address, and we want to buy our instruments first.'

Wow! What a ROMANTIC visit!

Well, we headed towards Gulmandi, the famous and crowded market in Aurangabad. We reached there in auto rickshaw, and wandered while searching for the address. Finally we found it and I felt relieved. They bought some stuff, their medical stuff.

We then went to take some meal and Janvi ordered a kachori.

'That's it? I thought you were too hungry.' I asked her.

'Hmm. But if I ate too much suddenly then I might get a reaction, hence light meal. And you should also not eat too much, especially in this sun.' She said as usual, with her well maintaining behaviour.

Whatever, Bhumi and I ate full to *paisa vasul*, and then went to drink juice. I wished to take one glass of juice with two straws, for me and Janvi. But Bhumi was with us so I could not.

'If your work here is done, then shall we go to movie?' I asked them.

'Yeah, I wish, but Janvi won't come.' Bhumi said and I looked at her with confused look. She continued, '*Memsaheb ne kasam khai he*, that she would watch movie in theatre with her special one only. God knows, who her special one is! We are tired insisting her to watch movie with us.' She said and I got flattered.

'Really Janvi?' I asked her and she winked at me with a smile. *Sahich na…!!*, I thought.

We left the place and I was thinking about what Bhumi said. I felt like… soo… I felt sooo…… *bhaari*. And ashamed as I didn't swear something like that for her. 'That's it! Here onwards, I will not watch movie unless I see it with her.' I swore to myself.

We wandered in Gulmandi for some time. I liked the way Janvi was walking with me, wrapping her hand around my arm and, as I was taller than her, my shadow was covering her from the sun. Rather she was walking under my shadow all the time to avoid sun. I felt so *bhari* again as I was being her protector. And if she had to talk some thing, she used to pull my sleeve down so that I would come to her height and she could speak in my ear.

Bhumi had to go somewhere to meet one of her friends, so she took our leave for few hours. And we got some privacy.

'That was so sweet.' I started talking with Janvi.

'What?'

'That you swore about the movie.' I said while blushing.

'Hmm.' she said and rested on my arm.

'So? Shall we go for movie now?' I asked her as we were alone.

'No. I mean, I would love to but, it's already 12:45 and we have to leave at 3.'

'What? Why?' I asked quickly as thought of her going away from me ran into my mind and gave me an ache.

'You know, our hostel. We have to reach there before 7:30 and the route is of almost 3 and half hours.' She answered while clutching my arm.

'*Nahi yaar*! You are going so early.' I got upset.

'I know dear. That's why I want to spend this whole time with you alone.' She said and I pulled her close.

'Bittu, we are on street. Let's go some where to sit.' She said and tried to get away from me. 'And by the way deodorants are to spray on body, not to take bath with it.' She suggested while pushing me. I realized I had sprayed so much deo on me.

We decided to go to *Sambhaji udhyan*, a well-known garden near central bus stop. We took rickshaw and headed there. In auto rickshaw, she rested on my shoulder and while leaving a sigh she said, 'Oh God! I missed you like hell, Bittu.'

I ran my arm around her and made her comfortable to sit. Taking her into my arm, I hugged her from one side and rested my cheek on her head. Fragrance of her hair made me feel like heaven and reminded me the night I kissed her first time, the Valentine's night. I kissed her on forehead.

'Do you remember that night?' She asked me while holding me tightly.

'Wow, you just stole my whole sentence. How would I forget it? It is like the best night ever in my whole life.'

'Yeah, for me too, but what were you thinking there? How did you dare to kiss me?' She teased me.

'I didn't kiss you first. You hugged me and held me so tight. What would any normal guy do at this situation?' I defended myself.

'Oh really? But it doesn't mean to kiss me.' She said with sarcasm in her voice and making her eyes tiny.

'Ok baba, I dare to kiss you. You want to see how?' I said and turned my face towards her and she gave me naughty smile and pushed me back signaling and pointing towards driver and laughing silently. I gave her a 'whatever look' and pulled her again. I ran my fingers from her cheek to her neck so softly and she closed her eyes tilting her neck. I grabbed her, took her close to me and she clutched my shoulder. Then I looked at her lips, and resting my palm on her cheek, I ran my thumb on her lips to make the mood sexier. She came closer to me and uplifted her neck to touch my lips. I closed my eyes and was ready to kiss her…

'Ouch…', '*Bhenc***…' we both screamed as rickshaw bumped into a big pothole screwing the mood. I wished to complete my word for driver, but controlled myself. Then I deeply realized why people always abuse the government for roads. For that moment, I also hated government like hell.

Well, we reached the garden. As we entered, we could see the garden was crowded, as it was Sunday. Lots of kids were playing on lawn.

We crossed the small wooden bridge and headed to sit, where all the lovebirds preferred to sit. I saw the senior citizens sitting on benches keeping eye on their grandchildren playing. Few of them were enjoying the ride of small train inside the garden. There was a zoo and an aquarium too, but we did not want to waste our time in sight seeing or watching wild animals. We hardly had a few hours; we wanted that time for ourselves.

We got a place to sit. I remembered the time when I used to go there with Purvi, and we used to sit in section of couples. We were not even 18 then. And hence, what stress and fear it was to meet there, in alone far from home! I reminisced the situation when some random guys had caught us both once. We were just sitting and they came and asked us for our IDs in tough voice, and we almost cried there.

Actually, I was the one who almost cried. I chuckled on myself for how stupid and timid I was!

'So, what's up?' she asked so formally.

'What?' I reacted controlling my smile.

'Nothing, I just wanted to get you OUT of your memories. I am Janvi by the way. If you remember me.' She said sarcastically.

'Come on, Chiku. I was not in any memories, I was just thinking about the kiss which didn't happen in the rickshaw.' I defended.

'Hmm. By the way, may be you forgot, but still, hi, I am Janvi, your evil best friend first, who knows you very well.' She said while uplifting her left eyebrow and I didn't have any answer for this.

She removed her gaze from me to avoid me in anger, as I was thinking about Purvi when Janvi was with me. So, I put my arm around her and said, 'Sorry na, Chiku. You love me na?'

She sneered and said, 'Not at all.'

'Listen, yaar I am sorry. I love you. It just came into my mind.' I tried to convince her but she was not ready to get convinced, so I continued, 'Come on, yaar. We have just few hours to spend with each other, and you are wasting it in being angry. And also, your friend had slapped you on your butt. I had forgiven that.' I said something in my defense, and as soon as I said it, she turned towards me with mouth opening wide, and eyes shocked, 'What? Are you still on THAT?'

'How could I forget it? Even I'd never slap you or Purvi.'

'Bittu, I left talking with him as soon as you got angry, I don't even speak with him now.' She defended getting hyper.

'Oh really?' I asked in sarcasm.

'Yes.' She answered in same tone.

'Oh, really?' I asked in normal confirmation.

'YES. And even Bhumi, Pradnya, Sunil and Vinit had gone to trip yesterday, but I didn't. Just because of you, as Vinit was there. They went and I just wasted my day at hostel. They had fun and I got bored. They saw waterfall and I? I made water to fall from my eyes.'

'Ok, ok. But why are we fighting?'

'Because......, because...... I don't remember. But I was angry on you.' She said so stupidly but I loved it.

'Ok then. I am sorry. And I will never ever do it again.' I apologized while laughing inside.

'You better remember that.' She said still reminding why she was angry.

'Ok, baba. I will not do a single thing again, which will make you angry.' I said and ran my arm around her and she rested her head on my shoulder.

'Anyway, I am participating in dance competition in our annual function.' I gave her my news.

'Wow! But *nachna ata he kya tujhe*?' Still an angry voice.

'Well, I had danced once in Ganpati function, and though I am not doing it solo. My friend gave me one of our seniors' number. He is a part of the dance group, some 'sizzlers' dance group. I hope they will teach me there something.'

'What is 'sizzlers'?'

'I don't know the meaning. It is the name of that dance group.'

'Hmm, that's great, all the best for it. I would like to see you dancing.' She wished me.

We were talking and she got message from Bhumi, and she replied that she will meet her at Cidco bus stop at about 3 o'clock.

As soon as she typed 3 o'clock, my heart felt like crying. I saw time, it was 1:20pm, it meant we were having only one and half hour and 10 minutes left to spend together, out of which some we'll waste in looking for rickshaw and bus. And also, some of it I have already wasted in thinking about it.

She finished her message and looked at me, 'What happened?' She asked, while putting her palm on my cheek. Oh god! I felt like now I should join my heart to cry.

'You are going so early. I don't want you to go.' As soon as I finished my sentence, she came closer to me jumped up and kissed me wrapping her hand around my neck.

I held her from back and supported her. I pushed my tongue deep inside her throat and held her so tightly. She was holding me more firmly with every passing second. Slowly, slowly we got aware that we were in a public garden. Our hug became loose. She rested on my chest after kissing and hugged me.

'Bittu.' She said softly.

'Hmm?'

'Now you will never remember her here. Now this place is only in the memory of our first kiss in Aurangabad.' She said softly.

'What? You remember why were you angry then?'

'Do you want me to get angry again?' She said lifting her head and seeing into my eyes.

'No. I am sorry. I love you soooooo much.' I said and kissed on her forehead and wiped her tears.

'And, I hadn't forgotten then also, I just not wanted to spoil the time in fighting because of her. It was so meaningless.'

'Hmm, I know.' I said and we sat there holding each other's hand and looking towards our palms aimlessly, rubbing fingers and drawing some imaginary lines by it.

Time was running like in an Olympic race. We talked, we laughed, we teased, we fought, we went silent, and we teased again, then we kissed and we talked again.

Well, we sat there for an hour and decided to go to Osmanpura, the area where we spent our 11th and 12th standard days. We went from our classes and then towards my former rented flat, her hostel and the temple where we used to meet whenever she wanted to cry. We recalled our old memories and she refreshed every place, replaced Purvi from my memories, and created her own new memories.

Her mobile beeped due to Bhumi's message, and we saw the time. It was 2:45 already.

'Oh shit!' She screamed as she saw the time.

'What? That's it? Are you leaving me?' I started being emotional.

'Sorry, shona. I have to go let's go fast. Bhumi is waiting there.' She was panicking.

'Ok, ok. Don't panic. We still have time.' I tried to calm her down.

'No, we have to leave now. I hope we would get rickshaw soon.' She said while walking already, rather running.

We reached to Osmanpura circle and got an auto rickshaw. While in auto, I was depressed and she was panicking. I was looking at her and she was looking at watch. I was saying 'don't go', she was saying, '*bhaiyya tej chalao*'. I was holding her hand, she was showing me time. And, at last we reached to Cidco bus stop.

Bhumi was already there, standing in front of a bus that was going to Beed.

'Where have you been? I was waiting for you. Come on, this one is our bus.' She said and headed for the seats.

She went ahead and Janvi said bye to me, while holding my hand. Bhumi called her from window, asking to come fast. My heartbeat increased. I thought, why? Why, why, why? Why does clock has 3 on it. What if today's 3 o'clock was skipped? Why did today's 3 o'clock come so early? For that moment, I hated that 3 o'clock like hell. In fact, for sake of moment, I would have supported Pakistan in India Vs Pakistan match, but there was no single chance to forgive that 3 o'clock. (No, no I am kidding. I would not have supported Pak in India Vs Pak match.)

I just stared in her eyes, and pulling her hand, I went close to her, and kissed on her forehead. As soon as I kissed on her forehead and closed my eyes, Bhumi's yelling had gone silent, that announcer's mike had like broken suddenly and there were no announcements or noise of passengers anymore. All I could hear was, my fast heartbeats. With my kiss, she squeezed my hand and stood still. I had forgotten the place where we were standing, I did not care about people who were watching, and I did not fear anybody asking us for our IDs. I wasn't 16 or 17 anymore I was totally above 18. But in spite of these things, moreover I was thinking about Janvi, she was going. She was going to leave in few minutes or seconds. Hence, I didn't want to waste those last moments.

I opened my eyes and looked at her. Her eyes were wet already. Few tears dropped from her eyes making way to her feelings. She looked down and tied scarf to hide her expressions.

'Bittu, I love you so much.' She said softly, words hardly making their way from her mouth as she was silently sobbing.

'I love you too, Janvi.' I replied.

'And I HATE bus stops.' She said so angrily reminding me how she had cried at Ambad's bus stop and here also. I just smiled. She also smiled mixing her sob in it and wiping her tear, 'Keep smiling like that.' She added.

'Hmm.' I nodded and she started walking towards door.

She went and sat in the bus. Bhumi didn't say any thing. Janvi sat at window seat to watch me. Her bus started and she didn't even flip her eyelid. I started walking with the bus slowly, slowly. Bus was going reverse. Bus went out side the bus stop and stopped at a corner. I ran to see Janvi one more time again. I have already told you that 'Android' was yet to be invented in India, hence we had to wait so long to see each other as there were no social apps like today we have. And also, I had a Chinese mobile, so you can imagine my condition.

Well, I ran to see her again, but I didn't find her at her seat. I got scared. I ran to other side of bus but the bus left. I was looking in all windows, but I couldn't see her. And when bus left, I saw her right in front of me standing with her bag and Bhumi waving me 'hi, again.'

I got surprised and was smiling like a stupid. I ran towards her and hugged her. Bhumi went to washroom, and we sat at the platform.

'What, how? Why? Wh…' I was just happy, struggling with my words.

'Nothing, I just couldn't go further. Bhumi said that you love me so much.' She explained.

'What? How did she know?' I got shocked.

'According to her, at such situations, when a person kisses you on your forehead without any fear of people, then that's true love, and not lust. Kiss on lips means lust, while kiss on the forehead shows your love.'

'Yeah, she is absolutely right.' I said and kissed on her forehead again to prove that I love her so much.

'And what about your hostel?' I asked in care.

'We will get another bus, so that we could get few more minutes to spend together.'

Though the time of her departure was shifted by just half hour, but the step she took for me was worth a million for me. We never knew how to regret; hence we lived in the moment always.

****

After half hour she had left again for Beed. I was waiting for her call. It had been 8 o'clock. I had called her in bus but network had cut and she then messaged me after reaching at Beed.

But I was wondering whether she got entered in hostel or not, whether she could reach on time or not. I was calling her and she was cutting it.

After few minutes she picked up my call and talked to me. She seemed so pissed and hyper.

'What happened?' I asked.

'Nothing, this bloody damn rector, our hostel woman, she was not allowing us to enter in hostel.'

'Why? Were you late? I am so sorry yaar.' I felt like it happened because of me.

'No, Bittu. We were on time. But just she wanted to earn some money, bloody thief. She says we are not allowed to wander without permission. And we didn't give her application.' She spoke in high tone and anger for that woman.

'Hadn't you?' I asked, and Bhumi grabbed phone from her, 'We had Bittu, but at morning there was different woman, and this one says she didn't told her about our application. Is this our fault?' Bhumi screamed.

'Ok, ok. Calm down now. You are in your room now, right? Then what is the big deal. Forget it.' I tried to calm her down.

'It is a big deal. She was trying to extort money from us as a fine for it and that also without receipt. Bloody shameless, *uski maaki aankh, uski bhe...'* Bhumi was getting hyper.

'Hey, hey control. Even I don't abuse some one with mother's words yaar.'

'Ok, sorry. *Uski bhains ki pucnh, tichya nanachi tang*!' She continued anyway. I didn't know whether I should have laughed or cried at her situation.

'Wow, Bhumi. You've learnt some bad words in Marathi.' I said.

'Hmm, Janvi taught me *nanachi tang*.' She admitted

'*Sahich naa...!*' I said and laughed.

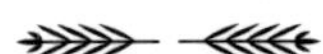

8. Things changed

❄ ❄ ❄

Well, finally I was relieved that they'd reached to their hostel on time. In these all, I had forgotten to call my senior for group dance competition. I dialed his number from my china phone.

'Hello?' A soft voice of a girl came from next side.

'Err, hello, myself Karan. Is this Amit's number? I want to talk him about dance competition.' I spoke somehow, while I could hear sound of counting like, 5, 6, 7, 8. She started calling Amit, and he came.

'Hello? Who is this?' He asked.

'Hello sir, I am Karan. My friend Akshay gave me your number. I wanted to participate in group dance.' I said.

'Umm, ok. We have already started practice, but still you can come tomorrow at 6 am. Do you know our hall?' He asked so gently.

'No sir.' I was still feeling awkward didn't know why.

'It's FF101, near MCA dept. in college. Ok?'

'Ok sir, I'll be there.'

'Hmm and two more things; first: DON'T BE LATE. And second: stop calling me sir.' He said and I was tensed about being late.

I called Janvi to say good night, but she didn't pick up. She then sent me a message, 'can't talk. Busy now.'

'Ok. Had dinner?' I replied.

'Hmm. Gud ni8.'

'gud night.'

'oye?' She replied so fast.

'what?'

' .. ' she replied and I got smile here. I kissed my phone and replied,

' .. '

****

I slept while thinking about the whole day. Her face was stuck to my eyes. It was in front of me all the time. I just couldn't help it. I was reminding the way she came to me at bus stop, the way she walked with me on the street and the *kiss we missed* and kiss we did. After every few minutes, I was repeating the same scene again and again. Like, it had taped and played on repeat mode. I was smiling so foolishly. The night was passing in thinking about her and dreaming of her.

I wished she were with me. I wished she were sleeping with my hand as her pillow. I wished I could pat her and treat her like a baby. I wished to kiss her on her forehead because I love her, as Bhumi said (although I wanted to kiss her on lips too).

I closed my eyes and started picturing her, imagining that she was sleeping beside me. I could feel the fragrance of her hair flying on my face. I took a deep breath in feeling those things and with childish smile I hugged my pillow. I opened my eyes to kiss the pillow where I saw Mahi staring me weirdly. I just stood still in position, reminding something to give excuse for, but didn't recall anything.

'Do you want to go to bathroom? Or should I go outside for few minutes?' He asked me with that weird look, and continued, 'Dude, do whatever you want to do, just don't ruin my blanket or bed.'

I just stared in awkwardness and took my mobile to message Janvi.

'Wake me up at 5:30. Miss u so much.

..'

****

Well I woke up at 5:45am with her call. I had picked up her call in sleep and she started crying like a baby in sleepy voice, 'Aaaa, umhhm umhhm why did you pick up my call? Now wake up and hang my phone. I am so tired to press the red button.' She said. I always loved her childish cry and sleepy voice.

I went to college for dance practice. I searched for the hall and got entered. As much as I remember, I was just 7 minutes late for the practice. However, Amit made me swear that it was my first and last chance to be late.

'Anyway, it's your first day, but remember, this could be the last day if you come late again.' These were his exact words.

'Yes sir.' I nodded like a school student.

'I think you forgot both things I told you, listen again. First: never come late, and second: don't call me sir. You can call me 'bhaiya' and be comfortable.' He said and called another boy who was his junior but my senior, 'Rishabh, come here, this is Karan from F.E. teach him that Marathi song.' Rishabh took me with the bunch of boys who were with me in that song. He became my first dance teacher.

I was surrounded by strangers, to whom I had not even seen till then and I was going to dance with them. How would that be possible? I told my doubt to Rishabh to whom I started calling 'Rishabh bhai' later. He introduced me with other group members. Amit bhaiya, Amar bhaiya, Maddy bhai, were from last year. Harshit bhai, Ajit bhaiya, and Rishabh bhai were from second year. There were some girls too. In total, it was a group of 18 members including me. Rishabh bhai was impressed with my fast learning skill. And a girl to whom I'd rarely talked but she seemed so annoying, came to me and said, 'Listen you, my name is Pranjali. And I am also from first year. So please, please, PLEASE, for god's sake stop calling me 'didi'. I am not that old.' I didn't know whether I should have laughed on it or feel awkward. What would have I done? It was the outcome of my town!

Anyway, everything went well. While in break, Amit bhaiya told me that how old this group was, and Ganesh sir, founder of this dance group gave name 'Sizzlers' to this group. In no time, I became one of them. It was so pleasant to meet someone new and be a part of a group. The only time where I used to feel that I was junior was the water time. They used to say that they don't rag us and they will never, but at least as F.E. students we should respect them by bringing water for them.

****

I could rarely talk with Janvi as my schedule had become a bit busy. The time at which I used to call her was covered with dance practice now. And I had to bunk my last lecture for calling her.

I called her and she seemed so pissed off.

'Hey, what is wrong?' I asked.

'Nothing, just these unknown numbers! I hate it. I was trying to sleep and someone is calling me and when I pick it up no one talks from the other side.' She narrated.

'Ok. Can you tell me that number?'

'Leave it, don't worry...' she said and screamed suddenly, '... wait, wait, wait. Here it is. I think it is on waiting. I will pick it up and conference it. If again same thing happens, then you talk, ok?'

'Hmm.' I said and then she picked that call and switched to conference call.

'Hello? Who is this?' She started.

'Janvi, are you deaf? How many times I've called you.' Some guy talked from another side.

'I didn't get any voice here. May be you should have tried calling from some place where network comes.' She spoke like she recognized his voice.

'Ok, ok. I called you because...' He said and stopped.

'What?' she asked and then he changed his tone took a nosedive,

'I was clutching my hand. It was reminding me how strongly you squeezed it today. Were you really that much excited?' He said and suddenly my call cut. Obviously, she cut it.

I was so crashed. What did he just said? What was he talking about? Oh yes, he was Vinit. I recognized him. He was the one who pinches her in public, and...

What the fuck! His one sentence made me feel so terrible. Why Janvi was squeezing his hand? What did he mean? Does he still do those things? And Janvi started it too?

I was out of my control. I was so angry. So many thoughts came into my mind. I tried to call her back.

'*The number you have dialed is on another...*' I didn't even hear full sentence of that operator and cut. I knew she was talking with him. I was so freaking out. My hand started shivering due to anger, my breath became faster. She had told me that she doesn't talk to him now, so what was this all? Did she lie to me?

I was so angry when Janvi called me.

'What? You got time for me now?' I spoke in anger.

'Come on Bittu. First listen to me.'

'Why? Why should I listen to you? Ha? So that you will lie

something again?'

'No. You are misunderstanding. Listen to me first.' She sounded nervous.

'Janvi, you cut that call, it leads me to the truth. I don't think there is any explanation required now.' I was so angry, didn't even wish to hear her voice.

'Please, Bittuuu…' She was speaking and I cut her call.

I started picturing what must have happened, and how she would have squeezed his hand and why? I started imagining. She was calling and I was cutting her calls. After so many times of cutting her call I called her when she sent me a message,

'my bf Karan has fought with me again. He misunderstood something. I need my best friend to talk. Bittu I need you.'

Why? I mean, why I promised her about our best friendship. I always had to forget my anger with her this type of messages.

'BOL.' I said in anger.

'Listen na yaar. Please don't misunderstand. We were in lab…'

'Chiku, I don't want to hear about it. You said you needed your best friend hence I called you.'

'O K. Hmm. I understand. So, Bittu you know…?'

'No I don't know.' I interrupted as usual.

'Listen na. My boyfriend Karan, is such a stupid guy. He is angry on me just because of any other guy…'

'May be, he is angry because you might have lied to him. Or may've hidden something from him.' I said with a huff. She chuckled there and said, 'No, but he is not giving me a chance to explain. Will you please tell him that I didn't lie or hide anything? Actually, he didn't talk to me today. So I was in practical, and was texting him that I missed him so much, and there this guy, Vinit…'

'Who pinches you and slaps you and you squeeze his hand.' I interrupted.

'No! This guy, Vinit who was standing beside me… just for the sake of roll numbers… saw my phone… and to tease me… he started calling professor, to tell that I was using my phone in the middle of practicals. Therefore, to make him quiet, I shushed him and squeezed his hand. That's it. And I don't know why, but he just teases me always and flirts with me. And I guess that's why he was talking like that on phone then.' She narrated the story.

'Hmm, then why don't you tell him that you have your best friend and boyfriend too? And all these things have patented to me only.'

'I swear to mom, Bittu that's what I was telling him just now when you were on waiting.' She acknowledged and I imagined her taking her throat skin in pinch to swear.

'Yeah, Whatever!' I said, realizing my anger is going down.

'So, are we ok now?' She asked.

'I don't know. See, I had not told you to leave him as friend, but now I seriously think that you should not talk to him anymore. It's not like, I am commanding you something, but I just want to protect my relationship. I've never been angry with you like this. But since this guy came, I have fought with you twice because of him. I hope you understand.'

'Hmm, I do. And I promise I will do as you said. I love you so much Bittu.' She said and I got a smile.

'I love you too.' I said and continued with chuckle, 'Wow, its funny how you started to talk with your best friend and now you are talking with your boyfriend.'

'Am I? Really? I lovvee youuuuuu. Ummmahhh, muhhhhhha.' She said so cheerfully. I just love the way she says it. And I just HATE that guy.

****

I started feeling the difference in friendship and love. I was kind of enjoying it. I did come to realize the real meaning of different dialogues of different romantic movies. I started experiencing what really the every moment of every second of every minute of… every day is.

'I can't live without you. I always think about you, each and every moment of every second I think of you.' These types of dialogues were becoming a part of my life. There was no single second where I didn't think of her, not a single breath which I took without remembering her.

If I used to be free, I would think what she might be doing. If I used to be in dance practice, I used to think if she was here to watch me dancing. If I used to be in bed, I wished she was sleeping with me, hugging me and resting on my chest. If I used to watch a movie, I wished she was the heroine and I was her hero. Yeah, she was. If I used to eat a meal, I wished if she was feeding me. If I was in bathroom taking bath, I wished if she was there to give me my towel. And, if I was in toilet....

No, no! Nothing, I didn't wish anything there. I need my privacy there.

Everyday, every single moment I was dying to talk to her. I was not winning any competition in dreams now. I didn't want to be the rockstar with some electric guitar in my hand anymore. I didn't wish cheering fans of me. All I dreamt was about the night we spent together, the 14th Feb.'s night. The time we enjoyed together, the bus she left for me.

I couldn't help it. Her beautiful face was in front of my eyes all the time. Her big fishy eyes fixed in front of me. I used to recall our first kiss of that night. No romantic scene from any movie, none of the Imran Hashmi's kisses or any of the porn movie's scene was able to compare with that one kiss. It was priceless. Unbelievable, unforgettable, and it was so memorable.

I wished she were there when I was performing. I was practicing so hard. I requested her to come for my college's annual function to which they had named, 'Razzmatazz'. I don't know about studies, but we students are pretty much cool to title something. Right?

****

It was our performance day. She had arrived with Bhumi and Pradnya. I had only one guest pass, but I could not let them hang around somewhere outside. So one of my friends from Sizzlers gave me his pass and I took Pranjali's ID card to get one of them entry on it.

J.N.E.C. is really strict about its rules. They don't allow external students for gatherings or functions without permission. Anyhow, they entered and enjoyed a lot. 'Razzamatazz' is really such an awesome event of my college. The design and decoration of the whole stage and the surrounding was done so beautifully, by architecture department students. The lights and the special effects, the crowd handling final year students and the discipline committee and all the organizers made it look awesome. Moreover, of course, we performers made the night tremendously entertaining and enjoying.

Well, they enjoyed a lot in Razzmatazz and none other than,

we Sizzlers won the first prize.

After prize distribution finished we headed outside to drink juice. Bhumi had already told Manav that they were in Aurangabad. So till then he had arrived to meet them in Aurangabad.

I saw the time, it was 11:30 pm. I asked Janvi where they had planned to stay for the night. 'I thought you planned it.' She said with surprised eyes.

'What? No I didn't, I thought you.... Anyway, don't worry, I will figure out something.' I said somehow to avoid panic. I called Mahi and told him to go somewhere else for a night. I didn't tell him that I was bringing girls to our room.

Plus, I was not allowed to bring any guests to my hostel room. We were 6 people and my room was really small. It was just perfect for two people.

I took them from back gate, silently like thieves and entered the room. My heartbeat increased. I was so tensed. Not like, Ihaven't had a girl in my room before. But it was almost 2 years before. And we were 6 people including me, Janvi, Bhumi, Pradnya, Manav and his friend.

We entered and were relieved for a moment. Girls went to get fresh one by one. Manav told me that he would tell Bhumi at midnight that he loved her. But Ifeared my watchman. 'If he saw us or if he came to know that we were here tonight, then I would have to leave this hostel. We have to leave early in morning.' I told Manav. He thought for a while and decided to go to *Shirdi*. I was not that much sure about it, but he convinced me so hard, as he wanted to spend time with Bhumi. I had no other option.

I had already spent all my money on dance competition and monthly expenses. I had to borrow money from one of my friend, Vijay. I took money from him and we headed towards the railway station. *Chori-chori, chupkese* like thieves we got out again and some how half way by walking and half way by paying triple to rickshaw, we at last reached the station.

Manav collected money from all and went to get the tickets. Train was at about 2:30am. It was my first time at railway station in midnight. I enjoyed it a lot.

After some time I got a message from my friend that next day results would be out. I got tensed. I put my hand on my chest and started patting it. (All is well, all is well. No, no. Aal izz well, aal izz well, aal izz well.)

We had about an hour left for train to come. It was totally a secret trip. None of my friends or my family members knew about it. Not even Mahi.

I was kind of tensed about it. Already my father was opposing me to participate in dance as I had to bunk my classes for dance practice. Though I had participated. And after doing that, I was out for a trip without telling him. In addition to this, I had received message from my friend about result.

****

We were sitting in waiting room at railway station. Manav was busy with Bhumi, his friend was busy in his mobile. Janvi had to stay with Pradnya as she was a stranger and Janvi had brought her with them. And I was so tensed.

Janvi saw me tensed and came to ask me what the matter was. I told her all the things I was worried about.

'Don't worry shona. It's your lucky time now. See, you got the first prize in dancing. You will clear your exam too.' She consoled me.

'No, it's not like...'

'See, there is a saying, what we sow, is what you'll reap. So don't worry. You will clear it.'

'And what if I didn't sow anything?' I said with hopeless face.

'What do you mean?' She raised her voice a bit bouncing her eyebrows.

'I meant I know already that I will have 2 subjects back *definitely*.' I said so *confidently*, 'And it's not my lucky time. We had practiced so hard to win the competition, but I hadn't done sufficient study.'

'What? Are you kidding me?' She got a bit angry.

'Now why are you getting angry?'

'*Toh kya teri PUJA karu?*' She yelled with her horror face.

'Hey... I... um... listen...'

'WHAT? Stop struggling with your words and tell me that at least this time you were preparing good for exams from starting, when you already knew that you will get backlogs.' She was talking like my father.

I didn't know what to say. I felt like I was giving prelims of scolding of my father. I changed my expressions to as cute as I could and said, 'Chiku, my girlfriend is angry with me, I need my best…'

'Shut the fuck up! And stop making fake faces.' She screamed and continued, 'I am the best friend one who is talking right now, and I swear if you got backlogs I will screw you before aunty and uncle.' She said and I thought, may be I need a new best friend.

'Hey, look. Manav is sitting at wrong side. He is sitting at the north corner.' I made up something to distract her attention but didn't work. She gave me her famous angry look by making her big eyes so tiny.

'You'll never change.' She said and left the room in anger. I had to follow her as it was after midnight and we were at railway station. Moreover, India is such a safe place where a girl can 'obviously wander alone at night', right?

Manav saw me following her and got relieved and continued with Bhumi, thinking that it was our regular fight.

I went to her and she said, 'By the way, sitting on north side is ok. Sleeping is not allowed, because we burn dead people facing that side.'

'O…K.' I muttered wondering if she was forgetting her anger. She just gave me a look and then turning her face to west and closing eyes by folding her hands, she prayed something.

'Oh right, at this time sun would be to that side.' I said stupidly to start our normal conversation.

'Idiot, that's the side where Shirdi is. I was praying to *Sai baba*.'

'Ok, whatever. I am hungry. I'll get some samosas.' I went to get two plates samosa. I bought for both of us.

'I am not eating anything.' She said.

'Why? You were hungry, right? Due to our gathering you also might be empty stomach.'

'I just prayed *Sai baba*, and wished something for which I will go to Shirdi with bare feet and empty stomach.'

'Why?'

'You can't understand, leave it.'

'Whatever.' I said and ate both plates of samosas, as I can't control my hunger at all. It kills me.

'*Bhukkad*!' She said irritatingly while I was eating her plate too.

While I was eating my last bite, Janvi suddenly came closer to me and clutched my arm.

'What? Do you want to kiss me now?' I said with mouth full of samosa.

'Shut up!' She whispered, and signaled at my back side, 'Those two men were staring at us.' She said and I saw backward. They started heading towards us. As they were coming closer, Janvi was holding my hand so tightly in fear, 'Let's go inside.' She said and we started moving.

'Hey, you wait.' One of them screamed.

'Don't worry, aal izz well, aal izz well.' I started controlling myself from becoming panic.

'Will you SHUT UP?' She whispered.

'What? Did I say it out loud?' I said and saw backward, they were coming closer. Both of them were wearing same white T-shirt and both were well built and having military cut hairstyle. I saw they were wearing khaki pants and police shoes. I got relief. 'Don't worry, they are not bullies. They are police men.' I said to Janvi.

'What?' She seemed shocked, 'That's even worse!' She said in fear.

'Why?'

'What if they made us to call our parents?'

Uh oh! She has a point.

They came to us and asked for our tickets and ID cards. We showed them what they asked for. One of them started screaming in tough voice, 'They have built that waiting room here for passengers. People like you wander around at night inviting crime and then just blame us.'

'Sorry sir. We were here to buy samosas.' I said.

'Its ok, don't worry. Go inside and wait for your train.' Other one said relaxing us.

****

Our train came at 3 o'clock. I loved this 3 o'clock as I was going to travel with my love because of this 3am, unlike that 3pm which was taking my love away from me.

Train was barely filled. We got enough place to sit and sleep in train. Bhumi and Manav were a bit away from us all the time. I was with Janvi all the time, Pradnya was with us too.

Janvi rested on my shoulder to sleep. After little time I also fell asleep resting my cheek on her head.

After like an hour I got up due to some pinching. I saw Janvi was looking at me so angrily. Uh oh! Are results out? Or am I watching a dream? I didn't get it. Then she pointed towards my other shoulder. I saw Pradnya was sleeping on my other shoulder. I got why Janvi was upset. I told her that it wasn't my mistake by lip movements only. She then made her eyes tiny. To calm her down and not to make her more angry I started waking Pradnya up by flapping gently on her cheek. May be Janvi thought that I was patting her to make her comfortable to sleep and hence she got angrier. To take revenge of this, she leaned towards the other passenger to sleep on his thighs, who was absolutely stranger by the way. As soon as she put her head down on his thigh, he woke up as if he got some electric shock or something. I really wanted to laugh on his condition but moreover I was trying to wake Janvi up from his thigh. She opened her eyes and said with sarcasm, 'NO, no. You please carry on, with her.' Then looking at that strangers face suddenly she also felt that electric shock and jumped up to wake from that place up. She was looking at him and me with shocked eyes, and that fellow fell asleep again, as if nothing happened.

'I thought he was Manav.' She said by taking her head in both hands. Then looking again at me gave an angry look. Pradnya was still sleeping. I started blowing her head, like it was going to wake her up. Janvi walked away from there in anger and I quickly stood up to follow her. As I stood up suddenly, Pradnya fell down straight towards that stranger and fell on his thighs. He got an electric shock again, 'What the hell is wrong with you people?' He said.

Such a… what should I say, gay! Giving more importance to his sleep than a girl. Had any girl fallen on my thigh to sleep, I would've really enjoyed it, and acted like nothing happened by not opening my eyes.

'Shhhhh… *sone de na yaar.*' Pradnya said without opening her eyes and putting her forefinger on his lips.

I followed Janvi, she was going towards the door. 'Hey wait.

Are you really committing suicide for such a small reason?' I asked her by holding her hand and pulling her.

'Oh you wish so, I know. But you are not going to get rid of me so easily.' She said, 'I just came here so that you will get some privacy there.'

'Oh come on, Chiku. I didn't even know when she fell asleep on my shoulder.'

'You don't have to specifically mention about shoulder. Seems like you enjoyed it so much.' She said with folding her hands and bouncing her shoulders in air due to possessivnes. 'I don't want to listen anything. Now onwards you are sitting WITH ME, right here in all way. You better remember it.' She ordered me.

'What do you mean? I didn't do anything yaar. It wasn't my fault.'

'I am wandering here with an empty stomach and barefooted for you, and you are enjoying the trip with other girl? How dare you?' She screamed.

'Ok, I am sorry. But what did you wish for?'

'I am not supposed to tell that. Are you sitting with me or not?'

'Ok, ok.' I obeyed and took her close to me and sat there. I liked that she ordered me to sit with her. I knew it was possessiveness, but I loved it. It showed how much she wanted me. I kissed on her forehead and then she rested on my shoulder. There after whole the way we were sitting in door enjoying darkness of the night, stars shining bright, cold feel of breeze and the warmth of the each other.

****

After traveling of 5 to 6 hours we reached the temple. We went to get fresh and all of us had to take bath. After an hour of getting fresh, we were ready. But before going in the queue for paying a visit to God, we decided to take some meal. We all took our breakfast except Janvi.

'Are you serious? Its ok now, we are in Shirdi, you can eat something.' I tried to convince her but she refused it.

'I will not eat anything before seeing *Sai baba.*' She said.

I wished I would have also been empty stomach with her, but I really can't control my hunger.

Well, we ate and got into the queue of temple. After following each others step by step and stop by stop we were one line ahead in an hour. I was worried about Janvi as she was hungry. And in the middle of queue she felt weakness and fainted. We all could not stop with her in the middle of queue so I stopped with her and everyone else went forward so that other people would not get stuck with us. I lifted up Janvi in my arms and then carried her to a corner where they serve water. I insisted her to drink water but she refused it also. I wanted to scold her there but I couldn't.

We got into the queue after few minutes of rest. She was so weak. I was feeling guilty as she was doing it all for me. I asked her to put her feet on my feet and lean back on me whenever queue stops. So that she could get rest. We were walking like *'Do jism ek jaan.'* She put her feet on my feet and I was taking her totally on me. Half way we walked like any dance step and for the other half, I lifted her in my arms. I didn't care about people. She was walking all the way without eating or drinking anything for me, and had I not even taken care of her due to people then I would have ashamed of me.

I felt so proud of us. We were some how completing each other. She was fasting for me where ever I was unable to control my hunger. And she was weak because of it, I was supporting her and carrying her in my arms.

While I was walking with her by lifting her, she was resting on my chest with no care and fear, with a relaxing smile on her face. I would have stare at her with no limit of time.

After like three hours of line we got to see the statue of *Sai baba*, just for like two seconds and before we could worship or wish something, we, rather all of the worshiper were thrown out of the sanctum by the *pandits* and guards. '*Chalo chalo aage chalo. Ha bohat ho gaya chalo aage.*' This is what they were saying continuously.

****

Well, after coming out of the temple first thing I did was took Janvi to restaurant and fed her some food. Manav was planning to go to a Water Park; I refused as I was out of budget till then.

We took our mobile phones from lockers. I saw missed calls from Mahi, Rahul and Rohit dada. I called back Mahi first, he seemed so pissed off, 'What happened?' I dared to ask.

'Where are you? Just tell me where the hell you are.' He shouted.

'Wh… what's the matter? I am at my friend's room.' I lied to him.

'Tell me the truth, Bittu. Aren't you in Shirdi? And hadn't you brought girls last night to our room?' He asked.

'What? No! Who told you that?' I said with my hands shivering.

'Prashant told me about Shirdi, he had heard you while talking with Manav last night. And for your information, our watchman told me about girls and he also asked me to leave the room as soon as possible. What the hell you think you were doing? You know what…'

'No I don't know.' I said and poked out the tongue as I used my habit at wrong place.

'Don't be so cool, because, you know? Rohit will talk to you about this. Ok?' He said and cut the call.

Great! Now I will have to listen my brother's lecture, which was the worst. I got a bit tensed and switched my phone off, and decided better to forget about it till I reach Aurangabad again.

We took our lunch and headed back to Aurangabad. During the whole way back also I was sitting with Janvi near the door, talking about some personal things, some professional things. Some confessions and some apologies. I told her how I respect her love and her small and big things she does for me. I felt so lucky to have a best friend and a girlfriend like her.

We reached Aurangabad, Janvi called to one of her friends to live at her hostel for the night. I dropped them to her friend's hostel; it was 10 minutes away from my room. Manav left as well.

Somehow, with some fear and with some tension I headed to my hostel. I entered by back gate and went directly to my room. It was locked. I entered and switched on my phone. It started ringing due to call of my friend Vijay. He told me that results were already out at evening and he was trying to call me but my phone was off.

I called Janvi to tell her this.

'I miss you so much already.' She said as soon as she picked up the call.

'I miss you too. I want to ask you whether what you had wished for and for which thing you were empty stomach all the time.'

'No, I will tell you when it will come true. If I tell you now then it will not come true.' She said.

'Hmm, but if you had wished for my results then for your information results are out. You can tell me now.'

'Really? What is your result?' She asked cheerfully.

'No, first you tell me what you had wished for.'

'*Arre baba*, obviously for your good result. I had wished for you to get clear in your first semester examination. Now will you please tell me your result? I'm dying here.'

'Hmm. But actually right now I also don't know about it. Tomorrow I will get my mark sheet in college then I will tell you.' I said and she got sad that she would have to wait till morning. I was so tired to check result on internet cafe, so I convinced her somehow by some love drama. Then after some lovely chat, laughing at some sweet memories, fighting at why I let Pradnya sleep on my shoulder, and some drama to avoid that topic and to convince her again we were talking untill sleep parted us. Before that, we felt so many ummmmaaaaahhhs and muuuaahhhhs, and so many *'I love you'*s. I did all the girly things while talking which any boy fallen in love does. We talked about all the same things and topics, yet keeping it interesting. Then while talking, when my phone got hot and my ear got hurt and she fall asleep, I cut the call.

9. Oh my god!

❄ ❄ ❄

At the morning, I woke up and got ready early as Janvi was going to leave for Beed. I called her to meet at the bus stop. I left my room and headed towards the Cidco bus stop, but before that, I was stopped by watchman at the gate and asked whether who gave me authorization to bring guests in hostel and that too female. With some struggle with words, I could not give him a satisfactory answer. Then he asked me very gently to leave hostel in one week. Whatever! Who gives a shit? Well, Mahi does.

I chose to forget about it and headed towards bus stop. At the bus stop, I felt the same things again. This time, I hated the morning as it was taking her away from me.

I saw Janvi so sad. Bhumi and Pradnya were busy with themselves. Janvi was waiting for me with sad face. When I went to her, she said with a puppy face, '*Kitti ushir?* (How late?)'

'I am sorry Chiku. My watchman had caught me to talk.' I said.

Janvi and I got busy in our love emotions and emotional drama of, 'Please don't go.' 'Stay with me.' 'I love you,' 'I will miss you' and all that stuff.

The sadness on her pretty face was killing me. With every second of time as her departure was coming closer, her eyes were getting wet and wet. I just held her hand and she avoided to make eye contact, as it would have got more tears in her eyes.

This time I didn't kiss Janvi, but she was expecting it. I also wished to do so, but couldn't. That brought more tears in her eyes. Her bus arrived, Bhumi and Pradnya went ahead and Janvi made clutch of hands stronger and looked into my eyes. I wanted to kiss her. I don't know why but I didn't.

Why do we have this long distance between us? Why can't we stay in the same town? We always need to search for some reasons to meet each other. And we always cry in public at bus stop, for leaving each other behind.

'I love you so much, Bittu.' She said so softly while holding my hand tight and getting more tears in eyes.

'I love you too Janvi.' I said while wiping her tears.

'And.... I... I HATE BUS STOPS.' She said and I smiled with a drop falling from my eye.

She released my hand slowly, slowly and started heading towards bus. Our fingers were clutched together until she entered the bus. She sat in the bus with a crying face and tied a scarf to cover it.

Again, as bus was going reverse, I was also walking with her window slowly, slowly. Bus stopped at corner and I ran to see at her window. But, this time I could see her sitting at her place. She didn't come down. I was hoping her to come back. That's why I hadn't kissed her thinking that she would come back. But, she didn't.

Bus started moving again and headed to its destination. Slowly, slowly bus left and went out of my eye's reach.

****

Well, bus departed for its destination. I started moving towards my college. I took auto rickshaw and reached college. I saw all the first year students were in a queue for taking their mark sheets. I also got in queue and got my mark sheet.

As I got my mark sheet, I... I just got... frozen. I started laughing after a while on myself. I reminded how tough those two papers had gone. And I clearly got an example of how a miracle happens. I was damn sure that I will definitely fail in 'Applied science' and 'EEE' and other subjects were good, 'ECE', 'Engg. Maths.', my favorite one and 'Engg. Graphics'.

Was it the effect of Janvi's love that I got such result? Or was it Sai baba who gave me such result? I mean Janvi had fast for my result, and here was my result.

I mean I was sure that I will get KT in two subjects and there I had failed in THREE subjects! '*2 subjects pe ek subject free!*' It was the time when I got more faith in BAMU (Dr. Babasaheb Ambedkar Marathwada University) as I had passed in Applied Science and failed in Maths for the first time in history.

I took my phone to call Janvi; she picked it up and gave me another shock. 'Hey, I am in Aurangabad again. I could not go further. I got out from bus near bypass and now I am in a rickshaw.' She told.

I asked her to come to my college and cut her call as my mother's call was on waiting.

'Hello?' I said.

'*Kuthey tu?* (Where are you?)' My mother spoke in angry tone.

'I am in college.' I spoke while guessing why she was angry.

'Don't lie to me? Are you or were you in Shirdi?' She said and I got, that the anger about result was yet to arrive; first, I have to suffer from the previous matter.

'Wh…wh… what?' I asked instead of answering her question.

'What am I asking to you? Were you in Shirdi? And is Janvi with you?'

'No, Janvi is not with me.' I answered half-truth. In this way, I didn't lie to her.

'What about your result?' She asked, I meant my father made her ask as he was also angry with me and was avoiding a conversation with me.

'….' I had no words.

'Bittu, I am asking something.' She screamed.

'Hmm?'

'Are you deaf? What about your result?'

'I… I … got backlogs.' I avoided mentioning the number.

'Get your back packed and come here as soon as possible and today itself. Your father will see you.' She said and cut the call. *Did she say your father would sue you?*

Aal izz well, aal izz well, aal izz well. What else could I have done? Except making my heart fool by patting it as *baba Rancho* said. I was waiting for Janvi. I really needed her there with me to control me. She arrived and she was panicing more than me.

'What happened? Why are you so tensed?' I asked her.

'Yes. Aunty had called me too while I was in rickshaw. And I could not lie to her when she yelled at me.' She narrated.

'What?'

'I am sorry! But good news is now you have a company to get scolded.' She said with childish expression and biting her forefinger.

I wanted to be happy, as Janvi had left another bus for me, but it was a different situation. I was a bit depressed due to result also. But the good news was I'd passed in Applied Science with **40** marks. May be it was the effect of just filling the pages with any technical sentences and not making any sense.

Well Janvi had her bag packed with her already. I went to my room to get my bag. I thought what should I pack in my bag? Should I pack just one dress or may I need whole luggage, as I didn't know when my parents were going to allow me to come back here. Or, even they will allow it or not.

I took my bag and we left for Ambad, back to home. While waiting for bus at bus stop my face had become like, '*Yeh duniya…. Yeh mehfil… mere kaam ki nahi, mere kaam ki nahi.*' And Janvi was like, '*Kar chale… hum fida… jaan-o-tann sathiyo… ab tumhare havale, watan sathiyo.*' We both were so sad and so tensed. There were other passengers who were looking at us and gave us a look, like '*koi mar gaya kya?*'

We sat in the bus. We didn't talk a word. When we sat in our seats, we just saw each other and thought who was more tensed. Bus started and headed towards its destination and my heartbeat raised like a goat's who is about to get *halal.*

'Please god, don't make it worse. I will even keep afast today…'

'NO, NO, NO Not at all!' I screamed as soon as Janvi was praying to god.

'Why? What happened?' She asked. Yeah! Obviously, she was not aware of the effect of her first fast she had for me. I didn't say anything and just took out my mark sheet to show her.

'What the hell!' She got more tensed knowing that now the drama, I mean the war which we were heading for, was going to be more oppressive and vicious. She just stared at me in old Hindi movie's sad look and went silent again.

'Do you have that song from 3 idiots?' I asked her as my phone's battery was dead.

'Which? Oh… All is well.' She said and nodded, and gave me a sarcastic smile, but didn't give her phone.

'I am so tensed yaar.' I said.

'Me too, but I am even more tensed of laughing.' She said.

'What do you mean?' I asked.

'I mean, whenever someone scolds me in front of me, I can't control myself, I start to laugh.'

'Yeah, I've seen that. If you laugh in front of me then I will also start laughing.' I said with a stressed face.

'Don't worry, you know what…'

'No I don't.'

'Listen na! You know what I do for avoiding that? I just start biting my forefinger so that it will hurt me and bring tears in my eyes.' She said with glowing face as if she was teaching me something big knowledge thing. Well, at that time it was an important one too.

'Hmm I will try that. But you please don't have any kind of fast or something.' I said with hands folded in front of her.

'I am having one right now. Don't worry, it will be alright…' As she was saying something, I took her close and kissed her on lips, by digging my tongue deep into her mouth. And after that kiss she got shocked and shy. By looking around checking if someone saw us kissing, she covered her face and asked, 'What was that?' She said and I loved the way she shieded. But it wasn't the right time for romance.

'I kissed you to break your fast.' I admitted.

'WHAT? You…. You…. You...' She screamed and started crying like a baby. But she had no words for me either.

'Now just shut up, ok. I have experienced effect of your fast; I don't want this one to be worst.' I said and she just looked at me with that angry and sulky face.

Well, I know it wasn't the time for romance, but she was angry on me so to calm her down I took her close and tried to hug her but she pushed me away in anger. Then I took her hand in my hand and she slapped on my hand. So then, I tried to take her phone as mine was dead, but she looked at me with tiny red eyes. I just gave her a puppy look and said, 'Someone is angry on me. I don't know whether it is my best friend or girlfriend. But whoever it is, I need the other one to talk, as my ass is going to be kicked after some time anyhow.'

She just stared at me and then becoming calm, she rested on my shoulder. I kissed on her forehead and hugged her.

'I love you so much, my Chikkkkki' I said.

'And I hate you.' She said while punching on my thigh.

****

Well, we reached at Ambad, and headed towards my home sweet home, which after few minutes was going to be a battlefield.

With every step ahead towards my home, my heart was screaming, 'Hey stop, stop. Stop killing me. I can't run faster now. Please go back to Aurangabad.'

'Ha Ha Ha, now your death is near. Run! Run like hell for your life.' Mind teased.

'Why are you getting so happy? You are also not going to be safe.' Heart said.

'Oh right, I had forgotten that.' Mind.

'Aal izz well, aal izz well...' Heart started praying to baba Rancho.

'*Lakadi ki kathi, kathi pe ghoda, ghode ki duum pe jo mara hatoda... dauda, dauda, dauda ghoda duum uthake dauda...*'

'Why the fuck are you singing that song?' Heart asked, irritated.

'I don't know! Well, your *all is well* was not working for me, so I came up with this song.' Mind replied.

I was in front of my house now. I opened the gate slowly. Its opening sound reminded me the scene of horror movie. That sound made me more afraid and produced goose bumps on my body.

'What happened?' Janvi asked, as if she didn't know what the matter was.

I just looked at her and said, '*Puri fatt gayi hai yaar.*'

'Hmm.' She replied and signaled me to go first.

'No, no, after you. Ladies first please.' I said and she headed to go inside. I stopped her and said, 'Right leg first, please.' I wanted it to be as positive as possible.

My mother opened door. I felt like I was getting a heart attack. It would not have been this much scary if any one of the things could be deleted. Like, if I wouldn't have failed or had I informed them about my trip. Well, *ab bhugto.*

With every stair I was stepping on, I was reminding the bad deeds I did for which I would be screwed. I started counting, 1) I was in defaulter list last semester.

2) Papa had to pay my defaulter fine for hall ticket.

3) I had brought girls to my room.

4) I had gone to Shirdi without permission,

5) I had 3 backlogs.

Great! *Dene wala jab bhi deta hai, chhappar fadh ke deta hai!*

Well, I entered and went straight to kitchen. Janvi followed me like a calf. I guess she tried to give a smile to my father who was sitting on sofa in living room. I didn't get to see his reply. I wished but I had no guts to look at him.

I opened the fridge and took out a bottle of water. I asked Janvi if she wants it.

'No, thanks, it looks like now only you need it, because just now uncle gave me a good smile.' She said with pleased face and I got more tensed. I felt like I have to play this double wicket cricket all alone. I gulped down a bottle full of water.

My mother didn't look at me; neither even talked nor asked how I was. I felt like now I don't even have a match fixer umpire.

Janvi came to me and whispered in Marathi, 'Hee waadala purvichi shantata ahe. (This is the silence before storm. Or something like that.)' She whispered it so horribly. I got goose bumps. I just stared at her. I swallowed back the lump in my throat and stared at her with a terrified look.

We shared our gaze for few seconds and then broke down into laughter. Then realizing that condition was not funny and we should not laugh, we both put our forefingers in mouth and started biting it so hard while laughing. I couldn't work it out, I was still laughing so I put all my five fingers in my mouth.

'Bittu, come here.' My father called me in tough voice. His voice made me forget all my laughter and made me silent.

'Here it comes!'

'*Lakadi ki kathi, kathi pe ghoda.....*' Mind started singing.

'Oh, SHUT UP!' I yelled at myself.

I went into the living room with shivers going up and down through my body and touched my father's feet. Janvi copied the same. I touched my mother's feet and sat in front of my father.

Holy shit! Who told you to sit in front of the cannon in a battle? I thought.

'Janvi, sit here.' My mother said to Janvi signaling her to sit beside her. It was completely partial, I was alone in front of them and Janvi was sitting with the opposite team already, just because she was a girl? How India would progress if you do such partiality in girls and boys? I should not be the one and only who is being screwed up here.

'Hmm, tell me. Had you gone to Shirdi?' Papa asked gently to be sure.

'....' I didn't say anything and just kept looking at floor.

'Had you gone to SHIRDI?' He yelled a bit, as I wasn't saying anything.

'Hmm.' I said and nodded while clutching my hand and rubbing my fingers without any reason but in nervousness.

'Why? Don't you have your college and studies? Ha?' He started screaming at me, 'Why did you bunk your lectures for it?' He kept screaming angrily and I kept looking at floor.

'I am asking you something.' He yelled again. But what would have I answered to him. I had no explanation. What should have I said? I had girls as guest in my room and had no idea what to do, and Manav wanted to spend time with Bhumi hence we went to Shirdi? Impossible! I had plenty of reasons of being screwed and those were enough. I would have not mentioned this and increase my problem again. Therefore, I was just silent and avoided answering.

'And who the hell were those girls at your room in midnight? Have you totally lost your mind as well as shame?' He said getting more uptight and leaning forward from his place taking an aggressive posture.

I thought, now there is no chance to stay alive. He knows about girls too. Oh god! I am dead, I am very much dead!

I started shivering. I need help. Back up, I need back up! I looked at my co-soldier Janvi with a peep. I peeked at her and saw she was looking down at floor as well. But then, I saw she was biting her finger.

Oh god! Kill me, please kill me. Is she laughing? I wanted her to be at my side to support me, and not to do such things, which will eventually lead to my death. Had I been alone there I would have handled it all well.

I chose not to look at her.

'Who were those girls?' Papa screamed again.

'Those… those were her friends.' I said while pointing towards Janvi like a kid.

As soon as I pointed towards her, she popped up like a rat that saw a cat coming towards it. Papa just stared at her for a while and she swallowed back the lump in her throat and again looked down towards floor biting her finger.

'We trusted you. And you are giving us this as reward. We thought you would change after Purvi…' Papa kept talking and I got shocked like my indicators turned on like a bike when he mentioned Purvi. It is always shocking when a father mentions your girlfriend's name. He continued, '…but you are such a shameless person. Last night we scolded Rahul and Rohit because of you. They were telling us that you were in Shirdi and we scolded them for you. And now, how are we suppose to face them? How?' He asked angrily and I looked up somehow in his red eyes. I opened my mouth to answer, but then closed it again as he might have thought that I was retorting. It's always tough to handle such situation where parents ask us something and we can't answer as it would be retorting and if we answer back, the scolding increases. Retorting is directly proportional to getting more screwed up.

We all kept silent for a while, as I was not answering. That silence was killing me either. But, suddenly from past, papa recalled something and continued again, 'Last semester your H.O.D. had called me to meet in college for your defaulters. I had to pay your defaulter fine for your absentees in college and still you are wandering out side bunking your college? Have you totally lost your shame? Can't you see that you are ruining your career?' He yelled and I heard small chuckling. Obviously, it was Janvi. I wished I could thrust a giant pillow in her mouth down to her throat as her finger was not working it well. She chuckled again and this time I got my lips curved a bit. I put my lips in between my teeth to stop from laughing.

'*Lakadi ki kathi, kathi pe ghoda, ghode ki dum pe jo mara hatoda….*'

Stop singing, stop singing, stop it and for god's sake don't laugh. I thought to myself. I also started biting my finger to stop laughing. I hate you Janvi, I hate you. Please stop laughing. My father is angry like hell, his eyes have red like blood, please don't laugh. I started controlling myself.

'Bittu, have you really gone shameless? Stop biting your finger and don't act like a girl.' My mother screamed in between.

'No, I am not a girl. I am a boy. Yes! I am a boy. In fact, I am a man. Ask Janvi and Purvi about it.' I thought to myself.

'Dude, do you really think this is the good time to debate about that?' My heart interrupted, and I got my focus on genuine topic.

'There is no need or any output talking with him. He has become shameless.' My father said with irritated face. 'Tell me at least this time your attendance is above 90%.' He asked.

'No, but they just need 75% to not to get in defaulter's list.' I said like a hopeless.

'So does your attendance fill at least 75%?' He asked again and, I had to look to my favorite spot again, that floor. He saw my reaction and continued, 'Great! Puja kara yachi ata! (Should I worship him now!)' Papa said angrily to my mother, and Janvi couldn't control her chuckling.

'You didn't attend your college in last semester, I had to pay your defaulter's fine, and this time also you didn't attend your college? What were you doing? Ha? Dancing with girls, and wandering with them?' He yelled at me and I felt proud of myself for a while by hearing that.

'We won the dance competition and got first prize.' I defended myself.

'Great! But *tere first prize ka kya achaar dalu mai?*' He said getting irritated and continued, 'And you have got a backlog, I haven't said anything about it yet.' Uh oh! He thinks I have one backlog. It means, *picture abhi baki hai mere dost. Abhi toh party shuru hui hai!*

'Show me your mark sheet.' He asked for my mark sheet and I skipped a heartbeat. I saw Janvi, she was continuously biting her finger. I opened my bag and took out my mark sheet, and with shivering hands gave it to him. Papa saw the mark sheet and went silent. He rested back at sofa rubbing his forehead. I felt so guilty. Not guilty because I had three backlogs, but because I had made him tensed as well as sad. I made him sad and disappointed by scoring great marks in 10th, 12th and AIEEE. Why? Why had I scored good marks in those exams? That made his expectations to rise like Mount Everest.

'Enough. Now onwards you two will never meet.' My mother made an exposure in between.

'What? Aai, it's not her fault at all.' I defended Janvi and she tried to stop her silent laughing.

'What do you think Janvi? Are we not angry with you? We are livid with you both. We are just hiding this because you are like my daughter. But had your mother been well, I would have informed it to her too. But I don't want to give her stress. She will not be able to handle stress.' Aai said to Janvi and Janvi stopped her chuckling. Aai continued, 'And your father is so tensed in caring of her; it would be really great if you focus on your mother's disease and your father's struggle instead of wandering with boys and passing their time.' My mother spoke with wide eyes to Janvi.

Wow! Mother's are really great. Till now in this whole drama Janvi was continuously chuckling and my mother's one sentence made her not only to stop her chuckling but also made her cry. As soon as Aai finished her sentence, few tears rolled down from Janvi's eyes.

'Aai, why are you scolding her?' I felt so pity for her.

'I am not scolding her Bittu. I am talking softly and seriously. You both are not kids anymore to wander and to have fun together. There are people outside who watch us. What would they think? After didi's marriage, you both have met so many times, haven't you? Why do you always go to Aurangabad to meet him, ha Janvi? Don't you have your college? Your father doesn't scold you, that does not mean that you free to do whatever you want to.' Aai was unstoppable, 'Here after I don't want to hear that you had gone to Aurangabad to meet Bittu. And you Bittu, if I heard that you bunk your even one lecture, then I will… I will never see you and I will do something to myself.' In this way, *Aai ne last ball pe sixer mara.*

All the singing and biting fingers and '*lakadi ki kathi…*' had stopped like a death silence. Janvi was crying silently. I was shocked that Aai really said that we could not meet again. Aai took Janvi close to console her, but made her to swear that she will never see me again. Hardly, if possible then we would meet for Diwali in Alandi.

Again, for few minutes we all were silent just sitting there. At the last of this all scene the conclusion was that, I must attend each and every lecture further and I can't dare to meet Janvi. Obviously, it was a tragedy for us. I was so broken inside. Aai had made us to swear on her that we will obey what she said. I saw Janvi with a sad face, she didn't look at me. She was still looking down but now with wet eyes. Not because we could not meet further, but due to what Aai said about her mother.

****

After about 20 minutes of silence, Janvi tried to take our leave to go to Beed. Aai scolded her again, 'Don't be oversmart. It's already 5 o'clock now. You will be late. There is no need to go now. Stay here for the night. You can leave tomorrow.'

The situation of my house had become as if some one died, just because I had failed in three subjects. I had to stay silent like a thief in jail as the jailor had all the evidence against me. Till dinner, I tried so many times to share a gaze with Janvi but she always refused and ignored me.

Aai was continuously having a watch on me. I was not able to speak with Janvi. She was right in front of me and acting like a total stranger. I felt like I was under house arrest or some one had put a *Gulab jamun* in front of me, and god gifted me diabetes. I mean she was there and I was unable to make even an eye contact.

We took our dinner as if we were eating at somebody's funeral. After dinner, Aai and Janvi were watching their serial on TV. I picked up my phone and messaged Janvi. I typed, 'you are in front of me and still I miss you.' I just typed it and remembered the oath given by my mother. I deleted the message. Again, after some time when I was unable to control myself from talking with Janvi, I typed, 'hi' and deleted again.

'Talk to me.' and deleted.

'At least once look at me.' deleted as well.

'I love y..' deleted before it could complete. Finally I typed our code word for love you,

‘ ’
..

I was about to send it to Janvi and she got a call from her mother. I knew she would go to bedroom for talking with her so I headed there before her. She picked up the call and came into bedroom; I saw her and saw the tears in her eyes which fell down before she could speak anything on phone.

'I miss you so much mommy.' She said while crying. I thought she would complain to her mother about Aai but she didn't. She said that she was crying because she was missing home so much and she was at hostel. Her phone cut after a long talk with her mother and father.

I went to her and wanted to hug her and wipe her tears. I took her close to me and hugged her. Her face was burried in my arms. She didn't hug me back. She wanted to though. She then took herself out of my arms when I was going to kiss her on her forehead. She went two steps ahead and realized that I was going to kiss her which I missed. She stood there silently sobbing. I went to her and pecked on her forehead. I applied my lips like for couple of minutes. She silently felt that closing her eyes and went to the living room.

****

The whole night I slept alone in the bedroom, rather I should say that I was awake alone. I was staring at the ceiling aimlessly. It was the first time after 14th Feb. when I was sleeping there. It killed me more. Because last time when I was at the same place, it was the starting of our love. The place where I rested was the place of my first kiss with Janvi. I missed her so much while I was sleeping on the floor intentionally to recall all the memories of that night. I closed my eyes and started feeling her. A couple of drops rolled down from my eyes. I was missing her so much. It's easy to survive in someone's memories when they are far away from you. But when your loved one is right in front of you and you still miss her, that's more difficult to accept.

I was feeling so lonely. I had no reason to laugh or be happy. I had no tragedy before this. I had never cried alone like this. If there was a bad news somewhere or whenever I had fought with Purvi, there was Janvi to console me always. But now, I was totally alone.

****

At the morning after getting ready and again listening mom-dad's words and reminding my oath, I was free to go to Aurangabad. Janvi and I, we both left together.

We reached the bus stop. We were together but still felt alone.

I was dying, as I hadn't seen Janvi like this ever before..

We were at bus stop but I wasn't waiting for bus. I was waiting for Janvi to talk to me. I was hoping a smile, which will cheer me up again. I was waiting for her to look at me once. I was staring at her, she lifted up her head, looked at me. I got happy, as she opened her mouth to say something.

'Bye, Bittu.... Here is my bus. And please don't call me ever.' She said while going towards the bus. I got shocked as suddenly she was leaving me. I felt like my heart was crying. A strong lightning ran through my chest as she said don't call her ever. But I had no time to think about all this stuff. She was moving so fast. I ran to stop her. She was heading towards bus so fast. I held her hand when she was about to board that bus. She stood at the door. I clutched her hand tightly and she stood like a statue. I was hoping her to see back to me but she didn't. She left my hand and went straight to sit there.

I froze in shock that she left just like that! Without saying anything, without any greeting. Neither any wishes of love nor any 'miss you' stuff. I was hopping at least for 'dot dot'. But I didn't get that either.

Her bus started and left the bus stop I was looking at the bus until it went out of my sight. It didn't even stop at entrance corner. She didn't come out of the bus. She was really going. And so she did. I went to platform with wet eyes and sat on the bench.

That's it? Is it over? Can one result or one tragedy end up the relation just like that? I just sat there. I didn't get any of the noise from crowd or any announcements. Everything had gone blank. I was sitting there with my head in my hands and looking at the floor.

Why didn't I study well for exams? Why did I go to Shirdi? Why? I should have at least attended my lectures well. I kept thinking about possibilities.

She didn't even look at me while going. How could she do that? Didn't she get hurt while going without talking to me?

'I HATE bus stops.' I heard a soft voice.

I left a sigh and stood up to see my bus and stood still. Wait! What did I just heard? I looked back quickly and I saw Janvi sitting beside my bag. I started smiling like a kid naively. I was so happy to see her again. She was looking at me with wet eyes. 'And I love YOU.' She added and smiled with a drop falling from her eye.

****

'I love you Bittu. But…' she stopped while talking.

'What? What is the matter? Look I am sorry for what Aai said yesterday. She was angry.'

'I know Bittu. But whatever she said I will never forget. May be she was right. I should really concentrate on studies as well as my mother's disease. Yesterday, when…' she said and stopped to wipe her tears, '… when I talked to my mommy, I could not control my tears. And dad told me that in last week she had fallen down so many times by headache and getting giddy and become unconscious. I don't want it to be worse because of us. And also you've failed in three subjects because of me…'

'No, it wasn't your fault.'

'It doesn't matter Bittu. Whenever people will see, they will think only that you've failed; no one will ask you the reason. I don't want to be the reason to spoil your career. May be I would not have come to realize this, had it not been understood by your mother. Or had she not scolded me.'

She was talking so seriously. She had heard from her father last night that how her mother's condition was becoming critical. She told me that her mother's treatment had extended and her dosage had also increased. She didn't want to be the reason of stress to her mother or our families.

She had decided to break this relationship. She was crying while saying that but she thought this was the only option. I tried to convince her so hard but I was helpless. Had it not been about her mother and her health I would have forced a lot, but I had no option too.

We decided to stick to our oaths my mother gave us last night and try to forget each other.

I was hoping to be best friends at least, she said, 'I will always be your best friend. No one can apart us. Even if god came down and told me to leave your friendship then I will dare him to make me do so. You cannot get rid of my friendship so easily. However, we just cannot call and talk anymore. Whenever you will need me, I will always be there. I PROMISE! But we can't meet now anymore.'

She said and left while crying again. We took our buses and left the bus stop. That's it! Once there, at the same place we had talked about starting our relationship and same there, we talked about breaking it. Our buses left and headed to our destinations.

She went to south and I went to north.

10. Two weeks without her

* * *

It had been two weeks since then we had no contact. No calls, no messages. In her case no miss call, no reply. My ears were dying to hear her voice. Whatever it would be, even if she would abuse me it was ok, I just wanted to hear her voice once. Life had become empty like space. There was nothing to do about, except to miss her. There was nothing to think about except to miss her. There was nothing to talk about except how much I was missing her. There was nothing .... Nothing....
Anyways it would go so long.

My old boring routine was back again. I was snoozing alarms again. My attendance might have increased in these days but I was never present mentally in class. I had started day dreaming again. I was missing her like hell. Already we were having long distance relationship and now in that relationship we were not allowed to talk or meet. Things were only becoming worse. And we both were suffering in those conditions.

After every minute, I used to see at my phone to check whether I missed her call or message. I was waiting for her call like the 40 marks.

She didn't call me. So I used to dial her number to call her, but before I could complete that call I always had to cut it off. I was missing her so much. My mouth was hurting, it had no one to talk in these days. I was dying to say 'I love you', I was so used to saying it. My mobile charged to optimum. It rarely needed to charge and recharge in these days. The shopkeeper of the mobile store was also missing me as I had not gone to him in these two weeks to recharge my phone.

My phone's call history used to be full with her missed calls and dialed calls. But now it had received calls of my home and mobile companies only. Even my friends didn't call me as they used to be on waiting for like hours previously. So they had left calling me and wasting their time.

When I used to wake up in morning and go to bathroom for getting fresh and brushing, I used to miss her there, as now I had no one to tell whether what her shona was doing. When I went to have breakfast, I was dying to ask her whether what I should order today, as she used to talk to me there also till I finished my breakfast. Since last few months, I never had been this much alone.

Once in college I went to get a sign of professor on my journals. Professor signed it after pointing out so many mistakes but when he ended his sign and put two dots under it habitually, I was frozen. I stood looking at those dots. I was dying to see those dots at least. I felt like Janvi messaged me secretly that she loved me, as two dots were our three secret magical words.

'I love you too Chiku.' I said inside my heart.

I had to talk to her anyhow, but couldn't. My mother's word always stopped me. However, after all, I also belonged to Homo sapiens, a human being. I can't control my emotions. I had to release my emotional fall anywhere. So… that's why… I… I… I called Purvi to talk.

She didn't pick up my call. Actually my number had changed. Though I felt why I called her. It wasn't good for my ego. But you know na, '*Banduk se nikali hui goli, muh se nikli hui boli aur phone se nikla hua miss call, kabhi wapas nai aate.*' Whatever! Never mind.

Where was I? Hmm!

I was missing Janvi like hell. I remembered every thing. The trip that screwed us had left a sweet memory of three hour's of queue and romantic *darshan* of Sai baba. I remembered each and every second we spent together till that day.

I remembered every kiss and every hug. I was crying alone remembering her wet eyes, which she made always at bus stops while leaving. Her face -with a scarf wrapped on it - and her wet red eyes were impossible to erase from my mind.

I started thinking, 'Would she also be missing me? What if she is forgetting me to move on? It has been two weeks and she hadn't called me.

May be she would have also dialed my number thousands of

times and cut it off like me.' I thought.

The worst thing was that I was continuously remembering her childish laugh and her effort to start crying by biting her finger. It was killing me more. I had no idea how to turn crying face into laugh, she hadn't taught me that.

I had become so…. So….. I had become so….
Ah! I have no words for me.

Dur hoke bhi tera aks mujhme,
Meri saanso me hi hai rawaan.
Tera naam lete hi band hoti,
Ye hichkiya hi hai gavah.

Rone ke liye gum bahaut hai,
Hasi ke liye bahana… dhundhata hu.
Palko ki diwaare dhak ke
Teri yaadon ka khajana… dhundhata hu.

Paas hone ka ehsaas, aur
Saath hone ka nasha chadhta hai.
Tu saath na hone ke sach pe,
Dil khudse hi ladh padata hai.

Kya karu mai, hai ye nadaan,
Kambakht ko na hai khabar.
Milke tuzse fir dubara,
Dhadakne ko hai besabar.

Tere jaanese tere aane tak,
Hai gaya jaise thum sa ye.
Ise chalane ke liye firase,
Koi dost purana…. Dhundhata hu.

Kyu dur tu, majbur tu,
Meri jindagi ka hai noor tu.
Awaaj tu, meri saans tu,
Mere hone ka ehsaas tu.

Tu hai khafa ya bewafa,
Tere aane ka na hai pata.
Meri jindagi, meri har khushi
Tere saath hi hai laapata.

Meri jindagi ka khushnumasa
Wo tarana... dhundhata hu.
Kho gayi jo meri hasi
Mai tera muskurana ... dhundhata hu

****

Though every day I was missing her like hell, Sunday was the exception. Because on Sunday there used to be no work or classes so on that day, I used to miss her more than like hell. I don't know the simile here. I can't compare it with anything. It was like... it was... like...

Ah, I told you! I can't compare it with any thing. I have no words.

So it was Sunday, and I had no work except to miss her. I chose to sleep till noon. I woke up due to a phone call. Initially, I got irritated as it broke my sweet sleep. *I was about to kill a terrorist entered in my college and save our principal by fighting with him without any weapon when he was having AK52.* You might be thinking why I was saving principal instead of any pretty girl. Well who knows, he might have a pretty daughter like Kareena in 3 Idiots.

But then I thought about the call which was waking me up,

Heart: What if it's Janvi?

Mind: No way!

Heart: Why?

Mind: She never gives you so long rings, she is always afraid of picking her call up and wasting her 60 paisa.

Heart: Logic! But what if she knew that I will cut her call and call her back, or what if she was missing me so much that she doesn't care about her balance anymore.

Mind: May be. But why are you asking me? Just wake up and pick the call.

Well I had to wake up, so I let that terrorist go on and I jumped up to pick the call. It was Bhumi's call; I thought may be Janvi was out of balance so she might have called from Bhumi's phone. I picked it up,

'Are you still sleeping?' It was Bhumi's voice, not Janvi.

'Hmm. Why did you call me?' I asked.

'Actually I am in Aurangabad and I want to meet you.'

'What?' I got surprised, 'Is Janvi with you?'

'No, I insisted her to come but she refused. By the way, I am at Canaught place, Cidco. I just bought a new mobile phone. Can you come here?'

'Ok, I'll be there in 15 minutes.' I said with a disappointment, as Janvi had not come.

I woke up and got fresh. Well this time I could get fresh in 10 minutes. Unlike previous days as tap problem of bathroom had been solved by changing room, rather changing hostel very *respectfully*.

I headed to the place where Bhumi was waiting for me. I saw her and she waved at me.

'Hi.' She said cheerfully, 'Actually, I was about to go but thought I should meet you.'

'Hmm.' I said with a smile, 'So what else?'

'Nothing I was just passing my time by copying pics from old phone to new one.' She said while showing her new Nokia C5-03. I saw she was forwarding the photos taken in Shirdi.

'Do you have those pics?' I said with happiness.

'Yes, I took it from Manav.' She winked.

'Can I see it?' I asked for her mobile. She handed it over to me and we sat there while watching those photos.

I was deeply lost in the memories of Shirdi and the time in train. I saw a photo of mine with Janvi and a drop was about to fall from my eye. I saw Pradnya's photo and reminded Janvi's lovely angry face.

'Did you guys fought?' Bhumi asked.

'What? Who?'

'Obviously, You and Janvi.'

'Why?'

'Nothing, I've just observed that she lives a bit lost and didn't talk too much.'

'Really?'

'Hmm, actually that's why I called you here. I want to know

what the matter with her is. I haven't seen her talking with you either since we came from Shirdi.'

She was enquiring and I was feeling pity about my and Janvi's condition. I told her how my parents scolded me and my mother's harsh words made Janvi feel guilty.

'Ok! So this is the whole thing. You know.'

'No, I don't know.' I said habitually.

'Sorry?'

I got my lips curved in memory of Janvi, - Listen na..- This is what she would have said.

'Nothing. You were saying…'

'Hmm, she was behaving like a haunted dog. Whenever we tried to speak with her, she just scolded all of us without any reason and fought with everybody. Just yesterday she fought with me just because I teased her by your name. And now she doesn't talk to me.' She narrated.

I was listening to Bhumi while I was looking at the photos. I kept changing photos and stopped at one photo. It was Janvi's. She was not alone, Bhumi and Pradnya were also with her but… there were other friends too, including Vinit.

'Where did you capture this?' I asked Bhumi showing her that photo.

'Oh, this one? We had gone to see waterfall at Kapildhar. Remember we had come here to buy our instruments? We had gone just a day before that day.' Bhumi said and I recall Janvi telling me that they all went to Kapildhar except her as Vinit was there.

'Was Janvi with you too?' I asked to clarify.

'No. It's a ghost in the photo.' She said sarcastically and continued while showing more pictures, 'Obviously! See, these pictures. We had lot of fun there.' She showed me all photos. I tried to control my anger as Janvi had lied to me. I didn't let Bhumi to know that I was angry. But inside, I was burning like hell. Bhumi was talking with me but I didn't hear a word. All the things regarding Vinit just kept picturing in front of my eyes. From the day I met him, I kept recalling the stuff about him. The pinching and slapping to Janvi, her very casual reaction on that behaviour, then his call on waiting, his sentence about squeezing hand in naughty tone, and at the same time Janvi had cut that call, and also now, I found out that she had lied me about going to Kapildhar with him. In addition to that, those pictures which I just saw. I felt so... so.... Fool. She lied to me! Why? Is he more important to her than me?

****

Well, Bhumi went back to Beed, but she gave me a reason to call Janvi. How could she lie to me? I had asked for one favor and she lied. I could not control myself and only one thing was running in my mind that Janvi was a liar.

I took my phone and dialed her number. I could not complete my call. Not because of my oath but because she had added my number to rejected list. I kept calling her. I didn't care of anything. I was frustrated, she had lied to me.

After so many calls, she took my number out of the reject list.

'Hello?' She picked up the call and I heard her voice after two weeks. I almost fainted there. A strong lighting passed through my heart as I heard her voice. My eyes suddenly got wet.

'Hello.' I spoke somehow.

'Why did you call me Bittu?' Why did she ask this?

'Hmm...? Nothing...' I said while controlling myself from being emotional, 'What is up with you?' I asked casually..

'Nothing, what else could I get here in this *bakwas* hostel and college? You tell me how did you call?' Why did she keep asking that? It was killing me more.

'So, now do I need a reason to call? Anyway, I was missing you. And I was just remembering the whole time we spent together. I could not control myself and called you. I feel so lucky to have you. I appreciate that how much you love me. I feel sorry that I could not do anything for you.'

'Hmm. But I also did nothing much for you.'

'You did. You have come here so many times for me, you have cried so many times for me. You had left so many buses for me, and you have also left your friends for me, like Vinit. And you didn't go to that Kapildhar with them as I would not feel good, right? You have done lots of things for me, haven't you?'

'Hmm, but let it be. It's not important.' She said. Didn't she get that I was speaking sarcastically?

'No, Janvi. It is important for me. I felt so ashamed of myself that I haven't done anything for you. You did so many things for me; even the most important thing is that you LIED to me.' I said with bit of anger.

'What? What's wrong with you?'

'Why? Don't you know? Have you really left friendship with Vinit?'

'Yes! But why are you asking me that now?'

'Didn't you go with them to Kapildhar? And lied to me?' My voice was becoming louder and my hands started shivering in anger.

'NO. Who told you this shit? I didn't lie to you.' Well she lied again.

'Oh please! Shut the fuck up. I saw your pictures with them and Vinit was there too. I don't care whether what did you guys do there. Bhumi told me that you had a bike trip. If you can lie to me then I can imagine at my level what the shit you might have done there.' I was totally out of control. I had no idea what I was speaking and at which level.

'Listen Bittu, if you can imagine at your level then do whatever you want. Already I am busy in studies and I don't want to waste my time.'

'Yeah, right! Now speaking with me is a waste of time. I was dying here to hear your voice and you didn't even call me once. I can now see that why. You have your substitution for me there already, don't you?' I was just yelling at her. But she didn't even try to calm me down.

'Listen Bittu, if you can't talk well then you better cut the call. And you don't tell me what should I do and what should I not. It's my life, and I will have friends which I want. What is this all shit? Who gave you the right?'

'YOU gave me. And by the way I didn't tell you to leave anyone's friendship unless he became the reason of fight between us. And you had lied previously also, that's why I am angry. And you are not even sorry? Great!'

'Oh, really? You obey my words that much? Then I am telling you to not to call me again, BYE.' She said and cut that call.

I tried to call her back so many times but she had added my number to reject list again and then switched off her phone.

What the fuck was this? I mean, she is the one who lied, she is the one who had hidden things and broke promise, and she is the one who gets angry! And cuts the call? GREAT!

I kept calling her as much I could and then at particular point I stopped calling her. I felt so alone and stupid again. Now I didn't care about Vinit and their bike trip anymore. But the thing that killing me was Janvi had lied to me. She had given more importance to him than me. I was feeling so suffocated. I could not digest the feeling of being at second number of preference on Janvi's list.

I was dying here to hear her voice, to see her once. Meanwhile, she was enjoying there with that bastard! I felt so shameful.

In these two weeks, I had missed her like hell and she had given me this as reward.

'See, you are talking your father's tongue.' Mind arrived.

'What do you mean?'

'I meant they have done lots of things for you, sacrificed so many pleasures for you. And what did you gave them as reward? A secret trip with a bunch of girls? A defaulter list? Three backlogs?' Mind was talking shit but it was right.

'Ok baba I am sorry. Leave me alone. This is not the time to listen lectures now. I am already...'

'What? What are you already? *Sach hamesha kadwa hota hai.* And I know it's not a time for lecture, but there is no wrong time for realization.'

'What realization?'

'TIT for TAT. You will come to know slowly, slowly. There is a simple rule of life. *Dharti gol hai, ghum fir kar wapas wohi aaoge. Gravity ka jhol hai, kitna bhi udo, akhir me niche hi gir jaoge.*' Mind continued with its shit.

'What the hell was that?' I got irritated.

'I don't know! It just rhymed so I added.' It replied stupidly.

I was so irritated with these thoughts, which were making me feel guilty where Janvi was the one who had made mistake. I wanted to scold her for her rude behaviour; I wanted to ask her if she had lost her shame as she was behaving like a shameless. But my mind was taking me to another world of explanation where I was the one who was responsible for all those things. While I was irritated with my mind, my phone rang.

My eyes rolled so fast to watch the screen. It must be Janvi's call, I thought. But I saw the number and stood silent. It was Purvi. After so many months, she had called me, and after so many months, I felt happy by seeing her number on my mobile screen. I was willing to speak with someone. I needed someone to release all my frustration. I was unable to bear all that anger. And Purvi had called me. What a great timing!

'Hey, how are you?' I spoke while clearing my throat and clearing my mind.

'I am sorry, who is this?'

A bunch of lightning ran through my whole body crushing my heart and squeezing my head making juice of my brain. What the hell she just asked? And why the hell she asked that? Oh god! Why didn't I ask that question before her, instead of asking her how she was? Why? Now she has a plus point in the battle of the egos.

'Err, actually you called me, so I think I should ask that question. Or you should know actually whom you are calling.' I tried to swing on her.

'Listen, I don't have time for this. I had seen your missed call hence I called you back. You had called me while I was busy. Tell me your name or I am hanging up the call.' She spoke with a wide and wild attitude. She had recognized my voice but though I don't know why she was doing this. But I got that her timing wasn't perfect to call me but my bad luck was. She had called me after seeing my missed call. She was winning the battle, what should have I said then.

'Listen, if you want to cut the call then just do it. Don't act like you didn't recognize me. And stop this shit. I hadn't called you. It was just a mistake. I was actually deleting your number from my list. Ok? Bye.' I said with same wild attitude and cut that call. But then again felt so alone. I wanted someone to talk about my heart's pain. I needed a friend to whom I can talk aimlessly and with no limit of time.

And here it comes! I won the ego war. Purvi called me back again.

'*Bol*.' I spoke with same attitude.

'What? You had called me. And you know you can't lie. Not at least to me. I still can catch your lie in a second. You had deleted my number long ago. Why had you called me?' She still rocked.

'Ok, but I had called you yesterday. How come you are calling me today? Obviously, because you also want to talk to me.' I swear, I do not know why I said that, and what I was talking.

'Hmm, ok. Bye then.' She said and unknowingly I screamed, 'NO, NO wait, wait, wait.' I screamed and poked out tongue as she completely got me.

'Why had you called me?'

'Nothing, I… I… just…. Never mind. What about your result?'

'What could it be? I have a habit of being first since childhood.'

'Wow, congrats!' (And fuck myself. The girl who used to cry for you, is a topper, and you? Having backlogs as same as your lucky number.) I thought.

Somehow, while talking with her, in next hour I told her about my new story and why I was upset and called her. She felt sorry for me but didn't forget to mention that it was just the starting of my pay back for all bad deeds.

'I don't think that you should get upset with her lying. You have a great experience of that, don't you?' She taunted me. Well I didn't feel bad of her teasing or sarcasm. I just felt good to talk with her. She continued,

'It's nothing new for me. I have seen worse than this. Have you forgotten the last two years?' She asked.

'I don't know. Have you?' I was confused.

'She is doing nothing new. She is just copying you by what you did with me.'

'Whatever! Leave it. What's up with you? Totally forgotten me?' I asked hoping to hear that she still misses me.

'Actually yes and no also.'

'What does that mean?'

'I've met someone. Someone just like you! He has voice like you, his behaviour is similar to yours, and his nature is much better than you. So I live in happiness with his nature and try to forget you. But his voice, his laugh and all those things don't let me to do so.' She narrated and I felt glad to hear that she was happy. (But not alone. Happy with someone else. Shit!)

'Hmm that's great! But do you really think that I… I…. was ….that bad to deserve this…?'

'Like, you don't know! You are a good guy, but you act stupid, as you did with me. And same thing is happening with you. TIT for TAT.' She said and I got a shock as I was just thinking of it few minutes earlier.

I got afraid; what if it was true. What if Janvi acted like that with me? What if she made me cry as I made Purvi previously? NO, NO! Janvi won't do that. She is my best friend. She will never make me cry. I was consoling myself. But had no answer for why had she behaved like that just before.

'Have I really hurt you that much?' I dared to ask. She left a sigh and ignored to answer it.

'I don't want to talk about it, Karan. I am happy in my life now, which is enough for me.'

'I… I am sorry if I did so.' I thought that was the time to apoligize her. She didn't reply to that, she did not say anything. After a silence of a minute, she cut that call.

I just put my phone down slowly and kept thinking about what did she said. I might have done some things wrong to her, but we had great time with each other. I thought…

11. Flashback again

* * *

2007-08

'Pritesh, I am so afraid yaar. I don't know what to do now. Please help me.' I said with scary face to my childhood close friend who was two steps ahead in these types of knowledge than me.

'What happened? Tell me first.' Pritesh said sitting on the bike in front of his house while closing his shirt's buttons as I had called him out and not even gave him time to wear his shirt.

'I think…. I think…. Purvi will get pregnant.' I said with sweaty forehead and running my hand through my hair in anxiety.

'WHAT? Are you serious?' He screamed jumping up from that bike and I nodded, 'Bhen****, *sala ball na bo***, fokat ka locha.*' He reacted in his regular style. 'What the hell happened and when the hell it happened?'

'I am just coming from her home. I met her and I came directly here to tell you.' I was so afraid.

'Abbe chu***, why didn't you use protection then? If you would have asked me first, I would have bought it for you.' He said lowering his voice down. Then he clutched my arm and took me to corner to speak privately about it.

'What? Buy what?' I asked stupidly.

'Condom!'

'What is that for?' I asked with an innocent face and he gave me an irritated look. Obviously, I was a geek then, and I had no knowledge about these things. That's why I had come to him.

'Tell me what happened and how?' He asked me and then I narrated him how I went there and I kissed her and I came back again. As soon as I finished my story, he asked me three times to confirm whether nothing anything happened. When I shook my head, he started laughing unstoppably. I didn't get it. I asked why he was laughing.

'You have a girlfriend, yet you are *kachha limbu* in these things.' He said and laughed again. I was confused. Then he started explaining me the knowledge about pregnancy, and how does a kiss mean nothing in that. Till then I was in the confusion that a kiss leads to pregnancy as I had seen in the Hindi movies, a heroine gets pregnant after first night by just cuddling and switching off the lights.

He vanished my misunderstanding about pregnancy and made my concept clear while explaining with the help of his hands.

His expressions, his actions and gestures he made with his fingers and hand helped me a lot to understand that concept deeply.

Anyhow, I got relieved from the fear of Purvi getting pregnant and was free to go home. As much as I remember that was the first time when Pritesh had taught me something important.

****

The kite of my first love had started flying in the sky already. She was the one who was holding the thread of the kite to take it higher and higher. I had become so skilled in entering into her house. It had become like a daily routine. We had holidays for S.S.C. prelims. As much as I remember, there was not a single day, which I spent without meeting her in those holidays.

Once I had understood the original concept of pregnancy, then I felt free to love her deeply. So many meets, so many kisses and so many cuddles had lead to a strong bond between us. We had taken a high step in a small town. Gossips started growing around us. I had become a rockstar lover as I was daily daring to enter her house as her parents used to go to their respective jobs. We had become the famous couple in school. Everyone had come to know about us except our parents. Our friends had started shouting my name whenever they used to see her anywhere, even if I was not around. She used to blush by those teasing and shouting of my name.

We used to talk for hours daily at her home. She used to make tea for us, as she had no idea about cooking anything except making tea. But I swear to god, that was the best tea I've ever drunk. That was the best time of my life. The teenage love! My first love! We had started dreaming about our future. I used to look at her as my wife.

But one day Pritesh doubted that how come she knows everything already about kissing and romance. He said that she must be so experienced in these things.

His doubt had started biting my heart. This thought was killing me. What if he was right? What if she is not loyal? What if she has already taken some training of all these things from another trainer? What if I was not the only person entering in her house like a thief? What if I was not the first person riding that bike? What if someone had already taken a test drive? How come we are of the same age and yet I know nothing when she is holding a degree in her hands about romance and all that stuff?

I was freaking out. Those thoughts were killing me. Hence, I had decided to ask her about it. I had decided to clear the things and make sure that she was loyal to me.

****

Next day I went to her home in thoughts of asking her about her loyalty and how she knows everything and was not freaked out about pregnancy.

I was in her colony, and making rounds of her house to make sure that no one is watching me. I entered in her house. As soon as I entered, she closed the door behind me and hugged me. I hugged her back in confusion that whether it was love or lust. I didn't know that.

'What happened? Karan, you look tensed and confused.' She asked while uplifting her face and trying to kiss me. I kissed her and that led me to remind what Pritesh said. For that moment, I thought he was right, because I was kissing like a geek and her kiss was like a professional. I couldn't take it more. I asked her to sit and said that I want to ask her something.

'Where did you learn to kiss?' I asked directly as I didn't wanted to be fooled around.

'What? What do you mean?'

'I mean, how do you know all this stuff about romance already, when I had no idea about how to kiss and, the freakiness of getting pregnant? Tell me, have you done it before with anyone except me?' I asked looking into her eyes.

'What? Karan, Jaanu what are you talking about? I love only

you.' She said putting her palm on my cheek.

'Purvi, this is not the answer of my question. Tell me the truth.'

'What truth? I haven't done it with anyone before. You are the first person who touched me, and will be the last one too.' She said while taking my hands in her hands and kissing them. I wanted to trust her, but the way she was convincing me was leading me again to that question. I was not satisfied with her explanation. She tried to convince me more and more. Then she told me that she had seen it in video clips in the mobile phone of her friend's brother.

'What video clips?' I asked her. She took out her phone -nokia 3100- and started showing me one of the clips she had taken secretly by Bluetooth.

She asked me to rest on the pillow and relax. Then she rested on my chest and said, 'Listen, this one video was taken by Bluetooth when I had forgotten my phone at Pallavi's home. She took it from her brother's cell phone. Otherwise I would not have known about it.' She explained already, as I would have asked more questions about it.

She asked me to sit back relax and she rested on my chest. She gave her phone in my hand and clicked on play. As soon as she pressed the play button, she hid herself in my arms and started laughing silently. I didn't understand what was going to happen and why she was hiding her face and laughing. I tried to look at her face, but she then covered it with bunch of her hair and avoided eye contact like she was shying.

I didn't get it. I tried to concentrate on video, thinking whether what that was. Video started, and I could see a man and a woman going into a house while kissing each other. There I came to know that Purvi took her kissing lessons with the help of that video. I could see that the way that woman was holding that man's shirt and collar and running her hand through his hair was the same way as Purvi used to do.

Well, the video continued further and Purvi's silent laughing increased. I didn't know why. I thought it looks like some funny incident was going to arrive in that video. So I kept watching further.

'Ok, that's it! Enough now…' Purvi said while giggling and trying to take phone from my hand to stop the video. She was just laughing and avoiding eye contact, which made me more curious to watch further. I didn't allow her to stop that video.

I grabbed her from my one hand and took phone away from her to watch further. As video went further, the romance and love of that couple was increasing and their clothes were decreasing. I was eagerly waiting for that funny incident which Purvi was laughing about. But till then, I had to take the pillow which I was resting on from my back to on my thighs to cover the unbelievable and unexpected increase of crust. I then continued to watch further.

I was watching the video and realized at particular point that this was something I had never seen before. What's happening? What are they doing?

And then that man threw that woman on bed, and…

OH MY GOD! OH MY GOD! OH MY GOD! I cannot believe this. They are…. They are really…. Shameless people… HOLY SHIT! What the hell was that? OH GOD! I can't believe this. MAN!!!! THEY SHOOT NAKED? THEY SHOOT NAKED??? They shoot naked!!!! Did you know that? Because I didn't!

I was so shocked. I felt like 100s of volt of current had passed through my body. I almost fainted in shock of watching a naked girl. My eyes were wide open by looking that. Purvi was still laughing and covering her face by hiding in my chest. I was struggling to manage the pillow on my thighs.

They shoot naked? I started shouting in my head. It was totally new for me. I had never seen something like that before. Holy shit! And why the hell that lady is screaming? Didn't she know that he was going to hurt her? Oh god! They really do that? Don't their parents scold them for being naked in front of camera? Or is it just me who is still a geek and immature.

I mean… I… umm…. Wh….

Holy crap! They shoot naked!!!

Ah I see! At particular point I realized, that is what Pritesh was trying to explain me with his hands and fingers while his pregnancy class!

But still, they shoot naked???

****

Purvi was still laughing. And I was… I don't know! I can't tell. I was shocked, I was laughing, I fainted, I was nervous, I was shy.

And most important I got anerection.

'Err…. Umm… I gotta go. Bye.' I said and jumped up from my place to go.

'Hey, wait. Are you seriously leaving?' She said and covered her mouth with her palm to stop laughing but couldn't control her shoulders from bouncing due to laugh.

'Hmm.' I said and headed towards the door while trying to not to laugh foolishly.

'Karan!' She tried to stop me.

'WHAT?'

'Nothing. But, jaan, are you taking that pillow with you too?' She said pointing towards the pillow, I was still holding. I had no answer. She then came close to me and took that pillow and threw it on the bed, and hugged me. I tried so hard to get away from her due to the crusts. She tried to give me a good-bye kiss, but I was not capable of that at that condition. I was still in the shock of watching a naked girl screaming like hell. It was my 10th prelims' days and I had watched a naked couple wrestling around in the bed. I should have watched an inspiring video about someone studying like, 'I will win', 'never give up', 'success is in your hands' and not the one with '*aah, ooh*' of those naked wrestlers. I ran out of the door and went out of the gate. She followed me till the door.

After five steps I came back again.

'Hey, can you give me your note book?' I asked her.

'Yeah! But of which subject?' She asked, like I was going to read that and prepare for exams. But who would tell her that I didn't ask it for study. I just wanted it to cover my censored portion so that I could go home and survive.

****

Well, I had seen something new, which lasted in my head for like a week. In the bed while sleeping, in the bathroom while taking bath, in the toilet while peeing or pooing, everywhere, I could only remember that. My fantasy level had also increased to a mature level. Then I had totally and truly understood the real concept of how do they get pregnant as I had attended a practical class by watching that video clip.

For next few days, Purvi and I were unable to control ourselves by silently laughing and giggling in class whenever our eyes used to meet. God! I loved those times.

But due to that distraction, I could not concentrate on studies and failed in prelims. Purvi took it more seriously than my parents. We had so less time to prepare for S.S.C. exams. So, there after we used to discuss about my problems regarding studies except extra romance and she used to take revision of it. After all, she was the first rank holder, and how could she let her love fail while she will be a topper, again. So, we studied like hell for our exams. Actually we were having the fear of exams too, but more than that one thing was bothering Purvi. If I could not score well in S.S.C. , then we might get parted by our different branches and may get different colleges too. Therefore, for the sake of our love we studied like hell and worked so hard which resulted in good marks for me, and even better for her.

****

Each day of the holiday had gone in the stress of admission to better college. Well I didn't care about my college or career that much. I didn't have to as there was Purvi and my father to be tensed about that. All I was thinking about was what if we didn't get admission in same college. I was feeling so alone already.

Her father had already decided something for her. He had fixed her admission in one of the Aurangabad's colleges where they teach students how to prepare for IIT examinations and make them work hard for it. It was a bit out of the city. Anyhow, I was just happy that she didn't go to another city and I had also got admission to same city but in different college.

I was with my dad that day. We were just out of my new college, -Deogiri College of Arts, Commerce and Science, Aurangabad- after doing all paper works and admission processes. We headed back to Ambad. While going back I was just looking the city and once we were out of it, I was trying to figure out whether where her college might be.

We reached out of the city; my father stopped the bike at corner and asked me to stand up in front of him.

'What happened?' I dared to ask.

'Listen to me very carefully now. I know you are so happy to get admission in this city. But let me tell you that I have controlled all my anger and raised my hopes on you. I know that your friend

Purvi is also in the same city.' He was trying to tell me something but I was not getting it, but as soon as he mentioned Purvi I got shocked and lifted my head in surprise, trying hard not to laugh. He continued, 'I know about you both and if this time you break my trust…'

'What are you talking about Papa? I don't know anything.' I tried to be as innocent as possible.

'Don't lie to me. I am a teacher, I see students like you everyday. So don't try to fool me. I have seen you following her to her house. You are just lucky that you have scored good marks; otherwise I would not have let you even stand in front of my door. Understood?' He scolded me and I had no choice except to nod my head. I couldn't lie to my father. I could never. Even if I tried so many times, but either I used to be unable or he used to catch my truth always.

****

Well, anyhow my new college life had started there. It took less than two days to find out where her college was. I used to live in Osmanpura area in a flat with my new friend Amey. Pritesh was also with me in same college but he had chosen to rent a room as he was in different classes.

It had been two months since I had talked her. I was missing her so much but I was controlling myself reminding what my father said. But once I had come to know where her college was, I couldn't control myself.

Pritesh helped me to find out the way to her college. We met her there and she gave me her new contact number. Well, then the unstoppable chain of calls started. I had found new safe telephone booths where I used to talk with her fearlessly as the city was new and no one was familiar enough to tell our parents.

I was dying to see Purvi. I told Pritesh about it.

'I hate this city. I miss my home.' I said to Pritesh.

'Really? You miss your home or her home?' He teased me.

'Either way meaning is the same. I miss her yaar! It has been two months since I met her personally.' I was boring Pritesh with my emotional drama where he gave me a plan to meet her.

'Ok, Ok. I know one place here in this city. You guys can meet there.' He told me about the *Sambhaji Udhyan*, also known as

Sidharth garden near central bus stand, but I was afraid of meeting her as I had heard and read in news paper about how do local political activists meddle into the privacy of 'love birds' and make them suffer. They even don't fear to harm them physically under the name of protection of Indian culture. But I was dying to meet her, so I was ready to take that risk after Pritesh promised me to be around us with two more friends to protect us.

I called Purvi and told her about meeting in Garden. She acknowledged and we planned to meet next day.

****

Well everything was set; we had planned it like we were going on a robbery. Pritesh's friends told me that they would be around us in the garden, but though if anybody catches us and try to threaten us then don't tell them that you are committed just tell them that you are cousins.

I went to pick Purvi from her college. Pritesh and his friends went ahead to garden. I was right in front of her college and waiting for her in rickshaw. I saw her coming towards me. The happiness of my heart reached to its top level. I got excited like hell. I could not control myself from staring her like a… like a… ah I don't know, I have no words for me.

I was just staring in happiness. It had been two months since I hadn't seen her. She had become prettier. Her hairstyle, her physique, and her beauty everything had changed. It was like, I was seeing her for the first time. I realized that I didn't even close my eyelid and I was staring her continuously.

She had let her hair fly free with air. I was seeing her for the first time in jeans and top as all the time I had seen her was either in the school uniform or in other Punjabi dresses. May be that's why I was feeling like I was seeing everything new. Her hair was flying with air and few of them were running on her cheek. She came closer, and gave me a lovely smile, and put the hair behind her ear with the help of her finger. Her eyes were sparkling in happiness. When she made curve of her lips to give me that lovely smile, I got totally lost in her there and then. She was smiling, she was shying moreover, she was driving me crazy.

Bass ek hi zalak jo dekhi teri

Jindaagi meri yun sambhalne lagi
Khuda aasmano me akela ho gaya
Apsara yun jameen pe jo chalne lagi

Fanah ho ke dil wahi tham gaya
Jindagi me jaise khushiyan chhayi
Muskurake usne muze dekh ke
Kaano ke pichhe jo latt sarkayi

Bhul gayi thi palke dhak jana jaise
Khuli ki khuli reh gayi thi jo aankhe
Usse dekh ke kuch aise laga
Mil gayi ho hasi jaise khud muskurake

Ek ek kadam jo badha meri or
Duriyan duriyo ki dur ho gayi
Khushine khushise khushi baat dali
Jindagi meri Kohinoor ho gayi.

Bijliya sir me kadakne lagi
Badalo me dhadkane garajne lagi
Baarishe hawa me hawa ho gayi
Khushi aasmano se barasne lagi.

****

Oh man! Kid, that's your girlfriend! I said to myself. The rickshaw driver started staring her, I saw that. Yep! That's my girlfriend! I said to myself so proudly.

'You look so different. I missed you so much.' I said as she came to me.

'I missed you too, like hell.' She said.

'Ahem, ahem, shall we go now?' Rickshaw driver interrupted while clearing his throat. He was clearly showing that he was jealous of me.

Well, we got into auto rickshaw and headed towards garden where Pritesh and his friends were already waiting to protect us. We were in rickshaw and I was not even out of the pleasant shock of seeing her yet, where she took my hand in her hand and rested on my shoulder.

'God! I missed you so much.' She said leaving a deep sigh.

'I know. And I missed your home.' I said and she punched my thigh while chuckling. I was just keeping an eye on driver through mirrors to see if he was watching us through any of the mirrors where Purvi kissed my hand. Holy shit! How? I mean how could I forget to kiss her? I blamed myself and started to take a deep breath.

Ok, ok. Its time to kiss now! You can kiss her. Don't worry, everything will be alright. I started to prepare myself as I was nervous due to the long gap of kissing. I was meeting her after so many days, and even more days had passed since we had kissed.

So, here it comes. I will take her face in my hand and....

I was just planning for a perfect kiss and there she turned my face with her hand and dragged my lips with her lips by lifting up her head and clutching my hair so tightly. I lost myself there for a while. Man! She was so fast. I felt like I'd broken my fast after so many days. My body had started sweating and getting hot. All of a sudden, I felt like I am getting fever. My whole body felt goose bumps all over. We had closed our eyes and feeling the kiss where I reminded about the driver. I didn't want to finish the kiss cause of some freaking jealous guy. So I opened my eyes and looked at him with a cross glance while not disturbing the kiss. I looked back at Purvi. She had her eyes closed still. So I looked back again at driver through side mirror and our eyes made a contact as he was peeking. He quickly looked further then but couldn't stop himself chuckling. Well, go to hell you freak! I have a girlfriend! I thought to myself.

We reached at Sambhaji Udhyan. Pritesh had already bought entry tickets for us. He took us inside. His friends were sitting inside on a bench. They winked at me. We kept moving further and reached to a section where there were lots of trees and bushes and so much privacy for couples. I saw there were few more lovers making strong bonding of their love. I got relief that at least we had company. I also saw that there were some guys dressed up like bullies wandering like a greedy shark rounding for meat.

We got a place to sit and Pritesh said that he would be around. We sat there and I felt like I am growing up. I was becoming a man.

I had girlfriend, I had my first kiss, I had entered in her house like a thief and we had planned our future together and here we were, meeting in a garden sitting in bushes like a grown up couple. I looked around and realized that we were the youngest couple there. I was a bit nervous too.

We kept talking. She had planned so many things about her career, about our future, about us. I just kept listening to her. I was totally lost in her. My eyes were just staring the beauty of her. Her voice was like feast for my ears. She was the perfect. She cared about me so much. She loved me so much. She was so sensitive and emotional about me. She was telling me how much she missed me. I felt so lucky to have her. I was like on top of the world.

She rested on my shoulder fearlessly. I could smell the fragrance of her hair. It reminded me the time we used to spend in her house with each other. I looked around and then making sure no one is watching us, I ran my arm around her and rested it on her shoulder. I saw at her face. She closed her eyes, and started feeling my touch. I could not stop my fingers from running on her cheek. As soon as I touched her soft and fair cheek, she took a long breath and tilted her neck to that side. I could hear the voice of her gasps. The sound of her increased breath was driving me crazy. She touched my hand softly, and then hooking up it with her fingers, she clutched it and turned her face towards me to look into my eyes with her heady and intoxicating glance.

I wanted to kiss her. I wanted to make her happy and surprise as she made me in the auto rickshaw. So I just grabbed her and pulled towards me. I took her face in my hand and looked into her eyes. 'I love you so much.' I said.

'I love you too, jaan.' She replied and closed her eyes. I closed my eyes and lifted up her head. I ran my tongue on my lips to make them ready to kiss. I made a pout to touch her lips…

'OK, THAT'S IT. NOW COME OUT.' I heard a tough voice as soon as I was going to rest my lips on hers. 'Come out of the trees and get your ass back here.' One of the four boys, who were almost 6 ft tall, well built, dark coloured and tough like a soldier shouted at us.

Holy shit! We are dead! We are very much dead! I thought to myself.

The lips with which I was going to kiss Purvi were now shivering like hell in fear. The eyes which were closed to feel the love were now wide open and rolling around in search of my bodyguards. The hands, which were holding her face, were shaking like hell with a head in between them.

'Come out here.' He shouted again, and I thought why I took risk to meet her here. Why I called her here? Why did I not go to any movie except to meet here? Why? I mean why did I take birth in this world?

We gathered ourselves and headed to the opposite side. 'Don't try to be smart. You can't run away. Just grab your ass back here.' He shouted again and one of them came from other side to trap us.

≈≈≈

'What's your name?' He asked in tough voice. I didn't answer him.

'Show us your IDs.' Other one took his chance to scold two little kids.

I was trying my best to not to fall down in weakness due to fear and trying hard to hold the ground with my shaking feet.

'Why should we show you our ID? Who the hell are you?' I dared to ask him by looking straight into his eyes.

Nah! I am lying. Actually, Purvi asked that question while I was looking at ground with no words coming out of my mouth.

'Well, we are from security department of the garden. And don't you re-question us.' He said feeling insulted.

'Well, then show us your ID card of garden security first.' Purvi said while folding arms.

'Umm… yeah.' I chorused but I don't think he heard me, as even I couldn't hear my voice.

I looked around and found that every one who was sitting there before were gone. May be we were the only fools who didn't get that sign of danger coming towards us.

'Do you really want to mess with us except showing your ID? Fine! Call that constable standing at gate.' He ordered one of his boys and I fainted.

'We don't have any ID card with us.' Purvi answered him.

'What are your names? Where are you from? Tell us your parents' number so that we could call them.' He said and I had to take help of Purvi to not to fall down.

'Er.. my… name is K…'

'Deepali. My name is Deepali and this is my cousin Ajay.' Purvi said before I could tell my real name and I recalled that Pritesh's friend had taught me to tell duplicate names and relation of cousins.

'So you are cousins? Tell me your parents contact number.' He forced.

Oh god! What should I do now? Where the hell are my bodyguards? You know what? I am firing them from their jobs of bodyguards, IF I survived out of this situation which I think is not going to happen.

'Hmm, write down the number.' Purvi said and I looked at her in fear. What the hell are you doing lady? Don't tell him the number. I shouted in my mind but she didn't hear it. She continued, '9…4…' Stop it! Don't tell them…I kept shouting in my mind but she was like deaf. '2…1…' Oh god! Such a stupid girl! God, my girlfriend is an IDIOT! '3…2…'

Oh right! Smart girl! She was telling him Pritesh's phone number who by the way should have been with us to save our asses. He will be here to save us very soon when that guy will call him. Thank god, my girlfriend is a GENIUS!

Well he dialed the number and cut that call, I don't know why. That was the chance to tell my friend that I was in trouble. Shit!

But as he cut that call I did realize that he wasn't the security guy.

'Hey! What's going on here?' Here they come. Thank god my bodyguards arrived. Pritesh's friend shouted at them and came towards us.

'What happened, Karan? Is there any problem?' Pritesh asked.

'Um… I… I am Ajay, I am not Karan!' I said as soon as he finished his question with uplifting my shoulders. 'And meet my cousin Deepali.' I corrected him and winked at Purvi like I did a big thing to save our butts.

Pritesh told us to leave while his friends were talking with those bullies.

'Come Deepali. Don't worry, I am with you.' The Ajay inside me said. (Please come with me lady Don. I need you to take care of me from those bullies.) The Karan inside me was freaking out.

Well we left and Pritesh and his friends took care of the situation, doesn't matter how and when. But the important thing was we were safe.

****

AFTER THREE MORE MONTHS, 2009

'Jaanu, why didn't you call me early in the morning? I was dying to wish you.' Purvi said with disappointment.

'I am sorry, jaan. None of the stores were opened to call from. And then I had to go to classes. Anyway, I knew you will never forget my birthday, so I wished myself from you. It's ok.'

'Hmm. Anyway, wish you many many, many happy returns of the day.'

'Thank you, so much Jaan.'

'Ok, I have a surprise for you. So I am coming there today after college.'

'What? Really? Well I guess I will be waiting for you eagerly.'

'I know that. I will be at your place by 5:30. You please don't go anywhere. I can't even contact you as you don't have a phone with you.'

'Don't worry; I will be waiting for you right in my apartment.' I said and saw Pritesh coming towards me on a bike. 'Ok listen, I have to go now. See you then, I will be waiting for you.'

'Wait, wait. Are you just hanging up like that?'

'Sorry! I got to go, jaan.'

'Aren't you forgetting something?' She said with a puppy voice.

'Umm, no.'

'Don't you want to say something?' Her voice getting cuter.

'Umm, take care.'

'And?'

'Have a nice day.' I was smiling over here.

'AND?' She said with more disappointment.

'And.... that's it na? Do study now.' I was torturing her and laughing on this side.

'KARAN! You always do that to me. I am not going to speak with you now.' She said like a kid. Till now Pritesh had come to me and was teasing me by making faces and lip movements.

'Ok baba, I... love... you. Happy?'

'Hmm, thank you! I love you too. See you soon.' She said happily.

'Ok, bye.' I said and hung up the phone as Pritesh was excitedly telling me to do so.

'WHAT?' I asked him as soon as I hung up the phone. He hugged me and wished me a happy birthday.

'I have two surprises for you. Come with me.' He said with an excitement and asked me to sit on the bike.

We headed towards his classes. We stopped at parking. He parked his bike and sat on it. He asked me to guess first whether what the surprise would be. I gave up so easily, as I didn't want to waste time and I was eagerly waiting to see the surprises.

He took out a small box from his bag and handed it over to me. I opened it up. It was a mobile phone. The one thing I was waiting for and he had given it to me. It was getting so troublesome to call from booths all the time and I had to wait till morning always to talk to Purvi.

'Oh my god! Thank you so much yaara.' I said with happiness and smiling like a kid. I mean, I was a kid, though!

'Don't thank me. I didn't buy it for you.'

'What do you mean?'

'Boy, I am not that rich to buy a phone as a gift. And that is also for a boy! Ha, if you were having a hole which I wanted, then there were chances that I would have bought a bunch of phones for you.'

'So who bought it?'

'Your parents. They gave it to my dad while he was coming here to meet me.' He said.

'Wow, it is so great.' I said while looking at phone, 'Anyway, then what is your other surprise?' I asked being so eager.

'Wait, wait. We are just waiting for the other surprise.' He said and pointed towards a girl who was coming towards us. I saw in the direction he was pointing.

'What the hell! Is she…?' I wanted to say, but I was not sure. I kept looking at her. My doubt got vanished when she came to us and said,

'Very, very happy birthday, Bittu.' Janvi said with a big ear-to-ear smile and sparkle in her eyes.

'Oh my god! What the hell are you doing here?' I asked her as it was totally surprising for me to see her. I was so happy.

'I am here to wish you a happy birthday.' She said.

I was happy like hell. I mean I had no contacts with Janvi after I came to Aurangabad. And then she suddenly shows up her face on my birthday. I mean that was the best surprise for me.

'Oh man! Pritesh, if you were a girl I would have kissed you right now for these wonderful surprises.' I said to Pritesh.

'Oh really? Behind Purvi's back?' He asked in sarcasm.

'Doesn't matter! I know you would not tell her.' I said and we laughed.

Pritesh saw the time and took our leave as he had to go to his lecture.

'You are not going to lecture?' I asked Janvi.

'Oh, so you want me to go?' She asked in fake anger.

'No! Tell me, how come you are here?'

'Actually I got a late admission in this institute. Last day I overheard Pritesh talking about you, so I introduced myself and asked him to bring you here.' She narrated, and continued, 'So, you and Purvi? Still working that relationship?'

'Yep! We love each other so much. I feel so lucky to have her.'

'Hmm, good for you.' She looked pissed.

'What happened?'

'Nothing.'

'Tell me.' I insisted.

'You know Bittu?...'

'No, I don't know.'

'Listen na!' She scolded me and continued, 'I have been here since last 3 months and one thing bothered me more that my very own best friend didn't even try to contact me.'

'I am sorry, I didn't know you were here, neither was I having a phone.' I said while showing her my new phone.

'Shut up! Don't give me any excuses. You had told me that you used to call Purvi from coin boxes and booths. Couldn't you call me even once? I guess you don't care for me. If you had cared for me, you would have done anything to meet me. But I guess you didn't get time from your Purvi.'

'Chiku, sorry na! Do you really want to fight with me on my birthday?' I tried to defend myself by taking advantage of the day of my birth.

'NO. But I know, only Sanjay cares about me. At least he had come here to meet me twice.'

'Of course! He is….'

'HEY, let me stop you right there.' She said raising her voice, I just put my hands up in surrender and tried to calm her down.

She said that she had to go to next lecture and she'll meet me at 4 after class.

She took my leave wishing me happy birthday again. As soon as she went I could not stop myself calling Purvi from my new phone.

****

I went to my apartment blissfully. I plugged my phone for charging. I was so happy. My birthday was getting better and better. I told my roommate Amey that Purvi would be there at evening.

After that incident in Sidharth Garden, I did not want to take risk of meeting outside. So there after either I used to go to her college with Pritesh as my bodyguard, or she used to come to my flat.

Well, I got fresh and looked myself in the mirror. 'Life is so good.' I said to myself while trying to set my curly hair. 'Man! This birthday is the best.' I said and a bunch of hair popped up like a clown doll from a surprise box from the spot where I was setting them. God! I hate my curly hair. I said and dismissed all my hair by running both hands through them. 'Ha! That's the way my girlfriend likes it.' I said and winked at my mirror image. 'I have a girlfriend!' I said excitedly to myself. And winking again I headed to the door. Then suddenly turning back to mirror, I looked at myself and said, 'You know what?' 'No I don't know.' 'I have a new mobile too.' I said and made a fake laugh like a villain from a Bollywood movie. Then again I turned back to door and before I could open it I reminded something again and went back to mirror, 'And one more thing, now your best friend is also with you boy!' I said and making some sound with tongue I headed to Amey's room.

I told him how today was one of the best day's of my life. He started teasing me about Purvi and the possibilities of things, which might happen after her arrival. I started blushing and dreaming about her. While I was dreaming about Purvi, we heard a strong and loud knock on the door. We both got startled and shocked and ran to open it.

'Hey,…err sorry boss. *Galti se bat gir gayi. Taklif nai dena chahta tha.*' A boy almost 20 year old with a cricket kit in his hands, said. I saw two bats dropped in our doorway.

'Wow, what a bat!' Amey said while taking one of them in his hand.

'Are you new here?' I asked that guy who was still holding that kit and struggling to not to drop it.

'Yes. We are just moving in here.' He said while trying to point towards the door next to our flat, which was still locked.

'Can I help you? Do you have keys?' I asked being polite.

'My friend has the keys of this flat; he is downstairs picking up our stuff.' He said and I took the stumps from his hands to make him comfortable. Now he was holding the *balls* only.

We introduced ourselves. He said his name was Mukram. While we were talking and waiting for keys, his friend arrived, with a big box in his hand. Anyone could tell that he was holding a TV. Mukram put his balls in his pocket and helped his friend with that box.

'Hey, I think I know you.' That other guy said as soon as he saw me.

'I…think so.' I said while remembering where I had seen him.

'You are Mahesh and Rohit's brother, right? I am Ganesh.' He offered a handshake.

'Yeah! I've seen you with Mahesh once. He calls you Ganu, right?' I said with a happiness of coincidence and shock inside my mind. The shock, of getting my elder brother's friends as my neighbour. Now how would I meet Purvi. I would have not saved my ass from the trail. The trail, which will lead from Purvi to me, from me to Ganu, from him to my brother, and then my father. I am going to die. I thought.

'Do you need any help?' I asked.

'No, its ok. We are not only two guys actually. We have lots of hands, downstairs.' He said and I could see the hands he was talking about were showing up one by one. Ganu opened the door and went to place the things on their places. I was counting the number of guys who were showing up one by one and were going to be our neighbours.

1,…2,…3, and 4, and 5. Oh wait, and 6! Six boys? Wow! Oh I am sorry, I forgot the first two, Mukram and Ganu. That means, 8 boys. Great!

They were doing their job of shifting. I saw the time. I remembered I had to go to meet Janvi.

I ran downstairs and headed towards her classes. She was already waiting for me in the parking. I went to her and she scolded me for coming late. After few minutes, I saw Pritesh waving me bye, bye. I waved him back and Janvi and I started walking towards her hostel.

We wandered for a while. She showed me where her hostel was. Then we went to eat some pani-puri. After some time she took me to a temple behind *peer bajar.* It was the temple of lord Shani, lord Ganesha, lord Mahadeva and lord Hanuman. She told me that ever since she had been in Aurangabad, she used to visit that temple. We sat there and kept talking. After few hours at 7:30, I dropped her to her mess, and headed towards my apartment.

****

As I was in front of my flat, I saw the door was already opened. One of the new neighbours was standing in their door and giving me a wicked smile raising his eyebrows. I didn't get it.

I went straight to my room crossing the hall. As soon as I entered in my room I got shocked. I saw Purvi standing in front of me with red eyes, no need to guess whether due to anger or due to crying. Both answers were true. Now I came to know why that guy was smiling at me. Oh god! I am dead! From both side I am dead!

'Why did you come here?' I shouted at Purvi as I was afraid of my brother knowing about her from his friend who was my neighbour now.

'What? I came here to meet you. It's your birthday.' She shouted back and I didn't know whether I should have scolded her again for being loud or say sorry for my mistake. I had totally forgotten about meeting Purvi.

'Didn't you get that I was not here due to some reason. The guys next to us are friends of my brother. If they came to know about you…'

'I don't care. I was waiting for you and you are two hours late.' She was pissed off, 'Where the hell have you been?' She said softly wiping her tears and looking at me in anger.

'Look, I am sorry. I totally forgot...'

'Oh great! You forgot.' She said and turned away while biting her lips to stop sobbing, 'You forgot me? Why? Who do you got there outside? Ha?' her voice becoming louder. There was no chance of telling Janvi's name at that condition. 'I was with my friend from college.'

'Oh really? Ok!' She stared at me for a while and I felt more suffocated than I ever felt in front of my father when he used to be angry with me.

'Couldn't you even call me once, you LIAR?' she shouted in anger and I closed the door so that my brother's friend next door would not listen.

'Don't scream. I had forgotten my phone while charging.' I defended myself while pointing towards phone.

'Oh please! Don't tell me that. Till yesterday you were not having phone though everything was alright. What happened today? Why didn't you call me from any coin box or STD booth?'

'Purvi don't scream.' I was panicking but I could not yell at her as she was waiting for me since two hours with some expectations and plans and now with two red and wet eyes.

'Then what the hell you want me to do?' She screamed again and threw a carry bag in anger, which she was holding. As she threw that bag I heard a happy birthday tone playing on piano. I looked down, there was a lovely greeting card opened up and playing that tone, rested on a new navy blue t-shirt dropped out of that bag. I felt so guilty. Moreover one thing scaring me was if that guy heard Purvi's words and if my father came to know about it then I... I... I was better being dead. While I was thinking about it, my eyes rolled at the corner of room, where I could see the box of cake smashed and half opened ruining the yummy chocolate cake within it.

I had to calm her down. So I ran towards her. I tried to pull her but she resisted, 'Just get lost.' She screamed again. She swept my hand and I tried to grab her. She pushed me and I caught her waist. I pulled her and hugged her. She was still trying to push me in anger, and punching me while sobbing silently.

'I am sorry. I love you jaan.' I whispered in her ear while holding her tight.

'No. Get the hell away from me and go to that bloody bitch.' She screamed like hell and I could hear a silent and continuous beeping as she screamed in my ear.

After few seconds I realized that she had mentioned a bitch. How the hell she knows about....

Oh! Pritesh!

'Listen jaan...'

'No you listen. I was waiting for you here and you were wandering with Janvi? That's how you love me? If you want her that much then why don't you leave me and go to hell with her.'

'For god's sake stop yelling.' I yelled at her. I know I was the one who was guilty, but I was worried about Ganu and the trail to my father.

'Don't you understand once? Ha?' I started scolding her, 'Now I don't care anything and dare you call her bitch again!' I said with big eyes and pointing a finger towards her. She went silent for a couple of seconds.

'You are yelling at me for her?' She said with a very broken feelings and a very innocent crying face.

'I am not, not only because of her. I know I hurt you. And I am sorry for that too. But it's not her fault at all. I just met her today...' I was explaining her but she didn't even listen to me. She picked up that bag, shirt, and greeting card. She pushed me away in anger and with wet face due to her tears; she walked away straight through my room and headed towards the door through the living room. I followed her. She stopped at the door. She looked at the dustbin, and with a strong force of anger, she threw that shirt and greeting card in trash. She left the apartment slamming the door behind her.

****

She left. I was sitting in my room, listening the happy birthday tone while wearing that new shirt. My phone beeped. I thought it was Purvi but it was Janvi's message about good night.

I didn't call Purvi as my ego was not allowing me to do so. I replied Janvi and continued on listening that happy birthday tone from that greeting card taken out of the trash.

'Fought with girlfriend, ha?' I heard a stranger's voice. I looked at door; there was that guy who was smiling at me before.

'Who are you?' I asked him.

'My name is Umesh. I saw your girlfriend arriving in excitement and going in anger. She is pretty.' He said and I wished if he was not Ganu's roommate.

'Did Ganu see her?'

'No, he was out for work. Why?' He asked me and I told him about the trail I was worried about. 'Don't worry man! And don't sit here like Devdas. Come with me.' He pulled me and took to their flat.

'Guys meet our neighbour.' He yelled taking focus of all his roommates. He started introducing me with his friends.

'This is Pradeep, we call him Chintu.' He said while pointing towards a well-built gym guy.

'Hello.' He offered me a handshake.

'Hi, I am Karan.'

'This is Sambhaji and that's Bhagya.' He introduced me with a guy who had personality like any south Indian actor.

'Hi, I am Karan again.'

'And that one is Sachin right beside Anil.'

'Hi, I am…'

'Karan. We know. Stop saying your name man! We know by heart already!' Anil said and they all laughed.

I had made some new friends. We kept talking for hours and they made me like one of their family members. I forgot all about fight with Purvi and tension about trail.

They told me that they used to do part time jobs and studied as well. Each one of them was crazy about cricket. They used to play cricket daily. Pradeep offered me to come and play next day but I refused as I had classes. I promised them I would play on Sunday.

****

Well, Purvi was angry for long time but couldn't carry her ego in front me as I was being rude to her even when I was the one who was guilty. Criminal actually, from her point of view.

She tried to maintain the relationship good from her side. But somehow, Janvi was affecting her brain. Somehow, she was becoming so possessive about her. Not only about her, but even if I spoke with any girl from class. Few of Janvi's friends had become my friends too. Her roommates, her classmates, we used to meet so many times in the temple behind *peer bazaar*. We used to sit there and talk for long time.

I always had to hide it from Purvi. I didn't want to hide that I meet Janvi and her friends but, it was for her own good. She would have reacted like a… like … a… what should I say?... a crazy woman.

That was Saturday evening. Janvi with her roommate was already waiting for me in the temple. I went there while talking on the phone with Purvi. They all started to tease me after her. I had to cut her call to talk with them.

'So, it looks like someone is having great plans for tomorrow.' Janvi started and I blushed.

'Come on. Nothing like that. She has hertest tomorrow. I don't know whether she would come to meet me or not.' I said.

'So why don't you go there to her college to meet her?' Sakshi, Janvi's friend with average personality, brown hair, slightly gray eyes and fair face with that geek spectacle on her just perfect nose, said.

'I can't go there. Actually I don't need to. Once we had decided to meet in Sidhart garden and what a problem we faced there! I can't even explain.' I said.

'Caught by bullies?' Sakshi guessed.

'Yep, and I don't want to let that happen again. I don't even want to remember that.'

'So where do you both meet then?' She enquired again.

'Well, Bittu lives in a flat with his friend. She comes there and I just don't know what these guys do. Ahem ahem.' Janvi tried to tease me by clearing her throat.

'Oho, that's great.' Sakshi said with a wicked smile.

'Why the hell are you enquiring so much by the way? You plan your tomorrow with…' Janvi was saying and Sakshi pinched her to stop saying her boyfriend's name, and Janvi laughed.

'What? With whom?' I tried to ask, 'Come on, you just asked me everything about Purvi and now you are hiding your secrets? That's not good Sakshi.'

'It's nothing, Karan.' She blushed.

'Come on. His name is, Suresh. One of her school friends.' Janvi answered. 'Oho, that's great too.' I replied with the same wicked smile. She just hid her face with her hair.

'She even knew all these things about you, which she just asked.' Janvi said, 'She was just trying to be polite and get you into the bottle to get her work done.' Janvi said and Sakshi punched her gently to make her quiet again.

'What work?' I asked and she shook her head. 'Come on, tell me.' I insisted.

'Should I tell?' Janvi said uplifting her hand like a student and Sakshi just looked at her tilting her head.

'Well,' Janvi continued, 'she wanted to ask you if she can meet Suresh in your flat.'

'*Bass?* That's it?' I asked, 'Looks like you also have an experience about bullies huh?' I said and she chuckled with a nod. 'Well, I have no problem with you *meeting* your boyfriend in my flat.' I acknowledged.....

****

... 'I, I don't think its right, Sakshi.' I said trying to get her away from me, and searching for my T-shirt.

'Its ok, Bittu. You don't feel guilty. If that moron doesn't think anything for me and if he has no value for my love, then why should I worry about him.' Sakshi said while removing her forearm, which was covering her from chest and trying to hug me again.

'I... I ... I don't understand. My mind is blank for now.' I said and she kissed me.

After that kiss, I was again. I was confused and my eyes rolled towards the navy blue T-shirt, which was lying on the ground beside my bed in my room. Within no second, I felt guilty like hell. What am I doing? I asked to myself.

'Karan...' Sakshi said resting her head on my chest and...

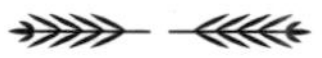

12. The truth (present)

* * *

My thoughts of past got distracted by Janvi's missed call. I just looked at the screen and started thinking.

Tit for tat? Really? Would it be like what Purvi said?

No, no! Janvi won't do that to me. But she just did it. Well, I don't care.

Before it will lead to that level, I will finish this relationship. Already she has fought with me because of another guy. She lied to me. She had promised me something and she broke it.

All the things kept running in my mind. I was deeply in those thoughts when my phone beeped. I saw the screen, it was a message from Janvi.

Why the hell she messaged me now? I opened the message. It said, 'gn'.

I saw the message and pressed the option button to delete her drama. I was still angry about what she had done and how she had talked to me. And if it was going to be tit for tat by my fate, then I must finish it now.

However, as I was about to press the delete button, I thought I missed something. I wished to see that message again. I went back and opened that message again. It was still, 'gn'

But then I scrolled it down, and it showed,

'gn ..'

Suddenly I felt my heart melting faster than ice. I could feel a sweet pain running through my chest as soon as I saw those two dots. I realized that how do even small things can mean a lot and make you happy. Those two dots had made me happy like nothing else. I was feeling like a.... like that... a... ah... I have no words.

Why? Why? Why? Why did she add those two dots at the last? I wanted to hate her. Why did she?

Was it a formal message or she did mean it with those dots?

Does she still remember those dots? Did she really mean she loves me or she just put those dots habitually?

I got to call her.

I was just… just getting freaked out. Although I was still mad at her but something deep inside me was stopping me from hating her.

I called her,

'Hmm?' She said so softly.

'What?' I asked in anger.

'What 'what'?'

'What did you message me?' I asked in rough voice.

'Good night! Why?' She replied so casually.

'And what about the dots?'

'Oh! You still remember?' She asked softly while sneering.

'Are you crying?'

'No!' Sneer again.

'Stop lying to me, ok?' I said in anger. As soon as I yelled at her, she busted into tears.

'I missed you so much Bittu…' She said and let her feelings fall from her eyes through tears.

Oh man! How could I get angry now? But inside my chest I was still carrying a fire due to anger about getting second preference in her life.

'Stop all your drama, ok? I am still mad at you and you haven't given me any answer regarding Vinit, neither have you apologized.'

'I didn't lie to you Bittu, trust me.' She spoke while crying. Though I had seen her photos with them there, I wanted to trust her.

'You are still lying. I have seen your pics.'

'I know, but I don't talk to him anymore. Trust me I swear. I was going to tell you about Kapildhar that day, but you recalled his stuff, which you were angry for, and I didn't want to make you angrier, that's why I just chose to hide it from you. I swear I didn't mean to, neither I talk to him anymore.'

'Oh really? You just clearly showed that I mean nothing to you. You gave him first priority than me. Moreover you scold me instead of saying sorry? What the hell was all that? You've even added my number to rejected list! How dare you? What the hell you think you are?' I was just getting hyper and angrier as while talking I was recalling the every other thing about her which was making me even more angry.

'It's not what you think Bittu. I didn't mean to hurt you. And he means nothing to me. I was just already in anger and frustration.'

'Stop all your drama Janvi.'

'Bittu, actually you called at wrong time. I was already angry and sad. I needed you, I wanted to talk to you but you started fighting with me. And I got hyper and angrier. I am sorry, I didn't mean to.' She was apologizing and crying. Her voice was melting my heart. All of a sudden, I thought to put that Vinit's topic aside and I should also let my feelings fall from my eyes. I had also missed her so much in these two weeks. I also didn't want to fight with her. I wanted to talk to her. I wanted to say 'love you' to her. I wanted to hold her and hug her.

'Why were you sad?' I asked keeping my voice down and closing my eyes to control tears, 'And don't lie to me.'

'No, I won't but promise me that you will not get angry'

'Why? What happened now? What did you do?' I said while getting worst ideas about why I would get angry.

'Promise me.'

'Ok, I promise.' I said and she took a deep breath to tell me something.

'I was so alone without you, Bittu. I missed you so much. But…' There it is. This 'but'! I hate these types of 'but's. '…but I needed to talk to someone. I needed you. And I couldn't talk to you. So, I called my friends to talk and to feel fresh. I called my old friends my classmates, but I could not talk to them as free as I was with you. So….'

'So…? Tell me.' I yelled while becoming eager.

'I… I called Sanjay. And please don't get angry.'

'What? You called your ex?' I shouted. Then I thought, 'Yeah! She also belongs to Homo sapiens like me.' I was not shouting because she called Sanjay, I was actually feeling insecure as she had chosen him as my substitution.

'Please don't get angry, Bittu.' She said and I realized that I had also called Purvi and she did nothing different.

'Hmm, I… I am not angry. What happened then?'

'Nothing...' She said and sobbed, 'He... he has added my number to blacklist.' She said and started crying again.

'Why are you crying? Does it still matter to you? Ha? You broke up with him. So leave all those things behind. Why do you care about it now?' I said being insecure as any boyfriend would be. She was still sobbing.

'What happened then? Did he say anything?'

'No, I didn't even get to talk to him.' She said and started crying again. I had no other option except to console her. I was her best friend first. I could not see her crying.

'Chiku... please don't cry. If you want, I can call him right now.' I said and waited for her reply but she didn't say anything. 'Shall I call him and make conference call so that you can talk to him?' I asked her proving that I am world's most idiot, stupid, fool and *chuu**** boyfriend who is calling his own girlfriend's ex, because she was crying for him.

Actually, that was the best friend material inside me, who was telling me to do so. I dialed his number but it was switched off. I swear it was switched off.

'Chiku, it's switched off. Do you have another number of his? May be he has changed it.' I asked her.

'Bittu...' she said softly and stopped while sobbing.

'Hmm?' I too said with a sob and a tear fell from my eye as I heard my name with that sweet voice and with that innocence after so many days.

'I love you so much....' She said followed by a big cry from her side and then followed from my side too.

'I love you too, Janvi.' I said rarely speaking correct words due to sobbing.

I forgot all my anger and frustration. I didn't even remind myself that bloody Vinit and those pics which Bhumi had shown me. I just focused on Janvi and those magical words coming for me from her sweet lips.

We both kept crying for couple of minutes and smiling while crying foolishly. I felt like I 'right clicked' on the monitor of our love and refreshed our relationship.

'Bittu... I want to hug you.' she said and I closed my eyes feeling that I was with her and taking her close into my arms.

'Bittu,...' She said softly.

'Hmm?' I said without opening my eyes.

'Wait. I think someone is on waiting. Its 3rd time it has beeped. I am taking that call.' She said and picked that call before I could reply, and as I was going to cut my call, she switched it to conference.

'*Ha, Dhiraj bol.*' She said to that other guy.

'Nothing, I was just worried about you. Are you ok?' He asked her showing care in his voice. But as a boyfriend, I thought he asked showing lust in his voice.

'Yeah! I am ok. Actually, feeling better now. I was just talking to Bittu. He is on conference.' She said cheerfully.

'What? Ok. So shall I cut my call?' He asked being polite. But I thought he asked being smart.

'No, wait... Bittu...' she stopped him and started talking wih me, 'the guy who is on conference is my childhood friend, Dhiraj. We were classmates in school.' She introduced.

'Hi, Bittu. How are you?'

'Err, actually fine, but my name is Karan.' Why? I mean can't she just introduce with my original name? I always have to add a sentence telling people my real name.

'Hmm, ok then. You people talk, I'll cut my call. Bye Bittu, bye Jaanu.' Anyhow he called me with that name. Didn't he hear me telling my real name? Whatever! It's good that he cut his call.

But wait! What did he said to Janvi? 'bye Jaanu?'

'Who was that guy?' I asked Janvi.

'My friend, I just told you na?' She answered.

'I heard that. But why was he worried about you?' I asked being possessive.

'I told you, I was so alone, missing you so much. I had called my old friends, and he is one of them. I had almost cried while talking with him as I was missing you. Hence he was worried about me.' She explained.

'Hmm.' I said. But I was so eager to ask her about why he called her Jaanu. I mean I used to call that to Purvi, as she was my girlfriend. How could he call Janvi that? I was burning inside, but avoided to ask her as I didn't want another fight. Don't these people have another time to call? Why do they always interrupt between perfect patch up and romance?

****

'Bittu, I have a news.' She said.

'What?'

'I spoke with my father and convinced him that these people here in my college are not that much good to teach us, so I wanted to attend extra tuitions. And he agreed.' She said excitedly.

'Hmm that's great. But why are you getting so excited about study?'

'Idiot, I am talking about tuitions in Aurangabad!' She almost shouted in happiness.

'What? Does that mean you are coming here to live? Please say yes. Please, please!'

'Yes! Yes, I am.' She said cheerfully and I got happy like never before.

'*Sahich naa…!!!!*' I almost shouted in happiness.

'I am coming there next week, and you will search for a room on rent or a girls' hostel for me.'

'Yep! I will. I love you sooooo much.' I shouted again in happiness.

She gave me a reason to live again. I was dying to see her. These last two weeks had taught me a lesson that I cannot live without her. And as I had heard those three magical words followed by my name from her lips after so many days, I did come to realize that I can't even forget her ever in the future too.

I started to search for a room where we both can live together. I searched so many places, but I could not find the place, where we both can live together, and which was not so expensive and also not so far from my college and her classes. The expense and distance from college was not that much big issue, but actually, Aurangabad or citizens of Aurangabad were not ready to accept a boy and a girl as roommates or flat mates.

That one week passed in just the excitement and the day dreaming about the future possibilities. I was so happy, so excited and bouncing in the dreams.

Finally, our long distance relationship was going to finish. We were going to see each other daily. We were going to wander with each other daily. I was happy like… like… a ….. you know,…. I

was happy like a.....
Ah, I can't even explain. I have no words.
Whatever they say about it is true, '*sabr ka fal meeeeeeeethaaa hota hai.*'

****

AFTER ONE WEEK

I was already at the Cidco bus stop waiting for Janvi to come. To come into my life again. And this time, not only in the life but also in the same city. I had searched a new room for me to stay. Only because it was close to her classes, so that we could meet daily, before and after my college. I had to lie to Mahi for that. It was Mahi's last month in Aurangabad as his college life was about to finish in a month. So I told him that after he leaves the room, it would be hard for me to find a new roommate or room. Therefore, I am changing the room now. He also agreed.

I was so excited about Janvi. She was finally coming to live almost with me. I stood up from my place as her bus arrived at bus stop. I prepared my heart to not to fail in extra happiness after seeing her. I prepared myself to feel the time stopped, as I would see her. I told my brain to get ready to see her hair flying in slow motion with air.

I was watching at the door of the bus. I saw Janvi coming out of the bus with a heavy bag. She came out of the bus and started struggling with the bag. I headed towards her to help her with her bag but then I saw a boy coming out of the bus picked up her bag and put it down. Such a nice guy! Helping her.
NO! Boys helping pretty girls can never be nice.

He was also holding a bag in his hands. Ha pulled out the handle of her bag and headed towards me. She gave me a cheerful and lovely smile. I felt like we were rebuilding our relationship as it was feeling new, new.

But wait! Why the hell that boy following her?

'Hiiii....!!' She said, so cheerfully and boy following her stopped in front of me. I gave him a wicked look. 'Dhiraj, this is Bittu. And Bittu, this is my old friend Dhiraj.' She introduced us.

'Hi, Bittu. How are you?' (KARAN!!!! MY NAME IS KARAN.) He offered me a handshake and I shouted in my mind.

'You guys talk, I'll just come.' Janvi said.

'Wait! Where are you going?' I stopped her as I thought I would not be comfortable with a gay. I mean with a guy holding such a girly bag.

'I'll just come!' She said while going towards women's washroom.

She left and I shared some awkward moments with that stranger.

'So! You are the one who is Janvi's best friend?' He started a formal conversation.

'Yep! Actually not only best friend, I am her boyfriend too.' I added.

'What? But I thought…' He said and stopped.

'What?'

'Nothing, it just, I know who her boyfriend is.' He said showing he has extra information.

'What do you mean?'

'I meant, I think you don't know, but her boyfriend is Sanjay, one of her relatives.' He answered, intentionally to make me feel down.

'I do know that, and that is past.' I said in frustration, 'Why the hell you bought such a girly bag? (YOU STUPID GAY!)'

'Actually it's not mine, these both bags are Janvi's.' He answered and I quickly tried to take that bag from him.

I saw Janvi coming towards us. We headed towards a rickshaw.

'Dhiraj, thank you so much for your help.' Janvi.

'Come on, Jaanu. It's ok!' He acted smart and my eyes popped out as I heard 'Jaanu' from his mouth again.

'Ok then, see you sometime.' Janvi wished him bye, bye.

'What? I am coming to drop you to your hostel.' He forced like an idiot. Didn't he get that she was trying to avoid him. She is saying THANK YOU! Get lost you moron.

'No, no please. Don't trouble yourself. I'll go with Bittu.'

'Yeah! We'll go together, you please don't trouble yourself.' I said while putting my arm around her.

'Come on, I have to tell uncle that you reached safe.' He forced again and Janvi had to agree as he mentioned her father there.

We sat in rickshaw and I intentionally sat in middle.

'Avishkar colony.' I said to rickshaw driver and he started the rickshaw.

Actually, her hostel was in N-5, but as he was with us, I didn't want him to know her hostel's address. Therefore, I was taking them to my room first.

We reached in front of my room.

'Where is hostel, Bittu?' Janvi asked me.

'Actually your roommate is in college now, and she has the key. So till then you stay here. We will go there at 8 o'clock.' I answered her.

While we were entering, my landlady came and enquired, 'Who are these people?'

'Err, this is my cousin Janvi and this is her BROTHER.' I introduced them and Janvi put her lips in between teeth to stop laughing. I told aunty that she was going to be there for an hour until her roommate comes.

'Ok then, I should leave now.' Finally, that moron took our leave, as he sensed why I made him Janvi's brother.

He left and we went inside my room. I just threw Janvi's bag on the bed and took her close to me. I hugged her so tight, '*Aaan... maz naak.* (my nose...)' She nasalized as her nose was crushed due to hug. I made my hug a bit loose and she hugged me back.

'I missed you sooo much.' I said and she shushed me and rested on me while closing her eyes and clutching my shoulder. We both felt our presence for a while and lost in the moments.

'Why the hell he calls you 'Jaanu'? No, no, wrong question. Actually, how can you allow him to do so and react normally on that?' I asked finally being impatient.

'What?'

'That moron, Dhiraj. Why do you allow him to call you 'jaanu'? You know I used to call that to Purvi.'

'Shona, what is my name?' She asked me.

'Janvi?'

'Hmm, so that is the short form of my name. Jaanu for Janvi.' She clarified.

'No, no, no. I can sense it. It is not as simple as it looks. Who is that guy? And this time if you want to not to fight, you better tell me the truth. I don't want any lies now.'

'Ok. But promise me you won't get angry again.' Here it comes.

'What? Oh great! Now another new story?'

'Promise me first.' She insisted.

'Ok, ok I promise.'

'Hmm. Listen I was going to tell you about this so early, but…'

'Janvi don't fool around. Just come straight to the point.' I was being impatient.

'Look Bittu, whatever I'd say, the truth is I love only you.'

'Janvi you are freaking me out now. Just tell me the truth.' I insisted her and she took a deep breath to start her story.

'He…. I mean, we…. Err…. He had proposed me twice in past…'

'WHAT? I knew there is something about that guy.' I almost shouted.

'Oh boy! You got angry on THAT part?' she said while putting her forefinger in between her teeth and raising eyebrows.

'What do you mean? What is it else?'

'I'll tell you but you better remember your promise that you would not get angry.'

'Janvi just tell me, the truth.' I shouted again.

'See you are getting angry.' She said while biting her finger.

'So, just tell me the truth and don't create any suspense.'

'*Chidu nakos na…!*' She said so innocently and I could not stop myself from being calm. I took her close to me, pecked her on her lips, we sat down and I assured her that I would not get angry if she finished it as soon as possible without creating any suspense. She started telling me the truth,

'I… err… I still love…. I mean I still like Sanjay.' She said and closed her eyes avoiding my eye contact and hid in my chest hugging me so strongly.

'WHAAAAT?' I shouted taking her away from me.

'Wait, it's not totally true. First listen to me.' She said but whatever she had said had made a fixed place in my mind. She still loves him?

'What is the total truth then? And how the hell it is connected to that moron Dhiraj?'

'*Chidu nakos na…*!! And why are you abusing him?'

'Oh, so you feel bad for him now!'

'Bittu, he means nothing to me. But you please calm down.

Listen to me.' She tried to calm me down but I was still shocked and her words about Sanjay were still running in my head making a strong noise like a railway engine. I just tried to calm myself down and she continued,

'Actually, I love you… but…' She was saying.

'Yeah! BUT.' I interrupted.

'Listen na! I mean, I love only you Bittu. That Dhiraj you were talking about… was… was…'

'Was what?' I asked being impatient.

'Actually, when I was with Sanjay, he was still dating another girl in his college and not behind my back. But anyhow I used to be jealous about it. I just never reacted on it thinking that he might say I am a narrow minded and can't even understand his friendship with that girl.' She completed half part in one breath.

'And?'

'And that's where, Dhiraj proposed me the second time. I didn't know what to do. I wanted to make Sanjay realize that how I feel when he wanders with other girl. So I….'

'Don't tell me you said 'yes' to Dhiraj at the same time.' I said with a surprised face.

'I didn't meant to but, I just… I just did it so that Sanjay would feel insecure and leave dating that girl.'

'Had you gone crazy? What were you thinking while dating two boys at the same time? Ha? Are you a slut?' I slept out a word in aggravation.

'Bittu… don't forget that you promised me you won't get angry.' She said trying to get into my arms and rest on my chest. 'And don't forget that I love you and you love me too.'

'Ok, ok.' I said trying to control my feelings, 'What happened then? Is that it or anything else is remaining?'

'Actually, I just used him for annoying Sanjay, but he didn't felt anything. And then when I met Sanjay at didi's marriage, I told him about Dhiraj to make him jealous. But it didn't work.'

'It means whatever cheap thing you did, resulted in nothing.'

'Not actually.' She said making herself comfortable in my arms. I rested back and ran my arm around her.

'Then?' I asked.

'He was annoyed and insecure too. But not for Dhiraj.'

'What do you mean?'

'He had a clue that Dhiraj was just an appendage, a substitute to make him feel insecure. He even supported my friendship with Dhiraj and told me more stories about that girl.' She said and I chuckled, she continued, 'He was actually feeling insecure about someone else.'

'Who?'

'He was just insecure and annoyed by my friendship with that guy and that's why we even fought in marriage. You know who he is.' She told me and looked in my eyes.

'Don't tell me. Me?' I said with a revelation. She just nodded.

'Wait a minute, is that why you guys broke up? Because he was feeling insecure about me?' I asked again.

'No, not actually. He was just feeling insecure because of our friendship but moreover he wanted to be friends with that girl and date her. So you were just a motive he made.' She confessed. I thought for a while and reminded all things she just said and clicked some points. Then taking her away from me and making her sit in front of me by clutching her arms I looked into her eyes.

'Janvi, tell me few things.' I stared in her eyes and started questioning her.

'Was it your idea to break up with him?' I asked and she looked down and shook her head silently.

'As you said, Dhiraj was just a substitute?' I asked and she nodded.

'Had he really called you that night for wishing happy valentines' day?' She shook again.

'But you were waiting for it. Right? And were still in love with him?' I asked and she didn't answer it. 'Answer me Janvi.' I shouted. She just nodded. At that moment, I felt insecure and possessive about him. And suddenly one thought ran into my mind. Was I also an appendage?

'Janvi,...' I touched her face with my palms and made her look up in my eyes, 'If you love me, tell me one thing. Whatever you said to me on 14th Feb., was the truth? Or you were just lying to me to make him possessive again?' I asked and she looked down. As soon as she looked down my anger started rising to its uncontrollable level. 'What am I asking to you? Was it a lie? Was I also the substitute to make him insecure and work your plan out?' I did not shout this time as she might have lied to me seeing that anger.

'I love you, Bittu.'

'THIS is NOT the answer of my question. Tell me, was I ….'

'Actually, I really love you, Bitt…'

'Don't fool around just tell me the truth.' I shouted being impatient as thought of being fooled and fraud made me angrier and I was losing my control.

'Bittu, listen to me first. I'll tell you the truth but just listen first.' She said and I just stared at her with eyes opened wide in anger. She continued, 'I really love you, Bittu. And I want nobody other than you. And you are the only person who understands me, who knows me better than anyone. You are my best friend, I won't lie to you. It is true that I love you, but the thing you just mentioned is also true.' She confessed and I just got the confirmation that I was being used by my own best friend. I looked around in frustration and pushed her away, so that I will not slap her.

'I agree that whatever happened was to make him possessive, whatever I did was to get my love back, but then….'

'Enough!' I shouted raising my hand. It was not bearable to me anymore. She would have told me to help her in that thing, but why did she lie?

****

What the fuck is this? Is my love story going to travel well for at least a moment? I thought to myself.

Every time it starts to grow well and romantically, some stupid things happen or some moron enters to spoil it or any stupid interference occurs to damage the mood.

What the fuck she just confessed?

I just stood there with empty words and slightly wet and shocked eyes. I got a big kick of pain through my chest right into my heart.

All of a sudden it was like someone stole all my thunder, all my glamour. I was feeling so foolish, such a stupid, chutya.., idiot guy who believed a girl and she was using me just as a substitute to forget her ex. I felt, such a chutya I am!

Yeah, here I could find lot of words for me!

What the fuck is this? So, she was saying that… that…. What the hell!! Why did she say THAT?!

Does it mean that all these days, whatever happened was a drama?

Was I or am I just a stupid substitute for her in her life? Was she just using me all these days to take revenge from Sanjay?

I was not getting anything. I felt like a fool there.

'Bittu…' She continued with some explanation, but I had no sense to hear her voice. I didn't even hear a word coming out of her mouth then. I was so angry, panicking and getting hyper.

'Let's go.' I said while taking her bag with one hand and pulling her out of my room by other hand.

I put that bag in anger to lock the door. After locking that door, I started walking towards stairs without asking her to follow me or to come with me. The next minute, we were on the road. I took the right turn and started walking faster. She was right behind me, trying to catch my speed and trying to say something, which I was not listening.

After taking another right turn, we were out of my colony. We headed towards Sidharth chowk, also known as Avishkar chowk. Crossing that small chowk, we headed straight towards the Saint Tukaram Natyagruh, known as Cidco theatre. While walking there, I had lost my sense. I didn't know how did all my feelings got cringed under my anger. We reached at the corner of Dharmveer Sambhaji School. I looked at the time; it was 8:50 pm.

'Walk faster, or your hostel's gate will get closed.' I said with loud arrogance.

'I will stay at your room then. I guess, that's why you had taken me there first, hadn't you?' She said and I got angrier after hearing her voice.

'YES, that's true. But now I don't think here after I want to see your face again. Actually, I personally think that I am not a supplement.' I said.

'Oh come on, Bittu. You are not. I love you so much. Please don't do this to me.' She said already starting trembling in her voice.

We reached in front of her hostel. I introduced her to her landlady and took off from there without saying good-bye to her.

I went outside the colony and sat on the bench in front of the theatre on road divider. I was damn angry and more frustrated. I covered my face in my palms and ran my hand through my hair. People were walking there after their dinner; some little kids were riding their bicycles. Few of the girls from same hostel were talking with their boyfriends on the stairs of theatre and wishing bye bye as the time was up. And, I was trying to overcome myself from what she had said and confessed.

'Bittu…' I heard her voice. She was standing in front of me.

'Go to your hostel. Or gate will be closed.' I said in anger and started walking back towards my room. She was calling my name but I didn't look back. She ran behind me and I had to stop, as I didn't want it to become a scene on the road. I took her back to her hostel and left her there.

I started to walk towards my place. 'Was 14th Feb.'s night preplanned by her to get distracted from Sanjay?' I started thinking as I was out of her colony.

I could not help myself but think about all the past. I was walking senselessly on the road. I don't know why but an auto driver abused me while I was walking on the road near the school. 'What about all those promises she made to me in Beed? Had she already said those to Sanjay? Or even she might have said that to Dhiraj at the same time.' My mind was running at its worst level while I was walking slowly and took turn towards Avishkar chowk.

'She lied to me about Vinit also.' I suddenly remembered that bastard too, 'Was he also the substitute for me or Sanjay in her life? And I am the foolish one.' I was thinking and my phone rang. I got distracted. I saw the screen; it was already showing Janvi's 5 missed calls. I cut that call and started walking. I crossed the chowk and my phone rang again. I cut it again and decided to ignore even if it beeped again.

'She lied about Dhiraj also. He still calls her jaanu.' My mind was not in my control now, it was digging deeper. 'Are they still in relationship and trying to fraud me?' I thought and my frustration level reached to its top. My heartbeats were louder, my breathing had become faster and my hands had started shivering like hell due to anger. All I could hear or think was just those names, Sanjay, Vinit, Dhiraj then me…. Sanjay, Dhiraj, Vinit and then me. I could not bear it.

When I reached my room, I just threw my cell phone as it was continuously showing her name on screen and I was not willing to see her again.

'I hate you, bitch.' I shouted in anger, and let my feeling and frustration fall from my eyes. I had decided to stick only with Janvi for my whole life. I accidently had broken up with Purvi and that I didn't want to do with Janvi. I thought we were so loyal to each other. I thought we would really end up well together. But no!

Here I had a bunch of dreams and future plans and there she had a bunch of boys in her BF list. And I was one of them as an appendage.

She stopped calling me and my phone went mum. I also fell asleep while thinking about her in anger.

****

I was half-asleep where I got awake with her call again. It showed 1:30 am on the watch. I was just about to forget those things in sleep, but her call reminded me all again. I cut her call with same resentment, and tried to sleep. After a minute, my phone beeped again. It was her message.

'hi, bittu. My boyfriend karan fought with me and is so angry. I'm so sad. I need my best friend to talk.'

Not again! I thought to myself. Why the hell on earth I promised her that thing about friendship? But I had to call her back. After all, I was her best friend first, doesn't matter how big a liar she was. Therefore, I dialed her number.

She picked up the call but I didn't speak anything as I was still angry.

'Bittu,...' She said with trembling voice followed by a barking of dogs, '... I want to see you right now. Please talk to me.'

'Listen, I don't want to talk anything. It would be better if you go and sleep and let me sleep.' I said arrogantly.

'Bittu I am coming to your room right now...' She said and I could hear the barking again.

'What? Look at the time.' I said, and she screamed as another dog barked, 'Where are you, Janvi?' I asked.

'Now, I am in front of that school, coming towards the Sidharth chowk.'

'WHAT?' I almost shouted, and jumped out of my bed, 'Have you gone crazy?' I said and quickly got out of my room, put on my slippers and started running towards Sidharth chowk.

'I got away from balcony. My roommate had showed me the path to get out even after gates are closed.' She was saying and I was running as fast as I could. It was after midnight, and totally dark outside. She was walking alone on the street. I reached at the chowk and saw her coming towards chowk with a shivering body and fear about dogs on her face. I cut that call and ran towards her.

'You are an idiot.' I scolded her, and she clutched my arm and wrapped her hand around it, as she was so afraid of dogs.

'Can we please fight in your room?' She said with that innocence and I could not carry my anger before it. We headed towards my room and she was walking faster than me, to get rid of those dogs.

'Don't worry, they won't harm you. They were with you to protect you.' I said, and within no second she replied, 'Put your theory about dogs with you. I just don't like them. I don't trust them.' I wanted to laugh on her condition but moreover I was angry on her.

Well, we reached to my room, which was already opened, as I did not get time to lock it. As soon as we entered the room, I pushed her away as I was still angry.

'Bittu, enough now. Please, talk to me.'

'What the hell were you thinking? Don't you get it? Why did you leave the hostel at this time? Do you've you any idea what could have happened to you by now?' I started to scold her.

'I wanted to see, you.' She said with her face down and eyes looking up towards me with that innocence in her voice, 'And in my defense, it was not my fault. Had you talked to me well and not got angry, I would have been safe, either here or in my hostel by now.' She said and I just wanted to slap her for her foolishness.

Actually, no! I wanted to hug her for what she did for me. But as I was still angry because of her confession, I wanted to scold her more.

'I really want to slap you now.' I said getting more aggravated.

'Slap me, hit me, punch me. Do whatever you want but please talk to me well. I can't take it now.' She said.

'Don't you…' I was saying something but stopped myself, 'Leave it.' I said and turned away to avoid her face.

'No, Bittu…' She said and took my hand and started to slap her with it, '…slap me if you want, but talk to me.' She was irritating me more with her that action. I was getting more annoyed and she was just trying to slap herself with my hand. I tried to release myself from her but she was not stopping. I warned her to leave my hand and stop that drama. I warned her to not to make any scene. But she was not listening to me. My annoyance got to its higher level and my anger was boiling my brain and was trying to pop it out.

SLAP! I pushed her away and slapped her on her left cheek making my hand loose. She went silent after that and really got what she wanted. The slap!

For few seconds she could not understand what happened then. And when she got her senses back, a drop rolled down to her cheek from her eye.

'You really slapped me.' She started sobbing. And I was really relieved for a bit.

'Yes, I did. And really now I am feeling so good.' I said, 'And now don't blame me for it. I just did what you asked me to do.'

She was a bit angry for it but she did not react more as it was her decision to slap her. She tried to control herself from what just happened and wiped her tears. She stood there just looking into my eyes.

'Are you happy now?' She asked me.

'Am I? Let me guess.' I started, 'My best friend first tells me that she loves a guy. Then she says that she broke up with him because she loves me. Then I trust her like a fool. Further, she gives more importance to another person and lies to me because of any other random guy. For him she fought with me too by the way! Then just when I think it's going to be alright now, another moron pops up and I come to know he was her bf too, like for a day or two. It was not enough to make me sick, so all these things come in front of me in a very dramatic way and yet I try to forget all things. And just then, she says that she still loves the first one to whom she had left for me? Like all these days I was just an appendage for him like everyone else.' I completed my story with a perfect sarcasm and started breathing fast as if I just ran a full marathon. She just kept looking at me and turned her face down, 'In addition to this...' I shouted again suddenly and she startled and lifted her face up, '... I don't even get to be angry or scold her, as I have promised her whether whatever would happen, I will be her best friend first.' I said with a furious face and she turned her face towards ground again. May be she was feeling guilty. May be she got what I was trying to say. May be she would cry now. I thought.

But no! I saw, she slowly took her hand up and put her forefinger in between her teeth and started biting it. Great! I just got more annoyed with it and turned around to avoid her.

She was now right behind me still biting her forefinger and I was.... I was... a...

Actually, I was right in front of her facing other side resting my hands on my waist and trying to control my laugh. I don't know how but her foolish act made me laugh where I was not allowed to laugh. How would I suppose to laugh there? I was angry. So I also had to put my finger in my mouth. She just saw that and started chuckling and then laughing like a monster. I also could not help it out and started to laugh. 'Shut up!' I said while laughing. She just ran and hugged me from behind taking her hands under my arms and resting on my shoulders clutching them tightly.

'That's why I love you so much, Bittu.' She said and chuckled followed by push from me. I pushed her away and tried to control my laugh.

Within a second, I do not know how but my frustration had lowered down but I was still angry. Why did she lie to me? She would have told me about it. Now she just broke my heart.

'Bittu...' She said controlling her laugh and sudden change in voice, 'Bittu, I know, it started in that way. To make him possessive I tried taking your help, as he was just insecure about our friendship. But on the next day I realized that whom am I fooling around? You were the perfect partner for me, we know each other, we like each other, no one ever can understand us as we do. I agree that it started with a lie but it is not a lie anymore. I really love you, Bittu.' She explained in a breath and I did not take efforts to understand what she just said. I did not need to. I was just looking at her and trying to get angry again. But her face, that beauty, the innocence did not allow me to get back to that posture again. My mind was telling me all the things she did and was making sense out of it for getting angry. But my heart was telling me just one thing, that I love her.

I was just staring at her. I took her hand and pulled her in my arms.

'I hate you.' I said and hugged her.

'I know, you can't.' She said and ran her hands on around me.

'I really do. I really hate you.' I said while taking her hair in my fist and pulling it to make her face up towards me. She looked up and I touched my lips to her and kissed her.

'If this is your hate, then I like it. Keep hating me always.' She said after resting on my chest.

She had lied to me so many times and yet I trusted her again. I don't know why. She had literally defrauded me. And yet, I was with her again.

'You lied to Janvi. So many times.' I said while hugging her, 'I don't know if I can trust you again.'

'I am sorry, Bittu. I was just being selfish. I know I should have talked to you about these things first. But I was afraid of losing you. I started it in wrong way but I really love you now, and I don't want to spoil it.'

'I don't know, what is going to happen further, but I don't want any lies now.' I said and she acknowledged.

Well it was a new start, (again) of our relationship. But yet, somewhere deep inside my heart I was still carrying a fear of being defrauded again. She slept in my room for that night.

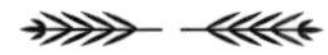

13. New life, new beginning

* * *

It was a start to the same life with a new beginning. All the detachments between us had drifted apart. All the misunderstandings and fights were finished. Now it was only us and our relation, which is never going to end.

'Hello.' I said with eyes full of sleep and trying to wake up by her call.

'Good morning.' She said in her sleepy voice, 'Wake up, I am getting ready for my class now.' She said and I opened my one eye hardly to see the time. It was 5:30 am.

'Hmm.' I said still with closed eyes and rested that phone on my ear, as I didn't have any sense to hold that phone too. I didn't know when I fell asleep again. No, actually I haven't even woke up to sleep again.

About half an hour later, I woke up startling with that ringtone which rang right into my ear with a loud sound almost going through my ear trying to make me deaf. 'A..Ah… I love you too.' I said without picking up the call and startling. It rang again. I picked it up and closed my eyes again.

'Still asleep?' She said with that disappointment.

'NO. I am awake, Chiki. I will be there to drop you within half hour.' I lied while trying to wake up.

'Half hour? See the time Bittu. I had called you half-hour ago. It is 6 already.' She said with her sulky voice. 'I am entering in my class. You wake up and get ready at least when I will come out.'

'Yup! I will.' I said with my sleepy voice again and she cut that call. This was one of our new routines. She went to the class in morning and I'd go to meet her. But unfortunately I slept again, lazily.

My phone kept ringing due to alarm and I kept snoozing it. I was asleep as usual. I was just dreaming about the house we would build after our marriage when I heard a knock on the door. I woke up from my place and headed to open the door. As soon as I woke up and stepped up ahead, I fell down as my leg was hooked up with college ID card and I fell right on the college bag. The room was totally messed up. I opened the door. Janvi showed her disappointed face as I was still sleeping. I hugged her as she entered in the room. She pushed me away, 'What is this *yaar*, Bittu?' She started to spit out her disappointment, 'I called you three times to wake you up and you are still sleeping.' She said and I tried to make her sit on the bed.

'I am sorry, sweetheart. I could not judge the time due to heavy sleep. I will just get ready and then drop you to your class.' I said while sliding my head on her lap and trying to sleep again.

'Move away.' She said annoyingly and tried to push me to wake me up again, 'Look at the time. My class is over. And what the hell is this all.' She said showing me the mess in my room. 'Yesterday I cleaned your room, and you made it again as it was.' She started to fold my blanket. 'Wake up, Bittu…' She said in anger and kicked me on my thigh. I just pulled her on the bed, wrapped her in my arms making her comfortable by resting her on me. She just kept looking into my eyes making her big fishy eyes tiny as usual. I made pout to kiss her and with no seconds, she closed her mouth by hiding her lips between the teeth. I kissed her closed mouth and she just got annoyed.

'Wake up you lazy boy. Go and brush your teeth.' She said while trying to get rid of my arms. I just smiled and woke up. I was searching for my brush; she handed it over to me and went to set my bed.

'Had great sleep?' My landlady asked me when I was heading towards washroom. She was cleaning the yard.

'Yes, aunty.' I said while rubbing my eyes.

'Who is in there?' She asked as she heard the flapping of bed sheet.

'Janvi, is cleaning my room. She just came from her class.' I answered. Till now, aunty also had got used to Janvi's daily meet to my room to wake me up.

'Boy, thank god she is here. Otherwise you would have left your room messed up daily.' She said.

'Thank me, aunty. I got her here.' I said and Janvi came out.

'Bittu, you haven't brushed yet.' Janvi yelled and I ran to washroom, as she might have got angry again. Watching my run on her yelling, aunty started laughing.

After few minutes, I took bath too. And when I entered in my room after bath, I felt like I've entered heaven. My room was never clean. She had turned all the messy things to heaven. She cleaned everything and was waiting with the breakfast, which she had brought. Man! I love her! I thought.

I threw my towel in sexy mood and headed towards her slowly, slowly with spark in my eyes and biting my lip. I went to her, pulled her in my arms and caught her waist to get her closer.

'Just PUT that bloody towel at its PLACE.' She scolded me, ruining my mood, 'Don't you get it? I just struggled so much to clean your mess, and within no second you are doing it again. Don't you feel any urge to clean by looking at this mess?' Oh god! I thought, how did my parents enter in her body, she sounded just like them. She was talking just like my mother. *Don't you get it; I just struggled to clean this room. And you are messing it again. Don't you feel anything about me before you mess it up again?*

'Nope.' I said leaving her and lifting that towel to put it in its 'right' place, 'I have a little angel to take care of me every day.' I said and thought she might get flattered, but she just stared at me and got annoyed again. She knew that answer already.

'Ok, baba. I am sorry. You know me, I am just like this.' I said taking her close and pecking her on cheek. She pushed me away gently and went to serve the breakfast without saying anything. But I could see that peck had worked, and her annoyance had lowered. I went to her when she was facing other side and wrapped my arms around her stomach. And rested on her. With my fingers, taking her hair to one side of her shoulder, I kissed on her neck.

'Bittu…' She smiled and tilted her head. I just succeeded to get that spark in her eyes back. Then resting on the bed we took our breakfast.

Life was so good. Just perfect. I just had to lie about Janvi to my parents. But nothing is new in that for a person who has fallen in love. She used to call me daily to wake me up and meet her before her class for a while just to see each other's face. But I was so lazy to wake up in the morning. She used to call me before entering in her class too. But I used to sleep then also. Then she used to come to my room after her class and scolded me daily like she did above. Our relation had taken off to the next level. This was the first time when Janvi and I were together for long time. My room was not a mess anymore. She was there to clean it daily. I really loved those two hours of morning when I used to wake up, watch Janvi scolding me, cleaning my room, hug her, and kiss her neck. Then, when she used to rest on me tilting her head and leaving her anger with a smile… Man! That was simply awesome.

Well, we took our breakfast. She then started reading her books while I was getting ready for my college.

'What is the plan for tomorrow?' I asked.

'Nothing, why?'

'It is Sunday tomorrow. Let's go somewhere.' I suggested.

'No, I can't.' She said with disappointment, 'I have a test tomorrow followed by an extra lecture at 3 o'clock.'

'What?' I was disappointed too, and wore my uniform.

'It's ok. We don't have to go anywhere now.' She said and got up from her place, 'We meet daily thrice. If we want we spend nights together…' she said and headed towards me, 'I am with you and you are with me. What else we need?' she came closer and helped me folding my sleeves. 'I like it like this.' She said and pecked me on my lips.

'Here, take your *mangalsutra*.' She handed me over my ID card.

'Oh man! I feel like those married men who go to work and their wives give them a peck to see them off, and that moment when they don't want to leave her behind.' I said and kissed her on her forehead.

'But you got to go, Shona. Those married men get paid for their jobs. But if you don't go, you would have to pay defaulter fine to college.'

'Hmm. I know, my bloody college!' I said with disappointment and rested my cheek on her head and hugged her. That fragrance of her hair was driving me crazy and was trying to stop me. But taking long breath I have to leave her behind. 'Anyways, see you at 5. You know where to put the key when you'll go to your hostel.' I said and headed to my college.

College was just a reason to stay in the same city with her now. The time between 10 to 5 o'clock was tough to pass. When I was a kid that time was fun as I used to be with Purvi then. This time I was leaving my heart behind me. Attending college was a compulsion, just to not be a defaulter student and just to complete the 75% attendance.

The daily timetable was changed again. This time it was like: Receive her call at 5:30 am, speak something in my sleep. Cut that call and go back to sleep again. Get another call from her at 6 and lie about I am awake. Listen her sweet sulky voice because we could not meet due to my sleep. Sleep again, (if I was really awake to speak on phone). Wake up with her knock on the door at 8 or 8:30. Hug her as soon as she enters in the room before she starts scolding me. Previously a hug used to work well, to calm her down. But when it became daily work, she used to get annoyed with it. Then listen some words of her anger due to late sleep and messy room. Try to silent her by kissing and locking her lips. Go to brush after a hide and seek with brush. Get fresh and take bath, feel like heaven as room used to be so cleaned and fresh within few minutes as she was there. Go to her in sexy mood and try to kiss her. But, she is still annoyed so first place the towel at its place and then hug her. Go to college after kissing her on her forehead. Try to be alive in college and survive hard. Call her in recess and ask if she had her lunch. Take lunch in few minutes and talk to her whole recess. Go late to next lecture; give a fake reason to professor that mess was crowded so I got late to have my lunch. Again, try to survive until 5. Once college was over, call her to meet, again.

At this time she used to be asleep and the time used to change, as at evening I used to be the boss. Call her to wake up and go to the room to get fresh. Get fresh and call her again to let her know that I have left to come to her hostel. She is still asleep. Reach in front of her hostel at 6. She is still asleep. Now, who is the boss?

Call her to scold her and take revenge of morning. Scold her as if she has done an *apology less* crime. Wait for her like for 45 minutes alone, sitting on the bench in front of the Cidco theatre. When she arrived, scold her again for being late. Calm down after seeing her fake cry and sulky sweet face and finger in between her teeth. Sit there talking on the serious issues like, what did you eat for lunch? When did you sleep? Facebook, movies etc. And, when bored, go for a walk towards 'Kala Ganpati' temple on Jalgaon road. Sit there till 8:30 and leave for her hostel. Sit in front of the hostel until 8:55 and then after drama of 'bye bye', 'I will miss you', 'I love you', get lost to room alone. Sometimes when the pain of leaving each other behind cannot bore, she used to stay at my room for night, by making any fake reason to tell landlady like time was up and gates were closed as she was studying in library and she could not judge the time due to heavy study.

Our Facebook accounts were not private anymore. We both used to know the passwords of each other's accounts. And that was one of the greatest mistakes of my life, including her.

Well, I was waiting for her in front of Cidco theatre. That day senior citizens filled every bench. As it was weekend, so many people were wandering with their kids. I saw the time again. I called her.

'Come on, yaar. See the time.'

'I will be there in just five minutes.' She said and I literally marked her words and started counting the five minutes. I came to know that in her watch, five minutes means whole one hour of normal watches, which we people on the earth use. I truly used to believe that she also belongs to planet earth as I know her since childhood. But, then I had started to doubt if she belongs to other planet or even other galaxy.

I saw her coming towards me and I started to walk without waiting for her to come with me. She was right behind me and I was walking faster as usual towards kala ganpati temple. I was taking advantage of great opportunity she had given me to get angry. We reached the temple and sat there after praying to Lord Ganesha. The statue of the Lord Ganesha in that temple is made of black stone, hence the name of temple.

We sat there and she started to try to calm me down. I was

not angry because she stood me up for more than an hour, but the way she used to struggle to calm myself down, was just the fun and the loveliest thing in my life I had experienced, for which I can live with her for my whole life.

But, that day she did not make more efforts to calm me down. 'Bittu, I said sorry to you. Are you going to talk with me or not?' She said with a wild attitude.

'No.' I answered in the same tone.

'Fine! Well, I won't tell you about the Facebook messages then.' She said sarcastically while trying to hide the message box. Well she was not actually hiding it. She was just playing with me.

'What is so special about it today?' I asked assuming that she got me.

'Just few messages from an old friend.' She said and her phone rang. She went to a side to talk to her father. I was being impatient about her facebook messages. So I logged in from my phone to her account. I saw the messages and the fake anger which I was trying to maintain yet, turned into real one. There was a chat with Dhiraj. Actually, I should say there was flirting with Dhiraj. I read all the chat and just got hyper.

What the hell is this again? Can't she just survive without any trouble to our relationship? Does these good going days not bearable to her? Why the hell does she keep doing this? I thought to myself.

She came back to me after cutting her call. She saw me and did not dare to ask whether what the matter was.

'So you read it.' She said with finger in her mouth already.

'I can understand him flirting with you. But what the hell were you doing flirting back? Have you lost your mind?' And, I started.

'What's wrong? We just chat for a while. It's not a big deal.'

'Janvi that guy is trying to steal you from me and you are flirting with him. It is a big deal.' And that went for long.

We started our fight again. I was trying to make sense by telling her that he is not a nice guy, he was trying to get her back to him. And moreover I can't survive without her if she left me.

But she was not able to understand anything. For her, he was just trying to be nice by asking her about her personal life and personal matters. And talking about sexual things was not a big deal as he was just clearing his doubts from a medical student. What the hell a dentist would know about sex? They are meant to check your teeth, not your private parts. And why the hell was he sharing his fake girlfriend's sex issues with my girlfriend?

Also for her, it was nothing that he was asking her figure size as he wanted to gift something to his fake girlfriend and Janvi answered it to help him for his fake girlfriend.

Output of this fight was that I was narrow-minded and did not understand her friendship with other guy. And moreover, if I perform with bunch of girls then how can I object on her chat? I tried to explain her that dance with some sincere and decent girls with a nature of sisters to me and chatting with a moron about some private things, flirting have big difference. For her sake I told her that if she feels uncomfortable with my dance group, I would not perform next time, I would not dance, I would just go to help them, and asked her if she would leave her friendship with that guy (again). The answer was unnecessary, because she had left talking with that moron already after our previous fight regarding him. But I was unaware that she just left talking with him, she had said nothing about chatting and flirting. So she had not broken her promise but just found another way to make me crazy, literally crazy.

I just left the place in frustration after her answers and did not even look back to her. I went ahead and stopped beside the corner to watch her go. Not to spy on her, but due to care about her. She got up from her place and headed towards her hostel. I followed her by a distance just to see if she reached safely. Dropping her to her hostel, I left for my room with same anger.

'Atleast he wd hav nt left me alone on street like dis.' Said her message as she entered in her hostel. I did not reply or neither told her that I had not left her alone on the street.

****

'Hey, beta. What happened?' I heard aunty's voice while I was in my room.

'Nothing aunty. I was in my library and could not judge the time so got late for my hostel and could not get in.' Janvi explained. I opened the door and saw her coming up stairs with a paper bag in her hand.

'I could not go to hostel when you are angry.' She said with that puppy face, 'I came from my mess, by bringing a parcel for our dinner.' She said and I just turned around, 'Why did you come here? Don't you have your other friends?' I said and headed towards my bed and kept the door open.

'Bittu, come on!' she said and pecked me after coming closer, 'You know what…'

'No, I don't know.' I said carrying my anger and she chuckled.

'Listen na!' Chuckle again, 'You've changed. So much. Previously you were not this possessive. Now a days you are getting angry too easily.'

'Oh, so you can see my anger only. Can't you see my love for you?'

'See… you are getting hyper again, and that also for no reason.' She tried to get me.

'Why would I not get angry yaar? Some bastard is trying to flirt with my girlfriend, he is trying to steal her from me and you want me to calm down?' I started shouting, 'I would have not got this much angry if he was flirting alone. But here you are also responding him. How am I not supposed to be hyper?'

'*Chidu nakos na…!*' She said with her finger in her teeth.

'I will not, if you'll be loyal with me.'

'Come on, Bittu.' She said and put that parcel down, 'I am loyal.'

'Oh yeah! I can see th…' I was shouting and was not getting calm. So she just locked my lips with hers, popping up and holding my neck. I tried to push her away in anger, '…that how lo…' and she grabbed me again and not let me complete my sentence. She locked my lips to stop my yelling. She did not leave my lips and slowly, slowly I calmed down.

When she realized that I am not angry anymore and calmed down, she removed her lips and stared in my eyes. After a couple of seconds, we both busted into laughter and hugged each other.

'I loved your way to make me quiet.' I said and she punched my chest followed by a chuckle.

'Listen Chiku, I know I have become so possessive. I also know that since we started our relation I am acting like a… like…. A…. ah…'

'You have no words for you, right?' She said and I chuckled.

'Hmm. But I know I get hyper easily, I don't know why?'

'I know. It is because you don't trust me.'

'No, I trust you. I really do. I just don't trust those guys I get angry about.'

'Oh really? You trust me?' She asked sarcastically.

'Obviously! Have I ever said anything regarding your friendship with other guys? I even don't say anything when you talk late night to one of your friend from C.O.E.P. and not also when you had went to meet one of them in hospital, and what about the calls of your college friends regarding lectures and notes and all that stuff? I never said anything about that.' I tried to explain.

'So, what is the deal with these guys?'

'It just… I just…I don't know. I just feel insecure when you talk to them. And by 'them' I meant, Dhiraj, Vinit and your ex.' I said and she just smiled, 'As a boy, I can sense that they are not good for my relationship with you. And I believe that Dhiraj is totally jealous of me and can do anything to steal you from me.'

'Oh come on, Bittu. It's nothing like that. And why the hell you keep adding Vinit?' She started again.

'Oh so you trust him more than me.' And I started again.

'NO. He is just my friend now. And why are you getting hyper again?'

'I don't know. But whenever I listen that name, I just… I just….' I stopped myself as I was being hyper again. I really hated that guy.

'Ok, ok. Calm down.' She said and pecked me.

'Sometimes I think, maybe I just reflect Purvi.'

'What do you mean?'

'I mean, she used to behave like this. Whenever I used to not pick up her call, whenever I used to meet you, whenever I used to miss you or even mention your name, she used to be out of control. And now, see. Who am I with now?' I explained, 'Yeah, this is it. You were my best friend and today I am with you leaving her behind. May be that's why I am insecure that they might steal you from me too.' I avoided saying –may be you'll go with them too- as I didn't want to hurt her and I was afraid if I said it and it happened to be happen.

'Don't worry, Shona. It is not going to happen. I am only yours.' She said and rested on me.

She tried to calm me down and told me to not to worry about it, but I was still feeling insecure. I just hate that guy and moreover I hate Janvi's friendship with him.

****

At the morning I woke up early as her ear ring was spiking my chest. I saw her sleeping with me resting her head on my chest and wrapping her arm around me. I set her hair back, which was spread on her face. Kissing on her forehead, I hugged her and she moaned taking me closer. I saw the time and I had to wake her up. I didn't want to but she had a test in her class. She used to wake up daily so early and was willing to sleep more on Sunday. But I woke her up and pushed her to sit from her place. She just rested on me keeping her eyes closed and sat there with me.

'Wake up, Janvi.' I said and pecked her lips.

'Hmm. Shhhh…' She said while wrapping her arms around my neck and not opening her eyes.

'Don't you have to study for your test?'

'Hmm. Shhh…' She said like a kid, and I remembered how I used to react when I was a kid and my parents used to wake me up on a Sunday morning. My mom used to offer us all the types of bribe like, great breakfast, more time to play, an extra biscuit, or chocolate if we woke up early. But it never worked for Sunday morning. I used to sleep until it used to be the time for 'Shaktiman' on DD channel.

'Ok, then. You want to sleep?' I asked her.

'Hmm.' She acknowledged in her sleepy voice.

'Hmm, sleep then.' I said and rested back taking her and kissed her on lips. She then woke up with that kiss, 'You just need the reasons to kiss me, don't you?' She said and looked at the time, 'What the hell! Why didn't you wake me up?' she said taking her head in between her hands and pushed me away to wake up.

'Great! Now suddenly I become the guilty.' I said and she came back and pecked me on the forehead.

'Obviously, you are.' She said and went to get fresh. She took bath and told me to go for bath. I went to washroom and came back fresh. I could see her sitting on the bed with those half wet hair, half of which, were left open to dry on her back and neck. And some of which were floating on her cheek and forehead as she was busy in book for test and not setting them up. I could not help it and kept staring at her. I went to her and slipped that bunch of hair behind. And by resting my palms on her cheek I lifted her face to peck on her lips. I pecked her and she kept reading again and put her hair again free to dry. I went from her behind and lifted her up. I sat on the bed and rested her on me. She was not distracting and kept reading without leaving that big Anatomy book. I wrapped my hands around her stomach and kissed her cheek. As soon as I kissed her, she lifted her shoulder, feeling a tickle. I saw her eyelid; there was a big scar on the corner of it, like it almost got her eye. I asked her what was the story behind that scar; she ignored telling that it was a long story and reprimanded to let her study. Well, then I kissed her that eyelid and got up to wear my cloths.

****

She was in her class filling paper with big answers in her test. I sat in my room getting bored and just looking at the time whether when her exam would finish and when would she come to my room. I saw the time and called her as soon as it showed me 3 o'clock. She did not pick it up. I was getting bored without her.

'R u still in exam?' I messaged her.

'I just finished my paper, now I am in class waiting for ma'm for next extra lecture.' She replied.

I was getting bored and then I again came to know that she was going to be late. I decided not to get bored alone. So I started sending her messages.

I : main duniya bhula dunga…. Teri chaahat mein.

She : I luv u 2. But what happnd suddenly 2 send this msg?

I : akele tanha… jiya na jaye tere bin.

tera hone laga hu,… khone laga hu, jabse mila hu.

She : Bittu, shona, why do you love me so much?

I : kaise bataye, kyu tujhko chahe, yara bata naa paye. Baate dilo ki, dekho jo baki aankhe tujhe samjhayein.

She: k I miss u 2. But I m in class now, bye. Cant talk.

I : zor ka jhatka haye zoro se laga, ha laga.

She: :D :D :D bye.

I : ab tere bin… ji lenge hum, zehar zindagi ka, pi lenge hum.

She: aww, then don't drink alone that poison, wait for me to come along. I cant let u die alone.
I : dil… sambhal ja zara… phir mohabbat karne chala hai tu.
She: Bittu I love u so much. Thnks fr cuming in my life. but I really gotta go now, I cant chat. Class is about to start. And don't miss me too much.
I : you know what?
She: no I don't know ;p
I : you go to your class leaving me alone. Aur main tab tak uske sath sota hu.
She: KISKE SATH?
I : hai ek, wo jo hamesha bed me mera sath kabhi nai chhodti.
She: WHO? Look, dare you to do something like that and I'll kill you.
I : where r u?
She: in class.
I : ok then, tu kar padhai, aur mai sota hu, (uske sath) taking her above me.
She: BITTYAAAAAAA, I'LL KILL YOU.
I : hahahahahah, arre baba I was talking abt my blanket. Hahahahah

She called me, (not a miss call) '*Chhichhundar*! I hate you. I ran out of my class for it. Now I can't even go back. Halkat!' she said so lovely, so sweetly I just wanted to kiss her.

****

Well, direction of sunrise and sunset doesn't change. Just like that, our life kept moving with same routine and with same love. But we all know that with every season sun rises a bit to north or a bit to south. Just like that, our behaviour's kept changing slightly, our love kept getting us back to the track and our egos, our friend circles, Facebook accounts kept leading us to fights. I loved those fights more. I know I was being more possessive than I was with Purvi, but yet I loved those fights as those used to work like a catalyst for my relationship. That effort which she used to convince me had lowered a bit but yet that effort was priceless.

Well, days kept passing just like that. PL started, exams started and exams over, but the love and fights did not change. I was feeling more insecure about her facebook friends. We had our passwords exchanged but I always tried to be calm as I did not want to steal her freedom and did not want another fight.

After exams, there were holidays but I did not spend too much time at home. I told my father that I have to attend the classes for M3 so I left home early and came back to Aurangabad, as she was alone there. I joined the Maths classes with the batch at the same time as her Anatomy class. She was happy that I came back early from home as she was becoming crazy alone. She hugged me at the very moment when she had come to receive me followed by tears rolling from her eyes. I could feel the pain she had felt when I was not with her. I promised her that I would never leave her alone.

My second year of engineering started and college life was changed. We were shifted properly to mechanical dept. now.

It was my result day. I was so tensed there. Moreover Janvi was tensed. She was at her hostel that night. I got a call from my friend that results are out. I downloaded the pdf file of result and looked hundreds of time to be sure. But I could not see my number in it.

I failed. I'd to drop a year.

I was speechless. All the things happened with me which a failed student experiences. My father scolded me on the phone, my brother wanted to abuse me in anger but he did not as my father stopped him in fear that I might attempt suicide. My mother just got nervous and tried to handle the situation and tried to make my father calm. I had no face to face them. Moreover Janvi was scared as they all would have blamed her for my bad result.

'Why did you do this Bittu?' She started, 'Am I the one distracting you from studies?'

'NO Janvi, you are not.'

'Then what the hell is this? You were an intelligent student how could you fail. You had scored well when you were with Purvi. You had maintained the relationship and studies too. What happened now? I guess I am the reason only. I should stay away from you.' She said almost trembling in her voice.

'Stop this nonsense. Do you want to live away from me? Can you live away?' I asked her, and she shook getting herself into my arms.

That was one of the toughest times of my life. Somehow, days kept passing and everyone just avoided that thing. I was still attending the M3 classes in confidence that I might get KT in revaluation.

14. Next Step

❄ ❄ ❄

Well, when someone dies we just cry for like ten days or a month hardly. Here I had just failed in graduation. The guilt of failure lived in our hearts only for a week. Then everything went well and we were back on the track.

The daily morning calls, her disappointed face, fight due to my sleep in morning and her not so punctual evenings were back. Dhiraj, Vinit and Sanjay did not leave my back as their topics also used to hop in between sometimes to spoil our mood and let the fight to get back on the track. But it also never mattered that much because the more I had become short tempered because of them, the more Janvi had become cool to calm me down by locking my lips, biting her finger, giving me that innocent look and with some new tricks. We were two best friends earlier, and then we became three. Lord Ganesha had joined our company.

She was having a small statue of Ganesha which her mother had given to her. She used to chat with it whenever she used to be not with me. Our daily meet to Kala Ganpati temple had given birth to more fate in Ganesha. We used to make him judge sometimes if our fight did not end early. Daily we used to go to pay a visit to him and I used to pray, 'Thanks for giving me such a wonderful best friend and wonderful life. I wished, may this happiness live last. And if possible, if possible, give her some sense to come on time at evening and not let me wait, so that we could spend some more time together.'

And I guess, she might use to wish that let me have some sense to wake up early in the morning to meet her. And some sense about cleaning my room daily before her arrival.

It had been a long time since I had gone to my home. I had skipped to go there in vacations also. Janvi was willing to go home for Dassehra. She told me she was missing her home so much and wanted to meet her mother. I just got upset with the feeling of letting her go home and live without her for few days. I would have not taken it well. I insisted her to not to go and stay in Aurangabad with me. She did not agree at first but after seeing my sulky face, and hearing that I had also avoided going home in vacations for her, she had no other option. She agreed to stay in Aurangabad for Dassehra.

I left her at her hostel at 9 pm that night. I headed towards my room. I was walking on the street where I got a call from my mother. I picked it up.

'Hello, Aai.' I spoke.

'Had dinner?' A typical mother's caring question to her child.

'Yes, just going to room from mess.' I lied about dinner as she would have questioned about it again and again asking whether why am I getting late for dinner and all that stuff about my health consciousness. We people on earth are so blessed with this person called mother. They don't know how to take care of themselves but never leave a chance to make any member of family healthy from sick. They would keep fast for you for weeks but if you missed your meal even once then they just can't bear it. All the important works of their lives would be thrown aside just to make your stomach full. I bet you, if mothers were the prime minister or president of this country, no Indian would sleep empty stomach.

'Hmm, what did you have in dinner?' Another question to be sure whether I am really full.

'Ah… umm… Potato and chapati.' That was what I could come up that fast.

'Go and get your dinner.' She caught me.

'Hmm.' I said and chuckled.

'You might have holiday to your class day after tomorrow.'

'Yes, why?'

'Can you come home tomorrow for Dassehra?' She asked.

'Umm… actually, it would be so hard to come for just one day. I will come next time for three to four days.' I tried to make a reason as I had made Janvi to stop in Aurangabad for me.

'Bittu, it has been a while since I have seen you. You had not stayed here long in your vacations too. Come home, everyone is going to be here for Dassehra.' She insisted and I could not say no to her.

'Ok, I will come.'

'Tomorrow.'

'Ok, I will come tomorrow.' I said while putting my hand on the forehead in stress of what should I say to Janvi now.

****

Next day, I woke up with Janvi's knock on the door. I hugged her as she came in and rested on her lap. She asked me about next day's planning and what should we do then.

'Tomorrow?' I got up from my place suddenly reminding that I was not going to be there for next day, as I had to leave for home on the same day.

'I don't know. We will figure out something at evening.' I avoided the topic for the moment, but couldn't tell her that I was going home as I had made her stop there. She got busy in folding my blanket and cleaning the room.

She went to her hostel after lunch and said that we will meet in the evening.

When she left for her hostel, I started to pack for my journey to home. While packing every shirt I was thinking whether what should I tell to Janvi for evening.

I left the city and was in a bus. I looked at the time and thought she might be sleeping at that time. Should I send her message about my departure? I thought so, but could not send her message.

After few hours, I was in Ambad. As soon as I reached there, I got a call from Janvi.

'Why didn't you wake me up?' She said with her sleepy tone. I just loved always whenever she used to speak like that.

'Actually I was with my friend. So I could not wake you up.' I lied.

'Ok, I will get ready and try not to be late today. You come till then.' She said followed by a yawn and I just scoffed hearing that she would not be late.

'Don't scoff idiot. What if she got early there? You are not there now.' My mind reminded me.

'Ah…a… I may not be able to meet you today. I am at my friend's room, doing some work.' I made an excuse while heading towards my home.

'Why? I will get so bored.' She said with that innocence and sulky voice.

'Sorry, shona. He needs my help.'

'I don't know anything. I want to meet you. I will come to your room then.' She insisted. And I just acknowledged for sake of moment thinking that I might handle it later when she would be in my room.

After cutting her call, I was in front of my home. I opened the gate and it sounded like a horror movie's door. I stepped up and started preparing myself for the scolding about result. It had been so many days to my result yet, it was the crime I did. If I say or do something very little thing wrong in these two days, it would screw me and result's topic may pop up to screw me more.

'Aal izz well…. Aal izz well… aal izz well…' Heart started.

'*Lakadi ki kathi, kathi pe ghoda,….*' So did the mind.

I entered in my home and everything went well for an hour. I met with everyone and sat on the sofa while watching TV. I tried to be as innocent as I could in front of my mother and brother, without doing any mistake. I was innocently watching TV without asking for remote to my brother or without arguing with him to change channel. My father arrived. As soon as he arrived and saw me watching TV he just gave a look to me, which told me what he wanted to say.

'See this shameless boy. He has failed in his college and he is watching TV so shamelessly instead of doing studies.' This is what his look told me. I got up from my place, touched his feet and went to bedroom to open any book to act as if I was reading.

About an hour later, I got call from Janvi again.

'I am waiting for you. Where are you?' She said disappointedly.

'Sorry, shona. I am stuck here. You don't wait for me and have your dinner.'

'NO. That's not going to happen. I am not eating without you.' She said like a kid. It made me more guilty. I did not know what to say.

'Janvi, listen to me. I don't know when I would come to the room. I am sorry. You please eat and don't wait for me.' I was convincing her and had to cut that call as my father entered in the room. I quickly put that book in my hand and opened any random page to act as if I was reading.

I messaged her, 'plz eat and sleep.'

'nt going to happen.' She replied.

About an hour later, again I got a message from her, 'I brought dinner. Try to come soon. I am waiting in your room'

'k. bt if I got late you plz eat n sleep.' I replied.

'I'll think about it.'

Well she slept that night without eating anything as I told her about another hour later that I was not going to come as I was in hospital with my friend.

****

In the morning, she called me as usual to wake me up. She was not having class that day due to Dassehra. I told her that I was still in hospital. She insisted to meet her. I had no answer for it. I lied to her that we would meet at evening. She hung up that call in anger. I tried to convince her but she did not pick up my call and switched off her phone.

I got her call at 4 again. I did not know what to tell her. I had to make some big excuse about my lies. Therefore, I decided to confess.

'Listen, Chiku. Actually my friend is not admitted in hospital…' I was searching something to convince her.

'Don't tell me that you lied.' She got angry before I could confess something. That made me suffocated. I thought for a while about confessing, 'Speak up.' She shouted from other side.

'Ah…. I … I mean , actually, you would have worried about me hence I did not tell you about it. But actually I am admitted in hospital, and not my friend.' I lied again.

'What? Why didn't you tell me first? Why the hell am I here for? Just to wander around with you?' She started to scold for this reason also.

'NO, I mean…'

'What the hell you meant?' she yelled again and I paused, 'Leave it. What happened to you and how are you now? NO, no. Tell me in which hospital you are first. I will come there right now.'

'I have less WBC. And I am in Ketki hospital near railway station.' I made up something and I don't know why I said that name.

'Railway station?'

'Yes.' I deliberately told her an address which was far from her hostel. .

'Ok, I will be there in few minutes.' She said and hung up the phone.

I was trying to call her back when my brother came to me and scolded as I was getting them late to go into the temple.

'Leave your phone and come with us. We are waiting for you.' He ordered. I followed him. 'I said leave your phone here. I know how *responsible* you are to carry phone in crowd.' He yelled again and made me leave my phone behind in house.

We headed towards the 'Matsyodari Devi temple'. A well-known temple of three goddesses. Every year people of whole district celebrated *Navratri* there. At the occasion of Dassehra, the crowd does not even let you stand. I could see the parking which had covered the whole road, and we had to struggle to find the place to park for few minutes.

We entered with the crowd and started to walk in the queue. The temple was still far from us. Not even in the temple, we were not even close to the stairs yet. All that climate of Dassehra made me to remind the every past year where I had gone there and struggled with that crowd. I remembered the time when I used to come by sitting on my father's shoulders to be safe from the crowd. We headed slowly, slowly towards stairs and reached in the temple after few hours. It took so long for us to get back in the parking. We got back to parking and I could see some of my childhood friends. I met them and wished them happy dassehra by exchanging those leaves, which meant to be gold for that day.

After coming home about four hours later, I ran to bedroom as my phone was ringing. I ran and saw it was Janvi's. I picked it up and could hear her, frustrated cum sulky voice.

'Where is that hospital Bittu?' She asked.

'Why? Where are you?'

'I am in auto rickshaw searching for that hospital for hours. I was calling you continuously but you did not pick up.' Holy shit! She had really left her hostel in search of that fake hospital.

'Why did you leave to search it. I would have met you tomorrow morning.' I said.

'Bittu, just tell me the exact address.' She said and someone asked her for phone, 'Bittu, talk to driver uncle and tell him exact address.' She said and handed over the phone to driver of rickshaw.

'Tell me the address beta.' He asked.

'Ketki hospital, uncle…' I was lying again and he cut me off in between.

'Beta, there is no such hospital. We searched everywhere, we asked everyone. There is no such hospital. We even went to N2 where there is a hospital named Kartiki hospital. But this girl could not find you there too.'

'Where are you now?' I asked.

'We are in front of Jaanaki hospital.' He said and I felt so guilty that Janvi had literally left to search for my lie.

'Uncle, can you please take her back to her place, please?' I asked him.

'Why? Where is that hospital?' By now, he had also got irritated with all the search of fake hospital.

'Actually, there is no such hospital. I was lying to her. Please pass the phone to her.' I said and grabbed my hair in tension.

'What happened, Bittu?' She asked.

'Chiku, I am really very sorry. Actually there is no such hospital. I was lying to you.' I said and waited for her response. There was silence on other side. 'Chiku, I am in Ambad, in my house. You please go back to your hostel.' I said and she just cut that call. Not need to tell in anger.

I tried to call her again but she did not pick it up. About half hour later, I got her call again. I picked it up and could hear her voice as if she had cried a lot and was still crying.

'I am sorry, Janvi. I did not mean to lie to you. I know you are angry…'

'I am not angry, Bittu. I am hurt. I am feeling all alone here. Why did you leave me alone?'

'I had to come here. I could not say no to Aai.' I said and unknowingly a drop rolled from my eye. 'I am sorry Chiku…' I said and started to cry with her.

'It was ok had you been here and did not meet me, but now that I know you are not even here, I am feeling so left out. I am feeling alone. I want you with me now.' She said hardly making correct pronunciations due to sobbing. She was crying continuously. I tried to calm her down and make her quiet, but it did not work. She was just insisting to meet me but it was not going to happen for that night. I promised her to arrive there next day as early as possible. She was not satisfied though. She refused to take dinner.

That night I was totally restless. I could not concentrate on anything. I was eagerly waiting for morning, so that I would go to her and console her, hug her, kiss her. I wanted to be with her as she was alone and crying for me, because of me. I was feeling so guilty.

****

In the morning when I woke up, I tried to get ready as fast as I could. I was packing my bag again for departure. My mother asked me to stay for another day there, but I refused. My father scolded me that there was not my college now as I had failed, so why I was hurrying to go there.

Somehow, I left my home and headed towards Aurangabad in a bus. While I was in bus, I was totally restless. I called Janvi to tell her that I was coming there. She got happy while crying again. I reached there at 5.30 . I was in auto rickshaw where I called her again to tell that I was coming. I told driver to drive fast as I was not able to bear that distance anymore. Rickshaw reached in front of Cidco theatre. I saw her already waiting for me in front of that theatre in a white sleeveless *kurti* with some flowers in black colour and some girly design on it. She was all dressed up and yet was not late that day.

I got out of rickshaw and put my hand in my pocket to take out money to pay him. I had not even paid him yet when Janvi ran towards me and hugged me on the road.

I just stood there with my wallet in one hand beside that rickshaw and my bag in other hand. I rolled my eyes around and saw that there were so many boys and girls sitting on the stairs of theatre staring us and some of the senior citizens sited on benches looked weirdly towards us. Some of the kids playing *gali cricket* started to chuckle after covering their mouth with their palms. And that auto driver stood silent without asking for his money.

'Janvi… people are watching.' I said while standing there in shock.

'I don't care. You don't know what I've felt in these two days.' She said and I felt guilty that I made her suffer. I did not care about people then. I dropped my bag on ground from my hand and hugged her tightly to let her feel that her Bittu was with her. I handed over the wallet to driver. He put it back in my pocket without disturbing our hug after taking his money. I hugged her and lifting her face with my hands resting them on her cheek and ears, I kissed her forehead.

'I think we should go to my room.' I suggested and lifted my bag. She acknowledged by saying ok and we headed towards my room.

****

We reached my room. My landlady welcomed us as soon as she saw us.

'Here you are. How are your parents at home?' Aunty asked.

'Good, they are good.' I said.

'Had you also gone with him to home, Janvi?' she asked.

'No aunty. I just met him now.'

'Ok. Well then, now that you both are here, don't go to your mess for dinner. I will cook something for you and you will have dinner with us.' She invited us. We both just nodded awkwardly and headed upstairs towards my room.

I opened it and we entered. Janvi did not give me chance to even remove my shoes and put that bag at its place. She closed the door and jumped to hug me. Rounding her arms around my neck, she hanged on me and kissed me. I supported her by lifting her in my arms and she ran her legs around my waist and hooked them. I could feel that she had really missed me so much.

After couple of minutes, I went to get fresh and we both had dinner with aunty and uncle in their house. Aunty had a son who was in Australia for his education. I always felt that aunty used to care for me as if looking her son's image in me.

After dinner, we both again came back to room. As it was already late, aunty suggested Janvi to stay at my room. As if, she was going to leave for her hostel.

Well, we both kept feeling our presence resting in each other's arm for hours. We kept talking, apologizing, crying and consoling each other.

I lifted her face to kiss her. I was about to kiss her when her phone rang. I took it and saw the screen showing Dhiraj's name. I saw the time; it was 1:30 am. I just stared at Janvi.

'He might have some important thing to say or any important work.' She explained before I could say anything. I cut that call and put that phone down. It started to ring again after a minute. How does that guy know which is the perfect time to spoil my mood? He always does it. Janvi took that phone and was about to receive it,

'Are you sure, you want to talk with him at this time?' I asked her.

'Bittu, it might be something important.' She said.

'First of all, you had promised me that you won't talk with him. And now you want to take his call almost at 2 am?'

'Bittu...'

'As if, for him the mornings are not enough to spoil my privacy now he is calling at this time too? Could he not call you in day time to speak about his *important* work?' I said sarcastically and she just stared at me. The call was about to cut where she picked it up.

She was talking with him and I just felt insulted. Her boyfriend is with her and she picks up the call of the person whom I hated most in this world as he was trying to spoil my relationship to get with her. I could not take it. After cutting that call, she told me that it was just a formal call to ask whether she had dinner or not. He was worrying about her.

'That's it? This was his important work for which you literally pushed me aside to talk with him.' I asked, starting to get angry. She just nodded and looked down. 'Why did you cut that call? Go speak with him more.' I said sarcastically.

'I thought you would get angry hence I cut it. Otherwise he was asking to talk with him more.' She said stupidly and started to dial his number.

'It was a sarcasm you idiot.' I shouted, and she startled.

'*Chidu nakos na...!*' She said making her face as innocent as possible and taking her finger to bite.

'Stop it right there.' I said and held her hand, 'This time it is not going to work.'

'Bittu, what is wrong with you? He is my friend. It's not like I ran away with him. It was just a call.'

'At 2 o'clock in the night?' I yelled.

'It's 1:50 am now and he called me at 1:30. Don't round it up to whole half hour.' She clarified. I just stared at her getting more frustrated, 'Bittu, it's not a big deal. Why do you hate him by the way?'

'Why do I hate him? Don't you get it; he is like a virus for my relationship.'

'He is a nice guy.'

'I can't believe this! Why? Why did I trust you? You are such a.... such a... a slut!'

As soon as I called slut to her, her expression changed to shock, and eyes and jaw opened wide.

'What the hell. What did you just call me?' She asked making her eyes tiny and rubbing her teeth.

'SLUT!' I answered her question.

'How dare you call me that again?' She said while making her eyes even tinier and pointing finger towards me.

'Because, you are a slut.'

'Just shut the fuck up.' She yelled.

'They are right. *Sach hamesha kadwa hota hai.*'

'Is that what your mom-dad taught you? Ha? Is this how you talk to a girl?'

'No, my parents taught me what you have seen till now, my good behaviour.'

'Oh really?' She asked sarcastically.

'Yes! Then what do you think, my father taught me all those things?' I said in anger and continued in sarcasm, 'Beta, Bittu speak after me, S-L-U-T, slut means JANVI.' I shouted her name in sarcasm.

'Who knows? You are such a... shameless guy. And STOP calling me that.' She yelled.

'Oh really? Then what about you? Loves to one, wander with other, tests another, and frauds everyone? That's why they have invented word slut for girls like you.'

'Now just SHUT UP. You know what...?'

'No I don't know.' I interrupted as usual, habitually and she clutched her head and grabbed her hair in frustration.

'Errggghhhh…. SHUT UP!' She yelled and continued, 'you know… you are… you are a…. you are a really bad boy.'

'Oh, thanks a lot.' I pulled my collar up to tease her more.

'You are a…. you know? You are a male slut.' She spoke so stupidly.

'Huh! Like there is a word, like that!' I….

'Tell me what do they call it?' She asked.

'Why should I?' I asked while staring her up to down and again back to up in attitude.

'Because, I am asking?'

'Who the hell you think you are?' I asked again overlooking her and she thought for a while and came up with,

'I am your best friend asking.'

'Huh! Like it's going to work this time.'

'You are breaking your promise.' She shouted.

This is great! I mean, she has broken her all promises and was telling me shit about promises. Who cares? Well, I do.

'I don't know the real word.' I said while ignoring her intentionally.

'Then you are a male slut.' She said again.

'Chiku, it's not even a word.'

'DO YOU KNOW THE REAL WORD?' She asked in her famous angry look. I just shook my head and she continued, 'Then I don't care. You are a very bad male slut.'

'OK, ok. I am. Fine? But can you tell me why? Because I can tell you about you. I can explain the whole list.'

'Erghhgg, you and your list!'

'Hey, it's not mine. It is your list. First Sanjay, then Dhiraj, then me, then Vinit, and then it was me again. And after all this stuff, still loves Sanjay but wanders with me.'

'Don't add Dhiraj or Vinit to the list. We were just friends.'

'What kind of friends were you, ha? You lied to because of them.'

'NOT because of THEM. I lied because of you, for you. Because you would have felt bad, you would have cried. You had become so possessive Bittu.'

'I didn't. And I don't cry. I was just lost in your words and promises.' I shouted and turned my tone to sarcastic level again,

'Bittu, I love only you, you are the only best friend of mine. You are my everything.... GHANTA!'

'What the hell is wrong with you? Stop making fun of me, and teasing me. And who told you all these bad words? You were not like this. I can't believe. You never used any bad word in your entire life and now... you have changed.'

Oh great! You are changed!

'I did change, because you are also no more like you were. You lied to me. Hide things from me and fraud me. Tell me one thing; have you done any course on defrauding?'

'NO, I didn't, but may be you did a course of bad words here.' She shouted again, and I started my sarcasm,

'Oh yes, I did. They taught us A for *Apples*, B for *Balls*, G for *Ghanta* and S for YOU.'

'S for what?'

'You! Slut.'

'SHUT UP...........' She yelled clutching her hair again, '... why the hell are you fighting with me again?'

'Oh, so now suddenly you became innocent like you don't know anything.' I said and sat on the bed.

'Bittu, can't we just get back to where we were.' She said trying to finish the fight.

'NO. I don't want to insult myself again. Who knows I might grab you and your *friend* would call again and you will leave me again to talk with him something *important*.' I said sarcastically. As I forced on the words 'friend and important' she got what I was trying to say. She just took that pillow behind her and threw it to hit me.

'Leave it.' She said while hitting me with that pillow.

'I can't. It is not the first time. I cannot trust you after so many incidents and still you are...' I was saying and she just took that pillow from my hand, threw that pillow behind, grabbed me, and locked my lips to make me quiet. Why does she do that? Her kiss makes me calm always.

But no. I was not going to let it be my weak point. I was not going to be calm that time. So I just kept quiet until she leaves my lips and started again as soon as she rested back, '...still you are doing the....' She again popped up from her place and tried to make me quiet again. I tried to push her but couldn't. Not because I was weaker or something like that, it was just I didn't want to. Actually, I liked that way to make me quiet. It had become my weak point.

'You don't trust me, do you?' She whispered after resting on my chest. I didn't answer for a while. Then scoffing there, I replied,

'How am I supposed to? You ask yourself, can I trust you?'

'Fine! You think I am a fraud. So I have a solution.'

'What? Leaving me behind alone and going out with them? So that whatever I think would be not just a thought and be real?' I said.

'You can't even think straight, can you?' She said uplifting her face and looking at me, 'I was talking about living together.' She said and pushed me back due to anger of my thought. 'I was saying that I would come here to live with you 24*7 so that you can put an eye on me and not get possessive or all *you* type.' She said spreading her hands and pointing towards whole me.

'What do you mean by *me* type?'

'You know, all possessive and, having doubts about me and my friends all the time and not trusting me.' She said and I scoffed, 'What? Don't you want to live with me?' she asked.

'You are literally talking about living in together.'

'Yeah! I am.' She said folding her hands and staring at me waiting for my answer. I just thought for a while without removing my gaze from her and tried to figure out whether she was bluffing or she was serious. There was only one way to know that.

'I am ready. You can move in tomorrow.' I said and she just unfolded her arms in shock that I was ready.

'Are you serious? What would you tell to aunty whether why am I living here with you? What about your parents and brothers if they came here to meet you?' She asked and I came to know that she was just bluffing.

'You leave it to me. I will handle that.' I bluffed to suffocate her. She again stared at me for couple of seconds and said, 'Ok. I will move in. Anyhow till now the people who were staring at us while hugging in front of theatre would have complained about me to my landlady.' She acknowledged and my mind ran to search the reasons to tell aunty, whether why I was getting a girl roommate.

We had taken a decision to live in together. Which was definitely the next step of our relationship.

15. Living in together

The daily morning calls of her to wake me up had stopped, as she was not a call away from me now. Those calls had changed to peck on the forehead as an alarm and a pinch on nose, if I snoozed it. The room was not a mess anymore, not even for night as she had moved in with me.

We had started the next step so excitedly. We were living together, we were eating together, we were laughing together, we were crying together. We were fighting together, we were sleeping together and we were waking up together.

We came to know so many different things about us, which we had not even known yet. Our so many habits, which we changed for each other's sake, our living styles and pasts, were becoming catalyst to our relationship.

Her that daily wake up kiss to my forehead, that spike of her earring to my chest, that grab of her arms to my neck and scratching of her nails. God! They were just making me fall for her more.

We unofficially became husband and wife. For the sake of old days and for the sake of our third best friend, Lord Ganesha, we had not left wandering in front of Cidco theatre and Kala Ganpati temple.

She told me the story of the scar on her eyelid. She got it when she was a kid by falling on the rock, which almost got her eye. After hearing that story, I woke up from my place and fell down at the corner of bed. The corner of that bed hurt me and it started bleeding. I looked in the mirror and instead of panicking or being afraid I started to laugh. It was almost close to my eye and when I cleaned the blood, it showed me a scar on my eyelid. I was happy that I got the same scar and at the same spot as my girlfriend has.

The life was good, but we are Homo sapiens. We get easily bored with our daily routines. There was nothing new after that live in relationship. The love, the romance, the kisses, the hugs, the cuddles, the morons, and the fights everything was the same. In fact, slowly we started to give more importance to other things like our future.

The wake up kiss started to fade after few weeks. The spiking of earrings started to flush with days as her sleeping close to me was also fading. Previously things, which were our favourite about each other, were starting to annoy us. The innocent laugh and her biting of finger when I used to be angry, started to irritate me, as it felt careless about my anger. All of a sudden, we both started to fight for every single and small thing for which earlier we would have compromised. That moron and his Facebook chat never left a chance to pop up and spoil our romance. I had started to call Purvi for each time when Janvi used to talk with Dhiraj, just to make her realize that how does it feel to me when she talks with other person, who tries to steal her from me.

But instead of realizing what I was trying to prove, she used to fight me back for that rascal. They say that in love, fights are necessary to increase your bond. I don't know if it was right. I didn't see that. I could just feel that with every fight we were together for nights only. The love and that romance were fading away.

I felt like I am losing her. I felt like my love story is going to its bitter end. I didn't want that to happen. I didn't want her away from me. I wanted the relation back to its track. So I decided to avoid fighting with her. But you know, sometimes things just don't happen in single way. I pointed out all the reasons of our fights and realized that Facebook, his chat and he were the only reason from my side to fight with her. So I just blocked him from her account. But it led to another fight again.

'Chiku it's getting worse.' I said.

'Why did you block him from my account?' She raised her voice asking for an explanation.

'I just blocked the reason of our fights. He is the one.'

'But why always my friends only? Have I ever said anything regarding your friends?'

'No. Because there is nobody who tries to get in between us and spoil our relationships. There is nobody who wants this relationship to be ended from my side. Why don't you understand that? Why is he so important to you?'

'He is not important to me Bittu. I just don't understand your nature against him. I just don't see any reason to hate him.'

'That is because he flirts with you and makes you laugh. Ask me how I feel when someone flirts with my girlfriend and she reacts normally to it.'

'Oh come on. Please don't start again.' She said like she had already annoyed with my nature.

'Right. Now you are annoyed with me. And may be my phase of time in your life has almost ended. Now I guess it's his turn to be your boyfriend.'

'Mind your language. Can't you even think once before talking anything like that?'

'Do you even think once before behaving like that?'

'Oh come on, grow up.'

'Listen, Chiku. I love you so much, and I don't want you to go away from me.'

'Who the hell said that I am going away from you? For god's sake leave it.'

'If you think I did a big crime by blocking him, then I have a solution. I will deactivate our accounts. Not only yours but also mine. I don't want anything and anybody except you.'

'Dare you do that, I won't talk with you. You are going crazy.'

'Yes, I am going crazy, moreover I am feeling insulted as my very own best friend giving more importance to other people.' I raised my voice.

'Oh great! Now there are people instead of one man. You are just unbelievable.'

'Chiku....' I was saying and she cut me off.

'Save it, for next fight. I am going to my class. And don't message me while I am in class.' She said and left the room in anger.

These types had also become the part of daily routine.

****

But however, the important and sweet thing was that we were together in spite of all those fights. Our fights were only for few hours. Every fight was breaking us apart slowly, slowly but, yet we were together. We understood each other and our egos were ruining our relationship.

Days kept passing and we kept trying to survive our relationship. And then it was the time for Diwali. I had decided to go to Alandi together, but Janvi refused. She said that she did not want my mother to have any doubt about us. She decided to go separately and act normal. She also told me that she was going to tell her mother about our relationship. I agreed to go separately.

Janvi left for Alandi before me. I left a day later. We reached to Alandi and I could see everyone had arrived this time. I saw Janvi and headed towards her to say 'hi'. But as soon as she saw me she walked into the house. I thought she might be trying to behave normal. But her normal act was going too normal. It had been several hours of my arrival and she had not talked to me yet. She had not even waved at me to say hi. She even avoided my eye contact.

While dinner, when everyone was sitting together Sanjay asked for a glass of water to her and she gave it to him. After him drinking that glass of water, I also asked for one for me to Janvi. She just avoided me and went ahead without looking at me. I felt insulted.

'Have you two fought with each other?' Sanjay asked. I just shook my head.

I went to her after dinner where she was in the room with her mother, 'Janvi, can I talk to you for a second?' I asked her but she avoided me again. Her mother went outside and Janvi was following her where I grabbed her hand.

'What is wrong with you?' I asked.

'Leave my hand.' She said without looking at me.

'What is this yaar? We had decided to act normal. You are acting too normal. It would make them to doubt us even more.'

'I said leave my hand, don't you understand?' She said angrily and her mother came back in.

I left her hand in anger and she went to other side, 'Don't trouble me again.'

'Am I troubling you?'

'Yes.'

'Who the hell you think you are?'

'Just go and don't trouble me.' She said arrogantly and I felt insulted again. I just took the towel, which hanged on the wall and threw it to hit her. It covered her face and she got annoyed. She hit me back with that towel and her mother kept smiling on our fight.

'Go to hell.' I said in anger and was about to leave the room, where Archana aunty, Janvi's mother stopped me.

She held my hand and made me sit with her. Janvi left the room.

'What the hell is wrong with her?' I started with aunty.

'Bittu, you know her well. She is just upset.' She said.

'But why the hell on earth always me? Why do I have to suffer all the time? Can't she fight with someone else when she is upset?'

'You are her best friend. Who else would understand her better than you?' she said and scoffed. 'Now you have to take care of her until she gets married.'

'What? You fixed her marriage? Is that why she us upset?' I got afraid.

'No! She is upset because of Sanjay. His marriage is fixed. And you might know her feelings about him.' She answered and I thought no one knew better than me. I even had to suffer from it.

'You knew about him?' I asked her.

'Yes, she tells me everything.' She said.

'Anything else did she tell you about?' I asked her being curious.

'No, why?'

'Nothing, so she is upset because of Sanjay?'

'Yes, when she arrived, we were talking about Sanjay's marriage. When she came to know that his marriage is fixed she just got upset and started acting weird.'

'Only with me, alone. I saw her behaving normal with or even good with others.'

'Come on, she might be angry because you came late.' She said and I scoffed again.

I started to think, Sanjay's marriage is fixed hence Janvi is upset. She was avoiding me. But why the hell was she doing this to me? Was she willing to get back with Sanjay again? Only one news about his marriage lets her forget about me and woke all the slept memories of Sanjay in her heart again? Had she been single after break up with him, it would have been bearable that she was getting upset. But she is not single, she was with me. Why the hell is she avoiding me?

I thought, whether she was trying to impress him again by avoiding me, as he was insecure about me.

'Bittu, listen. You know her very well. Since your childhood, whatever had happened to her, she shares with you. You are her only best friend. Do you want to get angry on her now? In my opinion, you should understand her as you do always. You should help her to overcome this situation.' She was saying and I just thought, *maine kya theka le rakha hai kya friendship ka? Why do I* always have to understand her. She continued, 'You already know about my disease. I don't know how much I am going to live even after operation...'

'Don't say that.'

'... What is not to say in that, it is true. But I always don't have to worry about Janvi. Because I know you are there to take care of her. She has earned a great friend like you. So just go, and for my sake, talk with her.'

'But you just saw, she is not talking with me well.'

'Well, then you might know how to handle her.' She said and patted me and asked me to go to her.

She had succeeded to wake the best friend inside me up. But I was still confused. I know I was her best friend first, but now I had no guts to console her for other people or her ex. Why the hell she was upset by his marriage when she was in a relationship with me.

But as you know now, I am a fool. I am a chu*** and I am her best friend. I had to console her.

She entered in the room. I just went to her,

'What are you still doing here?' She started again.

'Listen Chiku...'

'I told you already leave me alone.' She said and Archana aunty scolded her to behave.

'Mom, you stay out of it.' She said to her.

'What is wrong with you Janvi? I know you are upset....' I was saying and held her hand. Sanjay entered in the room and Janvi looked at him.

'Don't touch me.' Janvi said and pushed me with a jerk.

That was too much. I was not able to take it anymore. I had it with my insult. She was behaving as if I was torturing her by importuning her. By now, I had no doubt that she was doing it all because of and for Sanjay. I just left the room in anger pushing her intentionally towards Sanjay.

****

That Diwali was the worst for me. All the time Janvi kept ignoring me. I was feeling insulted and angry. Not only because she was upset for her ex, but I was even angry for me, when I had tried to console her being her best friend as a *chu****.

I was such a fool. I was trying to be her best friend ignoring the anger, but she was not even talking to me, just for Sanjay's sake.

We both came back to Aurangabad separately. After reaching to the room also, she was ignoring me. She was eating alone, living alone, studying alone, and sleeping alone. I tried so many times to talk with her but she was just fighting with me. What the hell had I done?

'Janvi, why the hell are you behaving like this to me?'

'Listen, I don't have time for this now. I have my studies and I want to be a doctor, without wasting any year.' She answered arrogantly.

'You will. But how the hell on earth is that concerned with this?'

'Bittu, please just mind your own business. I don't want to waste my whole year by...' she was saying but stopped.

'By what?'

'I don't want to waste my year like you did.'

'Do you mean to say that I am disturbing your studies?'

'Leave it. I don't want to talk about it. I have wasted my time here. Now I want to concentrate on my career.'

Wasted time? Relationship with me was a waste of time?

'Do you have any idea what are you talking about? I wasted your time?'

'Can't you understand? I don't want this argument. I have my studies to do.' She raised her voice.

'Hey, don't raise your voice against me.' I said angrily pointing finger towards her. 'For your information I had not come to you for this relationship. You had said first *I love you* to me. I didn't offer you this waste of time.'

'What do you think? Am I ....'

'Just shut the fuck up. You also know that you are arguing with me only because you want to get rid of the anger you are carrying in your mind about Sanjay and his marriage. And what do you think? If you study hereafter well then you will become doctor before his marriage, and get married with him?' I said arrogantly losing my patience. I had tried to be nice so many times and yet if she cannot behave nice with me then I have my attitude to screw her. I had wasted my year with her and she was talking that shit about wasting time with me, only because her ex was getting married hurting her ego.

'Oh shut up. You mind your own business with Purvi.'

'How the hell on earth is she linked to this now? Just let her live her own life.'

'Oh so now you are getting upset because I mentioned her name?'

'I am not like you to get upset because of ex. I love you. May be I *loved* you and that was the worst and biggest mistake of my life ever. And you know what? She was much better than you. You should not even take her name from your frivolous mouth; you are not even worth even to take her name.'

'Just go to hell with her then.' She yelled in frustration.

'Yeah I wish. But hell is full of people like you. And remember one thing; don't ever say that you love me again. I just hate liars like you.'

She just took her books and left the room to sit outside in the balcony to study.

The anger was so high that I was unable to feel any other feelings. I just went to her again, 'If you really have the guts, then go and spit out all this anger on Sanjay instead of abusing and annoying me. And stop lying about your love to innocent people like me.' I said lifting her face with my hand. She scoffed and said,

'You, and innocent? Tell this to that bitch, your Purvi.'

'Why the hell are you taking her name in our fight? How is it concerned with her by any angle?' I said and jerked her face.

'Oh, I am sorry.' She said sarcastically, 'I forgot that I should not take her name with my dirty mouth. I am not worth enough *na*.'

'Listen, I understand what is going on here. I know you are

upset by his wedding. But let me tell you, if you want him back just go for him. But for god's sake don't mention Purvi again.' I said folding my hands in front of her in frustration.

'If that was so easy, I would have gone to him yet... Anyhow I don't want to live with rascal like you.' She said and I just got shocked. Why the hell she said that?

I just could not bear that anger, she was behaving so crazy. It was not even my mistake except to trust her again and again. She was just getting crazier after that news, and was targeting me. I could not bear it. I just raised my hand and slapped her, right on her left cheek.

'Just go to hell with him. Who the hell wants to live with you? Even I am fed up now. You have crossed all your limits.' I said and left the place in anger leaving her alone in the room with a drop of tear rolling down from her eye and shutting that door behind me loudly.

All these days I was thinking that she had forgotten him, but she had not. I thought I was the one who gets angry easily on even small things and gets hyper for no reason, but no. I was right; she is worth of that anger.

I didn't go to room early in anger as I had no mood to face her worthless argument.

This type of behaviour lasted for days. She had gone crazy. She did not understand that whatever had gone she should leave it behind. But she was just behaving as if she was feeling jealousy because she had lost him totally now. I was nothing for her for that moment.

****

After that aimless fight, we used to stay away from each other. We did not try to convince each other. She was deep in her jealousy, and I was deep in my insult and ego.

That night we both were resting on the bed alone facing opposite sides. I was so restless to feel that she was right with me and yet I was not with her. I wanted to hug her but I was waiting for her to make me quiet by locking my lips, I was waiting for her to hide in my arms. I wanted her to....

I was thinking when I heard her sobs. She was crying and yet I ignored her. I had nothing to do with her anymore. I was done with the best friend thing or even with relationship.

Nah! I am lying. I thought so, but I could not help it out. I turned my face towards her. She was facing other side. I tried to grab her and turn her face to me, but she just jerked my hand and kept sobbing by facing other side. *If she really didn't want to face me, then why the hell was she sobbing so loudly? Just to get attention?*

I just got up and looked at her. She was looking in her phone. She had opened her Facebook account and was looking at Sanjay's picture, which he had uploaded. I felt possessive that my so-called girlfriend was crying by looking her ex's photo. But that was not the only reason to cry. Under that picture, she could see the notification telling, "Sanjay and Aditi have liked it.' Aditi was his that friend with whom he was going to marry and because of whom Janvi had tried to make him possessive by making out with me.

I could not bear my possessiveness. But moreover I was still her best friend. She had not said anything about friendship then, but I was feeling to do something to stop her cry.

I rested back and took out my phone. I opened her facebook account and liked that picture from her account. Now it showed, "You, Sanjay and Aditi liked this picture." It was not of worth. I unliked it again. I logged out. Then logging in from my account I liked it. Again logging in from her account I liked that picture for her. And then it showed, "You and Sanjay and 2 other friends ....." it was not worth yet. I logged out and logged in to my another account. It showed me, "Janvi and Sanjay and......"

I just took my phone and put it in front her face. I pointed towards that notification which I was trying to show her to stop her crying. She just stopped crying and took my phone without facing to me. I left my phone in her hand and rested back to my place facing other side.

'*Great! Chutya best friend ka ek aur chutiyapa.*' I thought to myself wiping the tear, which was trying to come out from my eye.

However, her crying had not stopped yet. I was just thinking what should I do more to stop her crying now? I thought to call Sanjay and let him talk with her. But I would have no answer to his question whether why are we both together at midnight.

I was just thinking some more options to make her calm and

in next minute, she hugged me from behind busting into tears and sobbing silently.

'I am sorry, Bittu.... I love you...' She barely pronounced the correct words due to sobbing, but that was enough to let the tears roll down from my eyes.

I just turned my face towards her. The anger was still trying to hop out from any corner of my brain but the feelings for her buried it under my love. I took her face in my palms and kissed on her forehead. Wiping her tears, I rested my lips on hers and hugged her tight enough to feel her heartbeats on my chest. She just ran her hands on my shoulders and grabbed them reminding me that she still had long nails.

After a couple of minutes of this emotional drama, I rested down and let her rest her head on my chest wrapping her hand around me and resting my hand on her to pat her to sleep. God! That was the feeling I was dying for since Diwali. All the anger and ego had left my heart, mind and thoughts for that moment with that one touch of her head on my chest.

****

It had been so many days. That night was just a onetime thing. She was still living as if something was missing. I had grown into her nature by then. I was just waiting to see my same old place in her heart again. But it was lost without any reason. I was suffering from someone else's mistake's punishment.

The meaningless fights had increased and the convincing nature of hers had lost somewhere. I had to get used to it. I had to get convinced by my own for her. I had to avoid my entire ego.

She had to leave for Beed for her submissions in her college. I had no idea whether she was going to come back again or not. She was at the bus stop waiting for her bus and I had refused to go with her to drop her. She had not even asked me to do so.

I was feeling restless in the room. I wanted to go to see her off. I wanted to stop her. But the conditions and the earlier days' behaviour of her was holding me behind. My mind was just stopping me saying that who the hell am I now, she has no priority for me in her life. My heart was not listening all these things. For it, those all things and all her mistakes never existed. It knew only one thing, that I loved her.

But it had been more than 2 hours till then. She might have gone by now, I thought. But when you are in love nothing is logical and your heart knows no boundaries. I could not control myself and left my room to see her of at the bus stop.

I reached there and I could see, she was still there waiting for me with wet eyes and a hope in her eyes that I would come. As soon as she saw me, she stood up from her place and wiped her tears. It had been so many days since we had experienced the drama at bus stops. The love story had come so far that it was almost at its edge of the end, but yet the feeling and the climate was nothing different. The surrounding and the yelling of people and that announcer of bus stand just stood still for that moment. I could still feel the heartbeat which used to increase in such situations.

She was leaving. She could have left yet, but she didn't. I went to her and she hugged me.

'*Kiti ushir kela yayla...*' She said.

'Haven't you got any bus yet?' I asked.

'I left three buses. I knew you would come.' She said and I felt proud of my decision, 'Bye.' She said.

'What? Wait....'

'No, I just wanted to see you. Now I have to go.' She said and started to head towards her bus. She just wanted to see me? What was so important in that one visit at the bust stop for which I had also come running all the way even after two hours? I mean she had left from the same room. We were living together since so many days. We were together for everything. Yet why was that so important to see each other at the bus stop?

'Chiku....' I called her and she looked behind with her wet eyes, '... I....' I wanted to say but that feeling was lost somewhere, my ego was stopping me, '...dot dot.' I said and she chuckled.

'And I hate bus stops.' She added wiping her tears.

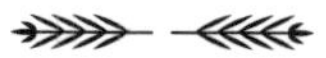

16. Things changed again.

✻ ✻ ✻

Again the lonely Aurangabad was haunting me. I had no roommate now. The bond was lost somewhere. I was missing her and I know she was missing me too. But there was something that was stopping us to call each other. Previously, we used to talk for hours without any topic and now....

Now I am afraid that if I call her and she starts fighting without any reason. Once or twice in a couple of days I had called her but the call would end in 5 minutes, as there was nothing to talk about and most of the time of those five minutes went in silence.

So many times she did not even pick my calls and so many times I did not call her back after her missed calls. She used to not to pick my calls and hence I used to not call her back. I used to not call her back on her missed calls and hence she used to not pick my calls. The cycle continued.

Slowly, slowly it felt awkward to talk with each other. Hence whenever I wanted to talk with her I used to message her on Facebook. I had sent so many messages but there was no reply from her side. I thought she might haven't logged in to her account, but then I could see the uploaded pictures and status on her timeline wall.

May be there was something called ego, stopping her. I was doing nothing different. I was waiting for her missed calls like as if it was my last day. But when she used to call me, something in my mind used to stop me and tell me that I should not call her back on only one missed call. I didn't want to let her feel that I was the one who was being needy.

Listening to my mind I used to not call her back and kept abusing myself. The heart used to get out of control and used to make my hands run towards the phone to dial her number. But this time maybe her mind used to overcome her heart and she used to not pick my call, just to take revenge of my behaviour and to show me that even she was not needy too.

I had not seen any notification for my messages I had sent her on facebook. I just did not understand it. I logged in from her account and checked whether she had opened my messages or not. There I could see that she had opened them and read it too. But she had intentionally marked them unread. I couldn't understand her behaviour.

While I was thinking about it, I saw the messages from Dhiraj in her inbox. That bastard had succeeded to get into her life again. He was taking advantage of her feelings about Sanjay and was trying to convince her that I was the one who was holding her back in spite of her happiness.

Janvi had also changed so much. She had shared so many things with him, which she used to share with me. She had chat with him as she used to chat with me earlier.

I just kept silent after reading her chat. There were some illogical messages and illogical replies to, that led to conclusion after thinking. It led me to think that she had deleted some of the messages. I just started thinking and making sense of the deleted messages.

My mind was running at its worst level. I had imagined to the cheapest level of my mind about those messages. I wanted to call her and ask her the truth. But by the time I was totally fed up of the fights. I did not call her. Instead of that, I stood still and I just imagined whether how the call would go if I asked her about Dhiraj's messages.

"*He is my friend,... you are such a possessive guy. You don't have brain..... such a narrow minded and cheap person you are Bittu!.... bla ... bla.... bla....*"

All her sentences started to make noise in my ears. I didn't even take efforts to dial her number.

While I was thinking about the fight, her inbox got a message from Dhiraj. I just read it but did not reply and marked it as unread. He kept messaging again and again and I could not control then.

'Stop messaging me. I don't want to talk with you. Good bye.' I replied him from her account. I felt a bit better after that reply. But he was such a *chipku.* He kept asking her continuously whether what had happened. I just blocked him and felt fresh again, as if I had won a war. I logged out from her account and put my phone down so that I would not call her and have another fight again.

I just rested on bed. There were few of her things still in my room. Her hair clutcher, hair bands, her dresses, and her pillow. I took that pillow and rested it on my chest. I was damn confused whether I was loving her or hating her. Whether I want to forget her or I want her back. After every minute, my feeling was changing.

I was getting angry with her, but moreover, I was missing her so much. I wanted to scold her and fight with her for her changed behaviour, but I had fear that she might leave me forever as she had another options, even for best friends too. I was not even sure now whether she thinks I was her only best friend.

I was thinking about her, (as if other times I do so much important work) when my phone beeped. It showed me her name. I just stopped to wait for another call, as I didn't want to seem needy. But that time she called again. I thought like I won the ego war, now she was the one who was needy. She had called me again.

'Hello.' I spoke with an attitude showing like I was very busy and her call disturbed me.

'What the hell you think you are?' She seemed so pissed.

'What happened?' I asked trying not to leave the attitude.

'How dare you to read my messages?'

'What? Who told you?'

'Bittu, you are really sick. Dhiraj had just called me and asked me whether what happened to me and why did I block him.' She explained and just woke up the psycho inside me which was trying to stay calm.

'So you agree that you still talk with that moron even after all these days.' I asked silently while rubbing my head.

'Yes, I talk with him and I will do whatever I want. Who the hell you think you are to interfere in my life? Dare you do something like that again and I will...'

'Janvi....' I interrupted to stop her before she could say something which she would regret later or which I would have made her regret. My anger was trying to rise and bury my kindness under it. But I was just trying to be calm as I did not want another fight. 'Chiku, I need my best friend. I think I've lost her somewhere. I think my girlfriend is angry, and she is so mad at me. I need my best friend to talk.....'

'Oh please!' She interrupted, 'Stop all this nonsense and grow up. I have so many things to do. I am not your best friend. You did nothing but just took my advantage all these days under the name of best friendship.' She said and I just could not help that psycho from waking up.

'What did you just say? I took your advantage?'

'Yes.'

'You mean to say whatever I did all these days was nothing. My friendship, my love was nothing for you?'

'Listen, I don't have time for another fight. I don't want to waste my time. I have studies to do. I had called you to tell you just stay away from my Facebook account and stop interfering in my life.'

'You don't have time? Right.' I said and ran my hand through my hair, 'I know, all the time you just chat with that bastard and talk with him, how would you get time then? Only when I want to talk with you, then you've to study. Great!' I said while trying to control my high respiration.

'I will do whatever I want. You are nobody to tell me anything. I will chat and talk with anyone I want.' She spoke arrogantly.

'Chiku, you are being arrogant unnecessarily. How could you forget all the things between us without any reason? What the hell is wrong with you? Do you even remember why you started hating me? I did nothing and you kept behaving....'

'I know how I am behaving. You just mind your own business.'

'After all those times we spent together, after all those lies you lied to me and after all the trust which I had on you, you are giving me this? Have you really forgotten my love?'

'Huh, love? Really? Do you even remember what you have done for me? Have you even done a single thing for me, which I would remember? It was just lust for you.'

I could not believe this. She was really speaking that. But it was not her mistake. She was just speaking whatever that bastard had lied her about me.

'You really think that I did nothing for you?' I said feeling like I was talking to stranger.

'You tell me, what have you done for me? Ha? Limitless kisses, meaningless sex, aimless fights and daily frustration. This does not mean that you love me. Anyone who would get a girl with him for living would do that just for physical....'

'JUST SHUT THE FUCK UP.' She had crossed the limit. I could not stop the psycho inside me anymore. 'Do you any idea what are you talking about? Just because that bastard has filled your thoughts with this type of shit, doesn't mean that you would believe whatever he says.'

'Nobody told me anything, I just.....'

'Oh please! I have read your chats. Don't tell me that you are saying this all alone. Don't you even understand now? He has succeeded to fill the poison in our relationship. He is taking advantage of your feelings and your loneliness. He is playing a game Janvi, wake up.' I was just yelling.

'Huh, nothing is new. You still fight with me because of my friends only. Whatever may happen only Dhiraj is responsible, right?' She said sarcastically.

'Chiku, he is playing with your mind. You have made a huge mistake by telling him about me, Sanjay, and Sanjay's marriage. He is taking you to him step by step, don't you get it?'

'I just don't want you in my life to interfere anymore. I will see my life and decide whether where I want to go and with whom I want to live.'

'Chiku I am your best friend. You got to trust me. I am telling you, that guy...'

'Huh, best friend!' She scoffed and continued, 'What did you do for me as a best friend? Took advantage of me? Made me clean your room, told me to leave my friends and spy on me by checking my fb account? You call that best friendship?'

'Why are you looking at the negative sides of the thing only?'

'Because there are no good sides. I don't even remember any. I just don't want you to interfere in my life again and if you don't understand that, I will block you forever and will not speak with you again.' She said and cut that call in anger.

I still don't understand what was wrong with her? Why the

hell she suddenly had started behaving like that? We were living so happily. Why the hell she has started to trust other people after hearing of Sanjay's marriage news? And why the hell on earth god created bastards like Dhiraj? They can't get a girlfriend by their own so they just steal others girls like a pathetic loser.

I wanted her back. But that was not happening. I wanted her to remind all our days and our friendship. I wanted to tell her that whatever might happen we are the only best friends for us. Whatever would it be, I was there for her, I wanted to tell her.

Main hu...
Main to hu ab bhi yahi,
Sath tere khada, banke saya.
Teri yaado ne jab bhi pukara...
Banke aansu, mai palko pe aaya.
Main hi main hu bass ik akela,
Tu hi toh hai jo mujhme samaya.
Jate jaate kyu bhuli lautana...
Dil jo mera tha tune churaya.

Jab...
Baarish, ghata banke tujhpe chhayegi...
Ik ik yaad tujhko satayegi.
Kisika sahara jab na mile...
Hoton pe mera hi naam paaygi.

Tab bhi..
Tere sath main hi rahunga,
Banke mitti ki khushbu mai aaunga.
Dhimi dhimi khushbu se tu muskana,
Khsusbu sang mujhe bhi, tujhme samana.

Jab...
Tu karegi raatbhar baate kissise,
To nind banke aankho me main hi aaunga,
Rakhegi jab takiye pe sir tu sone ko...
Banke lehar hava ki, tuze main sulaunga.

Hogi jab tu gehri nind me soyi soyi...
Aankho me sapana liye, usme hi khoyi khoyi.
Khwabo me tere tune kisiko bhi ho laya,
Mat bhulna khwab banke aankho me, main hi hu aaya.

Aisi koi jagah tu na payegi,
Jaha tere saath meri ruh na aayegi.
Bhale main mar jau, yaad banke aaunga.
Chahe tu chod jaaye, kafan banke jal jaunga.

****

Career is the most important thing in life. At a certain point you come to realize that. But, till then. It definitely gets too late.

You might have seen the 'Rockstar' movie of Ranbir Kapoor. There is a dialogue in that movie, *'tute hue dil se hi sangeet nikalta hai....'* very true. But in actual, it is not a *sangeet*. It is noise of *'pungi'* of the heart which, heart makes after it breaks.

My heart had also broken and I had decided to avoid it. But the most painful thing happened when I realized that I am not only losing my girlfriend, in fact I have lost my best friend too.

The most confusing time of the life is when our relationship goes at the edge of its end and it does not even fall off the cliff, nor itcomes back. It just seesaws with your emotions.

Your ego, your self-respect, your attitude, her ego, her attitude, her self-respect and her another best friend, everything keeps fucking you. Only to you, not to her.

At that time, when your relation is at the edge of cliff, nothing goes in your favour. If something marvellous is going to happen in your life, it just doesn't happen due to your new negative approach towards life.

She talks, she chats and she even wanders with a new guy which kills you even more. So to take revenge of it, and to feel a little less restless you decide to do the same to her. But you also have to wander with a guy. Not because you became gay or homo sexual suddenly, but something stops you from trusting the next girl you see as your very own best friend cum girlfriend has already defrauded you.

Sometimes in spite of all these things, you wander with other girls. But then, you let her know about it intentionally to make her jealous. However, here also things don't work in our favour. She gets so jealous that she blocks you after another fight and the other guy who was wandering with her lately, gets more advantage.

In this way also only you get fucked.

So, you cry, you cry, and you cry again and it becomes creepy.

Then you feel lonely again. You call all the girls from your past and you either flirt there (in which you suck by the way), or cry there, freaking them out.

Some of your well-wishers, good friends cannot bear your sulky face. So to cheer you up, they get their butts on work by buying drinks for you for the first time. And you then get more into her thoughts after boozing. You become all Devdas type. Your friends start their *bakchodi* about girls to let you feel good, but their every word just hurts you more thinking that whatever they are saying is true. Your girl is also nothing but a known and very own slut. You feel like shouting loudly by standing on the top of the highest building or in a stadium.

That is not enough for you to screw your life and career, so to fulfil the remaining quota; you walk alone on the road at midnight. You go to the centre of biggest square of the city. You look down, and take out your hands from your pockets. Taking a deep breath you squeeze your fist and then,

'I..... LOVE... YOU..... ERGHHHAAA...' a loud voice comes from your heart and mind which makes you scream in the square at 1:00 am. Not only in that square, in fact in every square on the way to your room and stadium nearby, and on the terrace waking up people and giving dogs chance to bark at you.

You see nothing in front of you. You imagine yourself in a mental asylum in next few days.

You become all the filmy type and you start thinking that all the movies and all the sad songs are written on you and about your situation only. Suddenly the very long and unstoppably very true dialogue from movie *'pyaar ka punchnaama'* becomes your favourite one.

When you see the romantic movie, which you used to like before, you start thinking, 'what a liar are those actors!' You even star hating the actress in that movie which was your favourite one.

Somewhere deep inside, you still love her more than you hate her. But your ego stops you from calling her. You just look at the phone screen waiting for her missed call like you wait for the **40** marks when a paper goes tough. Your heart says to call her but mind doesn't allow it. 'Why would I? She would call me.' This is what the motto of life becomes.

More than 16 hours of a day is spent in just looking at the screen after every minute to check whether she called you.

There is nothing you can do, so you just open the older chats, read it and smile with tearful eyes. You listen to your call recordings with her, which help you to feel like you are talking with her. But moreover you want to laugh on yourself after hearing your ugly voice in that recording. 'Oh my god! Do I sound that ugly?' you don't believe it is your voice.

Then you start dreaming with open eyes about her, wishing some miracle to happen and she would be as she used to be earlier.

But it just leads you to the shock therapy at the mental asylum. You believe that your admission in mental hospital is almost fixed now.

But then something happens and the woman who loves you unconditionally calls you. She cares for you, she asks you whether you had your meal, she could not bear your sulky voice and inspires you about your career. She reminds the hopes your father has. She reminds you what your father is doing to keep you satisfied and happy. And you reply with a smile to her, 'Yes mom. I will do my study and clear my exams this time.' You cut that call and see the couple walking on the street holding each other's hands, and a quick abuse spits out from your mouth for the whole gender of females.

17. Is this the end?

* * *

The studies kept distracting in such situations. But at some level in life you need to focus on your career. So I decided to forget that bitch who does not even care about me anymore and concentrate on my studies.

The whole PL I prepared like hell for my studies, forgetting my all the thirst and hunger and even sleep. It has been almost two weeks since I had any contact with Janvi. Neither I tried to call her, nor did she contact me. Slowly, slowly life was going on track and I was looking forward for exams only.

But how would god let that happen? He just doesn't feel entertaining when everything is going well. So to just spice it up a bit he gave an idea to that bastard Dhiraj to tease me by messaging on fb and texting in person. I just called him back to fight with him and to spit out all my frustration on him. There I get to know that he had not even talked or chat with Janvi since two weeks.

Why? I mean why on earth I called him? I was doing my preparation very well for my studies. Now I had to call her to ask her if she was ok. I hate myself for being so ..... so..... being so...

Ah... I don't know. I don't have words for me.

The frustration, the anger and the intimacy towards her was just making me crazy. I dialed her number but cut it off. 'The day after tomorrow is my exam. I don't want to get distracted.' I thought to myself. 'Focus, focus... focus.' I said to myself rubbing my head.

I just switched off my phone so that I would not get distracted. But you know, *dil hai ke manata nahi.*

My eyes were not sticking on the book. After every minute my eyes were rolling to see the phone, my hands were trying to run to grab the phone and call her.

I just closed that book and put it down. I looked at the phone and ran my hands to pick the phone. I took it and removed its battery. I threw the battery to one corner of room and put that phone in the bag, deep under the clothes.

But yet I knew that where the phone was, and yet I was unable to control myself from calling her.

I just got up from my place and took my books for study. I got out of my room and locked it. Putting the key at its place, I headed towards one of my friends' room to study.

'Vijay...' I said while knocking on the door of his room.

****

I stayed there for two whole days to study. And finally the day of exam came. Vijay and I, we both got ready to go for exams. There was not a single chapter or even a single line, which I missed. I had complete confidence that I would score more than 70 in that exam. Vijay took his stuff and we headed towards my room to take my hall-ticket. We were walking and revising some of the things, which might create the confusion in the exam. While we were revising, we reached to my room.

We could see from downstairs that my room was not locked. It was opened and a guy was standing in the door facing inside the room. We went upstairs and I could see that the guy who was standing in the door was none other than that bastard Dhiraj.

Great! I worked my ass out these days for exam and here I see his face just half hour before the exam. The perfect bad luck!

But the story wasn't finished yet. I headed further and I could see Janvi was in my room. All of a sudden I felt like I'd faint. When..... why... how.... why the hell she had come back? And why the hell with that moron?

All of a sudden my heart beats rose. I had no idea whether I was surprised or I was angry because she was with that moron in my room. I had no idea when she had arrived. It was 9:30 in the morning which led me to think that she must had come a day before, or at night.

Vijay told me to hurry as we were getting late for our exams. I just looked at Janvi controlling my confused feelings, and took my hall-ticket. I don't know how and when my breathing increased. I went towards door and stood there for a while.

I did not wish to leave the room. I did not wish to leave Janvi back alone with Dhiraj.

'Come on, Karan. We are getting late.' Vijay said again.

I just had to leave the room for the sake of exam. The worst time of my life where I was confused and I had to leave her back.

'Who was that guy?' Vijay asked.

'That was the one bastard...' I said with the hateful voice from the bottom of my heart.

'Dhiraj?' Vijay asked and I nodded.

'What the hell was he doing in your room?' He asked again.

I had no answer. I just took a deep breath and ran my hand through my hair. We reached the canteen for breakfast. Vijay ordered samosa and tea. I had no idea whether when he finished his samosa. I was just looking at the glass of tea aimlessly.

I had not even had a drink a sip of that tea. I just kept spinning that glass slowly, slowly thinking about Janvi while looking at the zero spot.

'Come on, finish your dish. Don't think about it. Let the paper finish. Once paper is finished then we will see that bastard.' Vijay said and I just got up from my place without eating anything.

'Why the hell she would have come with him again?' I started thinking while heading towards the main entrance of the college.

'Doesn't she know how much I hate that guy and her friendship with him?' I entered in college and was just walking like a robot, who has programmed to go into exam hall without knowing the surrounding. Vijay saw the hall no. And we headed towards the exam hall.

'Is he now that much close to her that she is not even wandering with him, but also taking him to our room!' I sat on my seat without having any idea of time.

Bell rang and that examiner distributed the question papers. I looked the questions and remembered all the answers. All the questions were familiar and well-practiced, even their answers were also familiar.

I started writing the answers. 'What if they had been in my room for whole night?' Suddenly this thought ran into my mind.

'What if they had kissed yet?' I could not concentrate on the exam. My hand just increased its trembling. I just held the bench tightly to control myself.

I looked at the watch and tried to concentrate on the exam.

The whole hall was covered with the pin-drop silence and my high respiration was spoiling the silence.

'Why the hell I left her behind alone with him? He is so cheap that he would not leave a chance to take her advantage in a lonely room.' This thought ran into my mind and I just could not write anything further on paper. His face and her arrogant nature just kept running in front of my eyes. I wanted to write the solutions in my papers but all I could do was imagine and picture them both together in my mind.

I could not bear that thing, neither could I forget it. I just kept trying to control my anger and frustration. More I was trying to be calm, more I was shivering, more I was trying to forget it and concentrate on my exam, more I was breathing heavy. I just clutched the question paper in my fist and kept looking down trying to avoid the imagination of them both having sex in my room.

I could feel that I was becoming more anxious and the psycho inside me was waking up. I looked at the time. It had been just 20 minutes and more than two and a half hour was yet to pass.

I tried to concentrate on my answer sheet. I tried hard to write the solutions avoiding their thoughts. But it just led to the trembling hands and the wet eyes. I wanted to scream like never before. I wanted to abuse loudly. I wanted to hit that bastard and moreover, I wanted to grab Janvi and slap her for making me psycho.

When I was with her, she used to flirt with him. And now when I am not with her and she was all alone with him..., what level she would have crossed yet? I could not even imagine.

Moreover, another thing was also bothering me that, they were in my room where I had all the memories of Janvi living with me. And now when I would go back there, I would not be able to even breathe in there.

I write as much as I could control myself in that completely silent hall. That silence was even killing me more as I could hear my heart screaming but I was unable to scream there.

After another terrible hour, I got up from my place and took my answer sheet. I had to leave the exam hall, as I would have died there if I had stopped for one more second.

I just started to run towards my room. I was on the second floor in my college. I just headed towards the stairs and just jumped skipping every 5 to 7 stairs to reach my room as soon as possible.

Once I was out of my college, I did not even stopped to breathe in way and kept running to reach my room sooner, and to catch them red handed. I had no idea why I was trying to catch them red handed and what I would have done after that. But I could not think any positive thing about her as she had changed and was behaving weirdly with me lately.

I reached to my room. I opened the gate and I could see from downstairs, he was still there. He was standing in the door where he was standing before. I just stopped there and took a breather. I went upstairs and entered in my room intentionally giving him a push.

'You came so early. Doesn't your paper supposed to end at 1?' Janvi asked.

'Why? You didn't get enough time with your *friend,* you whore?' I thought in my mind but did not say that, as I did not want to insult her in front of anyone else. 'Just leave.' I said to Dhiraj and he looked at me weirdly thinking what I was babbling.

'What? Bittu, what happened?' Janvi asked.

'I said JUST GET THE HELL OUT OF MY ROOM.' I shouted and Janvi stopped Dhiraj.

'Dhiraj wait. Just give us a moment.' She said and closed that door. She looked at me and came to know that I was out of her control. I was like a rabid dog, who was just barking and can sink teeth into her anytime.

I was just looking around in annoyance with pumping chest and bouncing shoulders due to high respiration and with the shaking hands rubbing my head and trying to make me quiet by running through my hair.

'What is wrong with you? What happened?' She asked and I just looked at her with blood red eyes and stood still. Trying to become quiet, I decided to give importance to my love first and forget the anger. I tried to be quiet. I looked down and left a sigh. Then looking back to her, I opened my arms and asked her to come to me. She just ran into my arms and hugged me.

I could feel the fragrance of her hair which I had missed in these days. I could feel her heartbeat which I had almost forgotten. I could feel her presence in my arms but yet I was not calm. Suddenly I recapped that the bastard was still standing outside the door.

She had tortured me all these days just for him and suddenly she hugs me like old days. I just could not get it. I slowly took her away from me. She was smiling by looking into my eyes. And her smile was not reminding me my love. All it could make me remind was the bastard standing outside the door and the time they might have spent together.

SLAP... SLAP.... SLAP. I slapped her three times nonstop pulling my hand loose.

I could not help myself from slapping her, as the anger was not gone yet. I had tried to forget the anger and feel her love but I couldn't. All I could feel was the suffocation I felt in exam hall.

'Have you lost your mind?' She said with wet eyes.

'YES...' I yelled, 'I don't trust you anymore. Who knows what you might have done while I was not here. You obviously seemed to enjoy the time with your *friend*.'

'Just mind your language. Do you have any idea what are you talking about?'

'What am I talking about? I am not that stupid to not see the things which are happening straight in front of my eyes. You have always fought me for him. You used to flirt with him and you almost left me because of him. Yet you want me to trust you with him standing in my room when I was not around. You are not that straight. I know you very well.'

'Bittu, you saw him. He did not even enter in the room. He was standing in the door all the time.' She tried to explain.

'Oh really? Like you are a *sati savitri* or something like that! I know you. When Sanjay was ignoring you, you had kissed me in my house even when there were other people around, and you want me to trust you with the guy all alone in my room for whom you literally forgot me and left me alone?'

'I don't believe this! Just go to hell!' She said and tried to open the door.

'Why, what happened now? You can't bear your *friend* standing alone out there?'

'For god's sake Stop it. What would he think if he heard your words?'

'Oh, so his thoughts are now important for you and even bothering you.' I had no idea what I was speaking and why? I had totally gone crazy. I would have not even needed any medical certificate to tell whether I was mental.

'Bittu, you just slapped me and yet I am trying to talk with you nicely. Just stop your nonsense, otherwise....'

'Otherwise what? You are not doing any favour on me by talking nicely. You have already spoken and behaved worst with me. And don't give me that shit about nice behaviour.'

She just opened the door and left the room slamming that door behind her. That moron was still standing in the door like a shameless. Had he lost all his shame? Such a cheap guy.

For a second I was trying to regret slapping her, but I found no regrets in my mind or heart at all. I thought whatever I did was right.

I was just suffocated in my room as I was in the same place where they might have done something. I did not care about her and where she'd gone. I just threw my pillow and bed sheets in anger and screamed loudly in my room.

****

'What happened, Bittu? Did you guys fought?' said Rupam on call, one of her friends from class who was in her hostel before.

'Why, who told you?' I asked trying to wake up from my place after almost two hours.

'Well she is here in my hostel, and she won't stop crying and abusing you. What happened?' She explained.

'Didn't she tell you?'

'Oh come on. Stop playing this. She says ask you and you say didn't she tell me. What is wrong with you guys?'

'There might be so many things wrong in me, that's why she has chosen that bastard Dhiraj.' I said and Rupam got the whole matter as she knew the condition well since we were living in together.

'Ohk... anyways. You don't worry about her. You concentrate on your studies and exams, till then she will live in my hostel.' She assured me and cut that call.

I could feel the anger about her still in my mind and was still suffocating.

****

The exams passed one by one horribly as I could not concentrate in studies due to the thought of her with him in a room. I had not even spoken with her in these days even when she was in same city. She had called me so many times but I didn't pick it up.

Previously when I was angry she used to give a missed call to me and I used to call her back. Then she started to get angry and I had to call to convince her, but she used not to pick those call. Then again, I fought with her and I used to not answer her calls. Then she went to Beed and there she totally forgot me and didn't answer my calls. And now, suddenly when she was in Aurangabad, I did not answer her calls. This cycle carries on.

I had asked Vijay to move in with me in my room as I could feel living there alone due to the thoughts of her and I had to study for my exams too. That day Rupam called me and told me about Janvi's departure. She said that Janvi was going to Beed again for her College work and would leave next morning. I just ignored the topic as I was still caring the anger about her and the pain of breaking heart.

****

I still remember that morning. That was the morning when she was going to Beed for exam preparations.

I was deep into my sleep in my bed when she came to my room. Vijay opened the door. It was 6 o'clock. She was going, so she had come to say bye. Vijay went back to bed and slept. She came inside, put some stuff in my room and said, 'Vijay, bye. I am going.' He was in sleep so he didn't respond her.

She came to my bed, and pulled my blanket, 'Bittu, I am going. Aren't you coming to see me off?' She asked while watching at Vijay's bed. He was still sleeping. I just shook my head. She just stared at me with blank face for a while. Then kneeling down towards me, she came closer. My eyes were open but when she came closer, I closed my eyes and turned my face to opposite side. My ego was stopping me.

She didn't wait for my response. She caught my ear tightly,

pulled it towards her, and as I was going to scream, she put her palm on my mouth and looked into my eyes very irritably. I still remember her big eyes, which she then softly changed to innocence. She then softly kissed on my forehead. She applied her lips on my forehead for long time.

'I would like to kiss you on lips.' She whispered in my ear. After completing that sentence, she smoothly got her lips towards mine, and stood still in front of me waiting for my response.

My heart was telling me to kiss her. However, my ego was not allowing me. So, I again turned to opposite side from her. After a couple of seconds, my cheek was wet due to a drop fallen from her eye. She waited for my response and then inserted into my blanket and bed. I just made some space for her to sleep, but didn't turn my face towards her side. She was feeling pain to go hence, she was controlling her ego otherwise she would have made me beg to kiss her. Suddenly she hugged me from my backside and held me so tightly.

Oh man! This time I could not stop myself for more than a couple of seconds. I quickly turned my face towards her and hugged her tightly, holding her close to my each cell of my body; I grabbed her lips in my teeth and kissed her. But this time, she didn't oppose me or didn't cry childish. Then for few minutes, she rested on my chest and at 6:30, she had to leave.

I wanted to say that I love her so much, please don't go. But, I didn't. She left my room, hoping that I would come with her, but I didn't. I even did not wake up from my bed. And she left. I knew she was hoping me to see her, but I didn't.

When she boarded the bus, she texted me, 'I got my bus. I am going. Ab tak soya hua hai kya?'

I read it but didn't reply. So, she sent me another message, 'Ok! Sleep. when u'll wake up, I'll be in college, so would be unable to speak with you.'

This time I replied, 'I'm not sleeping. I just not wanted to disturb or interrupt you and your Dhiraj, who might be sitting beside you right now. Enjoy his company.'

She: come on bittu. It's enough now. HE IS NOT WITH ME.

I: Then may be someone else, who I am yet to be known.

She: BYE. U cant change. I HATE YOU.

I : why should I change? You lied to me, you hurt me, you broke your promises one by one. Why should I change?
She : grow up yaar! I need my friends too. I cant be your prisoner all the time. How can I leave them?
I : I hadn't told you to leave them first. You had promised me that you want only bittu, no one else. But now u are ignoring me cause of him, who tried to break our relationship by poisoning it. how would I trust you?
She : fine! Don't trust me anymore and don't wait for me. I am leaving you. our relationship is over. I want my life and my freedom. I cant live with you.
I : first of all, I didn't take any of your freedom. I was just following my way to protect my relationship from those bastards, which by the way won now.
And second thing, I hadn't come to you, so you are free to go. GOOD BYE, GO TO HELL.

She didn't reply on this one. I waited for couple of minutes and then sent her another message.
I : what happened? Talking with him? Ok, ok! Sorry to disturb you both. Go ahead.
She: don't msg me ever again.

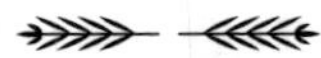

18. Worst two years

* * *

The break up is called so, because it breaks the relation. I mean it breaks the relationship only, not the feelings about each other. How great it would have been if someone could easily forget their loved ones right after the break up. But if that would be so easy, then people would have not called the feelings, 'falling in love'.. And we mostly get hurt in love hence they call it a falling in love, because every fall always hurts.

And it does not hurt when you've fallen. It hurts when you try to rise again. That's how I had fallen in love and was trying to forget her and get back on track again by rising up.

Earlier I was deeply angry with her and that anger was helping me to avoid calling her. But I had no cure for her memories. More I was remembering her, more I was getting angry. More I was getting angry, more I was missing her. More I was missing her, more I used to feel like talking with her. But whenever I used to dial her number, my ego would not allow me to complete the call.

My exams were over. I had packed my stuff to go to home. Before leaving for home, I decided to wander and go to 'Kala Ganpati' temple.

I was walking on the street and I reached to 'Avishkar chowk'. I could not understand that how, when I had studied for exam like hundred times and yet I forgot it, but some of her things that happened like barely once and yet I could not forget it even I tried harder to forget it.

I remebered the time when she had left her hostel, just to see me when I was angry at midnight. How much I was important for her that she did not care about anything and got out from balcony and had headed towards my room after midnight.

I kept walking trying to forget it. I kept walking towards the temple. I was right in front of the 'Dharmaveer Sambhaji high school.' I could see the dogs which had barked at her that night and felt the clutch of her hands to my arms due to fear of those dogs. It put a smile on my face remembering how timid she was and how she used to be afraid of dogs. But why the hell I was remembering her? We broke up our relationship. I should not think about her. I am supposed to forget her. I thought to myself and kept walking.

After going a little bit further, I had two paths. A right turn which was a short cut to the temple and a left turn which was long way but was going from the Cidco theatre. I decided to take the short one. I turned right and headed towards the temple. But after walking almost ten steps my legs stopped suddenly and were like forcing me to go back from another way. I turned back and started walking towards the Cidco theatre. I could see the benches were filled by some married couples who were keeping an eye on their kids playing, on bicycles around them and some girls from that hostel were walking on the street with their boyfriends. I felt so alone there after looking at those couples. I stood there for a while remembering the fight we used to have after her late arrival and feeling the hug she had given me when I had come after Dessehra. I closed my eyes standing in the middle of the road and took a deep breath. Living a sigh back, I opened my eyes, which were trying to get wet, but I did not allow them. I headed towards the temple and started putting my both hands in my pocket, slowly.

I reached the temple and sat there where we both used to sit regularly. I kept looking at the statue of Lord Ganesha continuously without blinking my eyes. I was fighting with him inside, for letting her go away from me.

While I was looking at the statue aimlessly, I could hear the silent fight of the boy and his girlfriend, who were sitting just beside me at some distance. It reminded me that bastard Dhiraj because of whom it all had its end.

No I won't let it end like this. I would not let that bastard succeed. I thought to myself. She is my best friend! She has to come back to me. She had promised me whether whatever would happen we would be best friends forever. I thought to myself and took out my phone.

I would say sorry. I would apologise to her and she would come back to me. It was just a fight. She has to come back. I thought. But I could not find a reason whether why I was going to apologise her.

I dialed her number. My ego was telling me to cut that call but I did not listen to it. I let that call complete. It started ringing. I was waiting for her to pick my call. I was a bit nervous. My heartbeats had risen. I was breathing faster. But she did not pick that call. I dialed again. Again it started to ring. My mind was asking me whether why I was calling her and why the hell I was going to apologise. I had done no mistakes. I should not be the one who would apologise. While thinking about it, my second call also got cut but she did not pick it up.

I dialed again. My mind was still stopping me from calling her. But I was not listening. My heart was telling me that it doesn't matter whether who made the mistake. If you love her then her presence in your life is more important than your ego. You should just go for it and talk to her. Even if she did a mistake, remember you love her more than her mistakes. You decide who is important for you, the person you love, or the mistake she did.

While I was listening to my heart, my call was cut. She cut it from other side. I just could not understand. I was the one who should be angry and still I was calling her and she was behaving like she was the queen of somewhere. I felt so insulted. I felt like why did I call her. I should have heard of my mind first instead of my heart. I felt like I want to throw that phone away in anger. I just looked up to the statue of Lord Ganesha. I abused him in my mind, I fought with him and I demanded him for the explanation whether why he is doing all this to me.

I just woke up from my place with anger about her and Ganesha. I did not stop there for a second then. I walked to my room the same way I had gone there. But on the whole way while coming back I felt angry for everyone. The kids that were playing there, the couples, which were sitting there. The girls who were wandering with their boyfriends, I felt pity about those boys. Poor boys don't have any idea what was going to happen in their life further. Only the dogs were for whom I did not felt anger. I liked them for barking at her. I felt like I should let all of them go to bite her.

I went to my room and took my stuff, which I had packed

already to go to Ambad. I left for Ambad at the very moment.

****

I was waiting for my bus at Cidco bus stand. The whole quota of her memories was not finished yet. How would I forget the drama at bus stand? I was waiting for my bus with the crowd at bus stop and that announcer was yelling after every minute to announce the bus numbers. I could see the bus arrive and stopped right in front of me. All the passengers ran to catch their seats. I read the bus name. It said 'Aurangabad –Beed'.

Why the hell all the things get attached to your memories when you are sad or you are frustrated or when you just broke up with your girlfriend? I mean, I was standing at the bus stop, where arrival of buses is quite normal. Not only normal, that's the only service they provide. Then why did I keep connecting things to her memories? I don't know. As soon as that bus stopped in front of me, I felt like it was a signal. Like Ganesha was telling me to board that bus and go to Beed to her. I remembered all the times when she had wet her eyes after arrival of that bus. I remembered all her looks she had given me with those wet eyes with the scarf tied on her face. I remembered holding her hands at such moments and the tight squeeze of a hug when the departure was close. I closed my eyes and felt like she was standing in front of me with wet eyes because her bus had arrived and I was looking into her eyes. I felt like I pulled her and applied my lips on her forehead for long time. I took a deep breath with eyes closed and left a sigh. 'I love you, Chiku...' I muttered. 'And I HATE BUS STOPS.' I could feel her saying those words with that annoyance. It curved my lips to smile.

I could not stop myself; I decided to board that bus. I took out my phone to call her and to tell her that I was coming to Beed. I dialed her number but she did not pick it up at first attempt I dialed it again.

'Don't you have any self-respect?' mind started to scold me, 'That bitch is not picking up your call and you are continuously calling her like you are the one who is pushy and needy.'

'Don't listen to it. Just go for it and remember that we love her.' My heart answered it.

She did not pick up the second call too. I dialed it again, this time becoming more restless and a bit angry.

'You still want to get insulted? Cut that call.' Mind ordered but I did not cut that call, neither did she pick up. I wanted to scream there loudly as I had been insulted again. Again I felt like I should have listened to my mind.

I took my bag and sat in the bus, which was going to Ambad. I did not feel like going to Beed then.

****

I reached my home and rested in the bedroom after dinner. More I was getting angry about her, more I was missing her. It was becoming more difficult to forget her and even to forgive her. How would I forget her, she is the one whom I had loved the most. And how would I forgive her when she had not even apologised for what she did. I was totally helpless. I was so pathetic. Nothing was in my favour.

I was trying to sleep. But as I said there was not a single place and not a single thing which was not making me to recall her. I was just at the place where we had our first kiss. The place where she had first time accepted her love. That was more torturing. Again my mind and my heart started to fight regarding calling her. And as I am a fool, I heard of my heart again. I dailed her number and I could hear the operator's voice, '*the number you have dialed, is on another call, please hold the line, or call again later.*' I looked at the time; it was 11:30 pm. I thought at this much late she must not be speaking with her family. And the second option which came into my mind was obviously the bastard's.

Nah! It was not like that. Actually first of all I thought that she must have been speaking with that bastard. But to be nice to myself I thought that she might even be speaking with her family members. But then I saw time and I concluded that she was not speaking with her family members. Now I used to get angry easily even for the smaller reasons, and there she was talking with that bastard. I kept calling her again. She did not pick up my single call. I kept calling again and again. But she had gone deaf for my calls. After 10 to 15 calls, I decided to listen to my mind and stop calling her. I had done with my insult again. I decided to stick with my mind and listen to it always, as heart was leading me only to the frustration and insult, and hurt.

But yet the volcano inside me had not slept. It was just like gushing to abuse them both and it was just not being quiet. There was a photo of Lord Ganesha in room, to which I kept looking in anger and being restless. 'Why the hell to me? Only I am the one who is getting hurt. Why are you doing this to me?' I asked him, but you know, statues and photos never talk. He did not answer me.

The time went passing like this only. There was not a single day where I did not try to forget her and succeed. I kept calling her daily and it kept telling me that either she was busy or she was on another call. The anger, love, irritation, restlessness and the frustration kept playing with my mind. Slowly, slowly there were only three people in this world to whom I hated most. That bastard Dhiraj, Janvi, and Ganesha. In this situation, days kept passing and my second year's first semester arrived.

****

I joined the college again and tried to concentrate on the studies seriously. I had a gap of one whole year, so after that one year I was feeling like a stranger in my college. Only thing where I could feel like home was my dance group 'Sizzlers'. There were some new faces for me this time. But when you are in Sizzlers, nobody is stranger for you. Here you could get everything. Lots of friends, big brothers, little sisters, seniors with the nature of your mother and the whole complete package of family.

We started our dance practice for the fresher's party. When I was in dance hall, or with Sizzlers, I didn't remember the time where I would have missed her like I used to. The time was going so well. I was toping in the class tests, I was attending the lectures, and I wasn't the defaulter student anymore. I felt like life was getting on the track. I thought I was moving on.

But life needed twists. How would it let you be happy forever? And especially when you are in love. So I was moving on and in between that sometimes I used to call her once or twice. But she still not used to pick my calls and put my phone on waiting.

Then there comes her birthday. I was awake that night. I wanted to call her too. But I did not. My ego was stopping me as usual. My mind was telling me, 'Suppose you would call her, and she might be speaking with that Dhiraj and did not pick up your call, then who would feel insulted?'

My heart was repeating its only thing saying you love her, you should go for her,.... bla....bla...bla.....

I was fed up of her nature and her arrogance of putting me on waiting. I decided to listen to my mind and not to call her.

I did not call her the whole day. Who knows, she might not even be waiting for my call. She might be wandering with that bastard as special birthday plans, I thought. I spend the day in college and in our dance practice.

While I was trying to sleep in my room, I got her call at 12:01 am. It surprised me as well as gave me a sweet shock. I picked up her call.

'Hey....'

'Why did not you call me?' Her first question.

'What?'

'It was my birthday and why did you not call me? The whole day I was waiting for your call. I thought and I knew you would call but you didn't. Why?' She said in a bit angry tone. I liked that at least she felt like she still has her right on me.

'Why should I call you?' I have no idea why I said that, 'All these days I kept calling you like a mental and you did not even pick once. Why the hell you think I would call you today? Who knows you might have been busy with that bastard and would have kept me on waiting again.'

'You know what....'

'No I don't know.' I said habitually.

'Oh shut up...' she said and it hurt me. This was not the thing which she used to say. But yeah, now she was not like she used to be, 'You know... you are so pathetic. I was waiting for your call today but you did not. You did not even message me. I think you have no value of me in your life now. Now it's over. I think I was a fool to wait for your call. Don't call me ever again.' She said and cut that call.

Great! According to her, NOW it was over? Just because I had not called her on that one day? Then what about the whole other days I used to call like thousands time except that one day? It means it doesn't matter whether I listen to my mind or to my heart, in both ways only I was going to get fucked.

I had to call her back. After all, I am the one who was *chutya*. I could control myself only for one day and that also the very wrong day. I could listen to my ego and carry my self-respect only for a day. Again I had become the dog who runs after the bone.

I kept calling her again and again, but she did not pick it up. I kept calling her until I fell asleep. But she did not pick it up. I felt like she was just retaining me from not calling her to call her again and again, as she might felt like losing her importance in someone's life. She might have felt losing her score about boys calling her as if they had gone mad for her, about whom she might have told stories to her friends.

I was so exhausted. The tiredness due to dance practice, the anger on myself for not calling her on that one day, the frustration about her behaviour, and the more anger about her for not picking my calls was just making me too suffocated. I was so restless and annoyed by her nature. All of a sudden, my all efforts of previous days of calling her had like gone wasted.

****

Well that gave me a lesson, no matter how much you love her, she would focus on the teeny-tiny hate you would have for her due to anger. No matter how much you struggle to talk with her, she would not keep that in mind. She would focus on the one day that you have not called her and will make you feel like a criminal.

I did not want to give her another chance to point a finger at me regarding my love. Hence, I kept calling her daily, many times. But it did not work. I kept being on her waiting calls. I started to hate myself for being so fussy about her calls. Why could not I ignore her like I had ignored Purvi? I thought to myself.

Many times she picked up calls just to abuse me and insult me. Whenever I called, she had nothing to say instead of reminding me how cheap I was to slap a girl, and not trust her. She even told me that now it was over and I should not bother her and stop calling her.

But you know how much I loved her. I could not help it from calling her, and this thing kept going for months.

****

It looked like all the misfortunes had fallen on me at the same time. I had dropped a year, I had that bastard in my story to screw my life, I had slapped her eventually, which led to our so-called break up. But it continued when our dance performance ended. We had practiced like hell for it, but yet we could not win that time. So many eyes had taken bath in tears for it.

I was not even balanced from these things when I got a call from Dhiraj to give an earthquake in my life.

I didn't pick up his call at first and avoided to get more frustrated than I was already. But I had to take his call after feeling like to abuse him.

'What's up, BITTU?' He started in a teasing tone.

'My name is Karan.' I said arrogantly.

'Oh come on! I can call you Bittu, like Janvi used to.' He said forcing on the words 'used to' as if he knew she doesn't talk to me anymore.

'Janvi can call me that. Who the hell are you? Just a pathetic loser who flirts with other's girlfriends.' I started to spit out my anger.

'Well I am Janvi's boyfriend in that case. I can call you that right?' He said and I felt like I'd fainted due to that. I mean all these days I was just assuming that in annoyance, but he just made the confirmation stealing all my leftover happiness and life.

'Boyfriend?' I just whispered rarely giving way to words out of my mouth.

'Yes! And, I have called you to tell you to stop calling her. Don't trouble her by calling or else it can give you a big trouble.'

'Go to hell. No one can stop me from calling her.' I said controlling myself from the shock and trying not to lose from him.

'Well I can tell you that. And for your information she told me to do so.' He said followed by a chuckle to tease me. 'Well Bittu, I wanted to say a big thanks to you.' He said waiting for my reply.

'Won't you ask why?' He asked after few seconds as I didn't say anything. 'Anyways, I will tell you.' He said and continued after clearing his throat, 'Actually, I wanted her in my life, but I could not have her due to that Sanjay, which by the way has no option to come back now. Then you came in between us. But lucky I am that you were so possessive about her that I did not to do anything except to flirt with her.'

'I had not come in between you, you did.' I said in anger while rubbing my teeth.

'Does it really matter? But I should say that it was really hard to make her forget you. But you made that easy for me. Thank you so much for not trusting her and for slapping her. It just made everything so simple for me.' He said and I could realise that he had really not entered in my room that day.

'I just kept silent and understood her all the time. Plus I stood out of your room for whole four hours. That really helped me to let her think how nice I was and how lusty you were.' He kept continuing his story. I was just listening him while abusing myself for not trusting Janvi. Suddenly I realised that I should turn on the call recorder and let Janvi hear all these things after this call, so that she would come to know that bastard's real face.

I turned on the call recording and he continued,

'Well anyways. Just wanted to thank you for all these things and warn you to stay away from her.' He said and cut that call.

'EERRRGGGHHHaaaa.....' I shouted in anger and threw my phone. Why the hell I didn't turn that recording on earlier.

I felt like I had lost my place in her life. I felt like who the hell he was to tell me something like that. I should be the one telling him to stay away from my Janvi.

I could not help it out. All of a sudden I felt like my mind is blowing in my head. From nowhere I could hear the voices of them both calling each other, Jaanu, shona, baby. I could not bear the imagination of Janvi saying him that she loves him. I just wanted to kill that bastard after picturing him with my Janvi. I wanted to cut his head out of his body. I wanted to decapitate him and chop his every part of body into pieces after imagining him saying, 'I love you Chiku and love you Jaanu.'

Not only this, I just wanted to burn them both alive after imagining her reply to it.

All of a sudden I felt myself sweating and shivering. I don't know from where and how, but I was feeling violent. I could not stop picturing them with each other.

All these days whatever I and Janvi had lived together.... all of a sudden I felt like he was living all those things with her.

I wanted to punch him right into his face and kick him between his legs till he dies. I was getting out of control I ran to gather my phone to call Janvi.

I dialed her number. It was on waiting. I just got more hyper. I wanted to throw that phone again, but I was helpless. I wanted to talk with her.

I kept calling her again and again. She just put my phone on waiting. I don't know when my sweaty face became wet with tears. I started crying helplessly, grabbing my hair.

I called her again. This time she picked my call and in no time she switched it to conference with that moron.

'Chiku...' I said with that sulky tone.

'Don't you understand? I am busy, I don't want to talk with you...' she said arrogantly.

'Please Chiku listen to me.' I continued with that cry, 'He is not good for you...'

'Oh, so you mean to say you are good, who doesn't even trust her and slaps her.' Dhiraj spoke from other side, letting my anger blow to my mind and making me feel like I should plunge into the phone and rip his heart out and crush it under my feet.

'Just shut the fuck off, you *madarch***.' I shouted.

'Bittu, behave yourself. Otherwise I will cut this call and you will again keep calling me like a creep but I will not pick it again.' She said more like intimidating me.

I had to keep calm on phone, just because I was the one who was helpless there. I wanted to shout but I could not as I wanted to talk with her. The ball was in her court, I could not even abuse that bastard.

'Please, Chiku... don't do this to me. How could you forget me?'

'You should have thought about it before showing scepticism in me.' She said showing how annoyed she was with me.

'I am sorry for that. I know I made a terrible mistake. But this bastard played a game with us Chiku..... you....'

'Last time I am warning you. Either you watch your tongue, or I am cutting this call.' She said and I just tried to control my anger by closing my eyes hard and biting my lips with the saliva trying to pop out due to crying. I never felt myself that much helpless ever in my life.

'I am sorry, Chiku.' I said with the loud sobs.

'Jaanu... I think we have talked something about your name.'

Dhiraj interrupted.

'Yes, I know.' Janvi said and continued, 'Listen, Karan. I don't want you to call me by that name. My name is Janvi, and you are nobody to talk me like that now.' She said and this time I just felt like dying alone as she had literally ripped my heart out.

'I... I ...am your best friend...' I wanted to say boyfriend, but I had lost that confidence.

'Huh, best friend?' She scoffed.

'Yes... that's what we had promised about.' I tried to remind her about our promise about friendship hoping that at least for that she would keep talking with me in future and I would apologise her.

'You should have thought about it before slapping me. And you know what...' she said and I wanted to say, "No, I don't know", but I didn't say it. But then I realised that she had also stopped for a while waiting for me to say that. I just smiled mixed with a sob and biting my lips. She continued, 'I don't care what you think about Dhiraj. But I trust him more than you. At least he will never harm me. You just used to think as if I was your slave...'

'NO, I don't used to think that.'

'Listen I just don't want you in my life again. Never ever. Just go to hell and never call me back.' She said and I started to beg her. I cried, I begged, I apologised her thousands of times but she was just rude.

She cut that call after getting annoyed with my sobs and sulky voice. She didn't feel like talking to a beggar who used to be everything for her once and who had slapped her.

****

I had not stopped crying. I had lost all my pride and self-respect. The only thing I wanted was her, back in my life. I felt like I have lost my whole life.

Ever since I had started to learn the things like talking, walking, eating and go to school or walk alone, I had Janvi in my life somewhere as a part of it, being as a friend, as a competitor, as an enemy with whom I used to fight. And in last few years I had not survived a single day without talking to her, without fighting with her, or without missing her. And now all of a sudden I felt very alone.

I had no idea how to live life like this. I had never lived this much alone ever. The pain of losing her as a girlfriend was not a big issue for me. The thing which was killing me more was some other bastard telling me to stay away from her and Janvi also had granted him to do so, as if he had won my place in her life.

How could she do that to me? How could she say that I never trusted her? I had trusted her all the time. I had trusted her nature, her behaviour, her friendship. She had told me that she would never leave me. I had trusted her so much that I had took her for granted thinking whatever would happen, she would never leave me alone. I had believed that whatever and however I would behave and fight with her, she would not go away from me. I trusted that after every big or small fight she would always jump to grab me and would lock my lips to make me quiet. I had belief that no matter how big the issue would be, she would make me calm by widening her fishy eyes and biting her finger.

I could not help and could not survive from that loneliness. I kept calling her repeatedly. It was suffocating me. The misery, the anger, the aggravation all the feelings were just mixing in my mind and choking me, as I was crying limitless.

I wanted to scream loudly, but had no energy left till then. I had no idea how to live that life all alone and what would come up in further. I just kept slapping myself for slapping her that day, and kept crying my eyes out like blood red.

My phone beeped. It was Janvi's message. I just took that phone with trembling hands. I had no energy left even to lift that phone. I took it and opened that message.

'plz bittu, listen to me. I cant come back. Forget me and don't call me ever again. And plzz, stop crying

..'

I saw and read that message like hundred times. My eyes were not rolling away from those dots she had put at the end of that message. Why the hell she had put those dots? What did she want to say?

Did she want me to forget her? Or she was still confusing me with those dots saying 'love you'?

****

Life had become so restless. Another semester just passed

like that. I believe that I might have forgotten hundred times to breathe, but I had never forgotten to miss her. I missed her every second, every moment. I missed her with every breath I took in and with every sigh I left out. Normally we flip our eyelid with every six seconds. But I had missed her six hundred times every time I blinked my eyelid.

They say if you miss someone then that person gets hiccups. I don't believe in it, as she would have died yet after getting limitless hiccups for every moment I missed her.

Moreover she had added my number to block list of her phone, as I had not left calling her yet. And that bastard also could not make me stop from calling her.

I had totally crossed all the limits of human being to call someone continuously and unstoppably. But moreover she had crossed the peak limit to disregard someone and putting him on hold intentionally to lead him to his death.

It had been so many days since I had smiled for any good reason. I had no motive left in my life. Missing her and crying for what she did to me was like the breathing work for me.

I truly believe that, had I called him this much, and then even Daud would have come to India and surrendered himself for my sake.

Osama Bin Laden would have come out of his grave and killed himself again after this many daily calls.

Had I worshiped any god this much, he would have come on earth and blessed me and granted me a boon to have anything I wanted. And I would have asked for Janvi to come back to me and never go away again ever.

I experienced the tremendous change in my behaviour; I had gained a very negative approach towards life. The filmy and dreamy guy had become so timid and always with a sulky face. I had not stopped dreaming. My dreams had become just violent now. I always used to dream about killing that moron in hundred ways. My life has only these goals now. Either get her back to me and never let go again, or think out the hundreds of ways to torture and kill that bastard.

Life was just passing like this with her thoughts and daily calls to her. And another semester passed.

****

I was in third year now, and yet I had only one wish, I wanted to talk with her. And lucky I am, she picked my call that day. That day arrived almost a year later.

'Have you gone out of your mind?' That's what I heard after all these days. But that also felt like a feast to me as I focused on her voice only, which made me happy and not on her words. 'Please stop calling me. I don't want to talk with you.' This is what she said further.

'Please, forgive me Janvi. Please come back to me. I was stupid; I was a jerk, then. Now I want you only.' I started my sentence with a nervous tone and ended with a cry and tears falling from my eyes.

'Try to understand, I can't come back to you. I have a boyfriend; I don't want to be the so-called slut again.'

'Please stop hurting me Janvi. Please..... I want you.' I said with sobs.

'You never trusted me. You slapped me. No matter how much I love you. I will not come back to you ever again.'

'What the fuck is this yaar? Don't you get it?' I started to shout, 'It has been more than a year I am trying to talk to you. It has been more than a year where I have called you every day like hundred times. And still you don't trust me?'

'Don't raise your voice against me. You have no rights on me now.' She said arrogantly.

'Why?' I didn't calm down. Instead of that my voice become louder with sulky tone, 'that *bhench*** has all rights on you now?'

'Bittu, watch your tongue, or else...'

'Or else? Or else what?' I shouted in anger wiping my tears, 'You would cut this call and never pick it again?' I said and waited for her reply, 'Just go to hell. I don't need you. You can't even understand why I used to fight with you?' I yelled again as she did not reply. But after this yelling also she did not say anything. I got afraid thinking that she might have cut that call. I looked at the screen. She hadn't cut that call.

'Hello?... hello....'I said with sulky voice and then busted into tears as I was helpless there. I had raised my voice but had a little fear in my heart about her cutting that call and torturing me for another year or even for life.

'Hello...?' I shouted again followed by a sneer and sobs.

'I am listening.' She said arrogantly, 'Finish your thing and then I will cut this call. And I don't want your calls on my phone ever again. You have your time; say whatever you want to say.' She said as if she had no effect on her of my crying voice and tortured feelings.

'Chiku...' I started softly controlling my anger, 'Don't you see? I used to fight with you because of this bastard and at the end, I am all alone and you are with him as I used to afraid of. That's what I used to tell you about, and now I am the one who is all alone.' I said with a poor face crying like hell.

'Is that it? Have you finished what you had to say?' She asked again in arrogance. She was feeling like a queen for whom a slave is crying.

I just felt like I was worshiping the god made of stone only. I could not bear her behaviour. It made me more frustrated. I felt like abusing them both. I felt like shouting at her, and so I did.

'Just go to hell with that *bhench***, you slut. Get lost. I don't need you. That *madarch*** Dhiraj, I will not leave him. I will kill you both...' I started shouting and abusing her, but before I could complete my sentence. She cut that call.

'Just go to hell. At last you showed your competence.' She said and cut that call showing me my place in her life.

As soon as she cut that call, I threw my phone in anger and yelled like never before. I sat slowly taking help of wall and put my head in between my knees while crying.

'I LOVE YOUUUUU....' I shouted.

Again I felt like all alone and helpless. The restlessness was not leaving my back. I had gone crazy. I wanted either to kill them both or commit suicide.

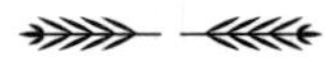

19. To the extreme

❄ ❄ ❄

The craziness was increasing and was leading me to more violence, but I was always confused between how much I loved her and how much was I angry with her. Because that evening also, I had talked with her in anger but when she had cut that call, I kept crying like hell for hours.

I decided to get her back in my life at any cost. Whatever would it take, I will get her back in my life, I swore.

I took my phone and started to call her. *'The number you have dialed is on another call. Please call after... The number you have dialed is busy...'*

She was obviously talking with that bastard. I dailed again, *'The number you have dialed is on another call. Please call after... The number you have dialed is busy...'*

That operator's voice was like a part of my life now, as all these days I had heard only to that operator. All these days my almost half time had gone in listening that operator's voice. I dialed again,

'The number you have dialed is on another call. Please call after... The number you have dialed is busy...'

The more I was hearing that self-operated message, more I was calling her.

'The number you have dialed is on another call. Please call after... The number you have dialed is busy...'

'The number you have dialed is on another call. Please call after... The number you have dialed is busy...'

With every time I heard that operator's voice, I reminded my love and anger. I dialed again.

'The number you have dialed is on another call. Please call after... The number you have dialed is busy...'

The more I was calling her, more she was ignoring me stubbornly. But I had decided that night, either she would pick up my call or I would die.

'The number you have dialed is on another call. Please call after… The number you have dialed is busy…'

'The number you have dialed is on another call. Please call after… The number you have dialed is busy…'

'The number you have dialed is on another call. Please call after… The number you have dialed is busy…'

I was counting my calls. It was almost three calls per minute on an average. Because she had added my number to reject list, every call used to cut so early.

'The number you have dialed is on another call. Please call after… The number you have dialed is busy…'

'The number you have dialed is on another call. Please call after… The number you have dialed is busy…'

Almost after half hour, I had reached near to hundred calls. I felt like I would definitely make century.

'The number you have dialed is on another call. Please call after… The number you have dialed is busy…'

'The number you have dialed is on another call. Please call after… The number you have dialed is busy…'

'The number you have dialed is on another call. Please call after… The number you have dialed is busy…'

And there I was. I had completed century, but yet she had not picked up my call. I was totally suffocated and wet due to sweat. But not only she was stubborn, I was the one too. I kept calling her again.

'The number you have dialed is on another call. Please call after… The number you have dialed is busy…'

'The number you have dialed is on another call. Please call after… The number you have dialed is busy…'

*'Bhench**, madarch**, aaj aar ya paar bhench**...'* I shouted abusing and kept redialling again. I just kept dialling and after an hour later I felt like I had become a robot. I had no idea what I was going to speak with her, but I just kept calling her.

'The number you have dialed is on another call. Please call after… The number you have dialed is busy…'

'The number you have dialed is on another call. Please call after… The number you have dialed is busy…'

But more I was calling her, more she was getting stronger to ignore my calls and to me. All these days she had been used to it. It was nothing new for her to ignore my calls now.

'The number you have dialed is on another call. Please call after… The number you have dialed is busy…'

I kept dialling, kept dialling, and kept dialling again.

'The number you have dialed is on another call. Please call after… The number you have dialed is busy…'

'The number you have dialed is on another call. Please call after… The number you have dialed is busy…'

'The number you have dialed is on another call. Please call after… The number you have dialed is busy…'

After three hours later, I saw in mirror and could see that my face my nose, my eyes, my head everything was wet and red. My phone's battery was about to die. I plugged it to charging and kept dialling her number again, again and again,

'The number you have dialed is on another call. Please call after… The number you have dialed is busy…'

And it continued. It continued until she cut that bastard's call and switched off her phone. She had cut his call in almost three and half hour and her phone kept ringing after that but she did not looked at it, neither had she picked it up.

Her phone went off due to continuous ringing, and till then it had been more than 8 hours.

I just left my phone as it was on my ear while I was rested on my bed with the tiredness of those calls. My body and especially head had become warm inside. My ears were swollen and lips were dry. I did not count the calls but it almost went 1250 because my speed of dialling had decreased after few hours. I just laughed at myself with that dejected face and swollen eyes.

We both were really obstinate. I had crossed the limit of calling and moreover she had crossed the limit to ignore someone. May be it was easy for her, as half of the time she was speaking on phone with that moron and half of the time she might have put phone on silent mode and slept peacefully, leaving me alone in torture.

****

I was not only calling her daily, I was taking all the efforts to get back to me. I wished to speak with her and remind her how we used to be together, I thought may be after reminding our good times she would come back to me. But she was not even picking up my call so it was hard to convince her to listen whole story like *Ramayana and Mahabharata*. I decided to send her a big message about her and my love.

I thought for a whole week, completed a history of 25 pages, and tried to write it in Marathi poetry. I would have sent her a passage too, but I remembered how my poems used to make her laugh and cry. I thought it might work if she felt it funny, and she might call me. And if she not felt it funny, she might felt it serious and it would remind her our days. Hence I wrote it in a Marathi poem...

It said…

When I miss you, my eyes get wet. My eyelashes take bath in tears. How could you leave me alone? Why did our love die for you?

When first time you called me your best friend, the art of this friendship took birth in my heart. At the very moment,

I decided to live for you. Whatever may happen I will not leave you.

I would cry for you, I would laugh with you.
Before you cry, I would wipe the tears too.

I survived my friendship as much as I could.
Seasons kept changing, changing your mood.
With that time, we went apart.
I survived with your memory in my heart.

New schedule of your life totally got you.
Silliness of future planning drives me through.
Contact with each other had almost broken up.
Slept heart in there was not even woken up.

One day when you called me suddenly,
That day became beautiful which used to be ugly.

You also used to wait for my call.
When we talked, you just forgot to all.
Talking about our love, there is nothing you need.
Not even meal, but you even forgot to flap eyelid.

When I saw you after so many days.
Drifted apart the distances between us anyways.
I met you as soon as I saw you with no fear.
I felt like my heartbeats just got clear.

What should I tell you about survival I did
My best friend was with me, what else I need?

Those days we had our company,
Are the unforgettable days of my life.
I wonder how you could forget that,
Stabbing my back with a knife.

Were you a liar then or you are lying now?
The drama you played about love was just 'wow'.

Where are those cries where are those tears?
Where are those hugs for every small fears?

You never loved me.
You never loved me, I was just an appendage.
Whenever you got hurt, I was the bandage.
Crossing the road, holding my hand.
For those small reasons, our fights were grand.

Walk of yours, holding my sleeve.
My smallest mistake too, you would never leave.
All these things just make me crazy.
I try to forget it being fake busy.

The pillow you used to make of my arm,
for your sleep.
That push you used to give me after kiss

without a bleep.

Those fights after pointing out each other's mistake.
That hide of yours in my arms giving fight a break.
All these things just make me crazy
I try to forget it being fake busy.

You never used to sleep alone when we were together. Watching you sleep in my arms, I used to wish that night should never pass and sun should never rise.

Sleeping you in my arms was just a prize.
I used to wish then, sun should never rise.
Watching you like that, I never even flip.
You used to sleep silent, stealing my sleep.

Such great opportunity, how would I miss.
Your brow used to invite me asking for a kiss.
Kissing your forehead was the best satisfaction.
It was the best feeling, giving me verification.

Verifying you are real and not just a dream,
In over happiness, my heart used to scream.

Moreover one thing I just could not wash away from my brain. You're that innocent face when I used to angry, that finger you used to bite to stop your silly laugh. It just kept picturing in front of my eyes. Please Janvi come back to me. Why did you leave me? I promise I will not get angry on you for any reason here after.

When I start getting angry and start screaming, just try to make me calm. That jump from your place to grab me, that hold of your arm around my neck to hug me, and that lock of your lips to make me quiet and stop me yelling, I can never forget. Why did not you try it one more time to calm me down. Am I not that much important to you now that you didn't calm me down and left me just like that?

Please Janvi, come back to my life.

I want to hug you, I want to kiss you.
I want to be with you, and not just miss you.

Kill me, hit me, punch me, slap me.
I am angry, jump to grab me.

Bite your finger, give me those smiles.
Leaving me alone, just don't go miles.

I'd have conquered, had it a mountain,
I'd have cured, if it was a disease.
But it's your mind, not giving me chance.
Listen to your heart and come to me please.

****

I could not write further. More I was writing, more I was remembering her. And more I was crying. I just sent that to her. With the hope of at least a positive reply. But didn't get any reply. I don't even know whether she got it and read it, whether she laughed on it or cried on it. Whether she felt it funny or she felt like reminding all our memories.

And finally my poem worked. I got a call from her after two days. As soon as I saw her name on my mobile's screen, my eyes automatically started getting wet; my lips got curved into a smile. I felt like I was heading towards the success of getting her back to me.

'Hello....' I picked up her call.

'Bittu..' She spoke from other side softly.

'I love you Janvi.... I love you so much.' I busted into tears, as I had no other jobs in those days other than crying all the year. I was kind of crying because I could not say 'I love you Chiku' too.

'Don't.' She said and I tried to understand what she was trying to say.

'What do you mean?'

'I am telling you last time; for god's sake forget me. I am not going to come back to you.' She said with a little sobs from her side too.

'No, you are lying. You also know that you still love me. Why are you doing this to me?' I said raising my voice with every word.

'I do... I love you too Bittu...' she said it and as soon as I heard it, I felt like flying. My ears were dying to hear those words from her mouth. All these two years, she had just tortured me and spoke arrogantly. It felt like heaven after hearing that with this much long gap.

'Then why don't you come back to me?' I said while sobbing and closing my eyes imagining her as if she was resting on my chest.

'Bittu.... I can't. And you also forget me.'

'NO, I also can't.' I said making that imaginary hug tight.

'Bittu, Dhiraj got a job yesterday... and first thing he did today was to talk with my mother about our marriage.' She told me that and my dream just broke. My eyes got wide open and my mouth was paused with no words making their way out.

'But.... but you said no to him, right?' I asked foolishly even I knew the answer.

'No Bittu. I had told him to speak with my mother whenever he gets the job, and so he did. So please forget me and focus on your career.'

'You are not leaving me. The marriage is not fixed yet. We can run away, Chiku. I can't live without you.' I started crying horribly.

'No, Bittu. I am requesting you last time. Forget me and leave these all things where they were. It would hurt you only.'

'No....' I was just crying.

'Good bye, Bittu. Don't call me again.'

'No, Janvi, wait.... I love you...' I was saying but she had cut that call already.

I just sat in my room with that red face and bloody red eyes. My mouth was filled with saliva due to non-stop crying. Had she or I died yet, we would have cried like for a month only. But I don't know how and why I was crying continuously that even after two years I could not forget her and could not help it from stop crying.

I had just lost everything. I was thinking to kill myself unstoppably. I was just thinking of killing myself when I got her message.

'plz bittu... move on. Don't keep crying. It hurts me too. I am not going to come back again. No matter how much we love each other, we don't trust each other anymore. The thing is gone. Plz forget me. And take care

Good bye

..'

To the reality

❄ ❄ ❄

The days kept passing but Karan's love and anger could not get to its end. More the days were passing more he was feeling lonely. More he was feeling lonely, more he wanted to talk with her. More he wanted to talk with her, more he was calling her. More he was calling her more he was getting frustrated and angry as she had not removed his number from her reject list. But he had gone crazy for her. All these days he had got used to of calling her unstoppably like a maniac.

'*The number you have dialed is on another call. Please call after... The number you have dialed is busy...*' It was the 53rd time in one and a half hour of that evening when Karan had heard that operator's voice. Nevertheless, he was dialling her number unstoppably as if he had gone crazy.

He dialed again, '*The number you have dialed is on another call. Please call after... the number you have dialed is busy...*'

His breathing had increased due to frustration. His eyes had become red like blood. Cheeks were wet due to tears and sweat. He was continuously calling her but she was not only cutting his call but also had kept him on waiting to torture him more.

Karan could not believe that the girl who was torturing him, leading him to craziness, or even suicide, was the same girl who was once ready to do anything for him, once who used to go crazy even if she didn't hear his voice in a day.

'*The number you have dialed is on another call. Please call after...*' He went crazy after hearing that sentence again.

'I HATE YOU JANVI...' He shouted and started punching to wall after throwing his phone which broke in 3 pieces.

'Why are you doing this to me?' He started crying horribly, running his hand through his hair and grabbing them, stretching them in frustration.

'NO. I don't hate you, I love you so much. Please, please talk to me.' He was crying, he was talking to himself while whimpering, sobbing.

He saw at small statue of Lord Ganesha with tearful eyes. 'Why are you doing this to me?' He asked and ran to gather the parts of his phone again. He assembled his phone with trembling hands and switched it on. 'Please, please, please talk to me. I LOVE YOU YAAR.' He yelled while dialling her number again. He was going crazy to talk to her.

'The number you have dialed is on another call. Please call after...'

'NO, NO, NO...' He shouted and started crying again. He saw at statue of Ganesha with dejected eyes. He was so helpless. Nothing worst could have happened in his life. He wished if he was dead. He knew that this type of condition comes in every one's love story. But he was going through worst. He was not only losing his girlfriend, he was losing his everything. She was not only his girlfriend; she was his best friend too. He had no other thing or person as important as her. In last two years, he had hurt all his relatives, all his friends just to be in touch with her. And now, she was also gone.

****

The words of Purvi kept running in his ears, 'Tit for Tat'. Karan opened his red eyes after sobbing unstoppably like for hour. The thing, which had happened to him and the sin which he had done by making Purvi alone and cry like hell, was not letting him rest happily.

He woke up from his bed with trembling body. His hair was so murky and dishevelled. All the parts of his body were so weak like they were unable to even handle their own weight. He was feeling sodark in front of his eyes. The room was as messy as it used to be before Janvi as his roommate. He was silent and kept looking at the zero spot aimlessly. Had he been sitting on road by now, he would have earned lots of money by the sympathy of people and alms. He was looking shoddy, but his very own best friend was not giving a hoot.

He thought, his very own best friend avoiding him for the sake of any other guy. He had done terrible mistake with Purvi and led her to limitless crying. He had done an inexcusable sin in his life by hurting Purvi and slapping Janvi. Moreover, he had failed in third year too. And now, the only girl who was very important for him was going to get married with other bastard. He had no motive left to live.

He got up from his place like an old man. Any 85 years old lady would have beaten him in this situation as he had become so weak. He started to walk out of his room. He did not feel like locking his room as there were so many important and priceless things that had already lost and stolen from him. He kept walking in the darkness of night on street. With every step he was walking he was reminding all the good time he had spent with Janvi.

He reached to the medical store. The medical shop boy asked him for what he wanted.

'A bottle of sleeping pills.' Karan said with his weak voice gulping down the saliva. The boy refused to give him the sleeping pills as he did not have any prescription of doctor. Karan begged him to give him the sleeping pills and put a thousand rupee note on his medical counter. The shop owner requested Karan to leave and placed that note in Karan's upper pocket. Karan could not help himself from getting disappointed.

As he was heading away from that medical store, all the other people and the shop owner kept staring at him with a fear and sympathy in their eyes. They had come to know whether what he was asking and for what purpose.

Karan headed towards another medical store. He kept walking like a beggar and put that thousand rupee note on the counter of medical store.

'I need a bottle of sleeping pills.' He requested.

'Do you have prescription of any doctor?' The lady at the store asked him. He had no answer for that question. He felt like his plan of suicide was going to fall flat at its face. He looked around in nuisance. He could see the ad of mass gainer capsules. He thought for a while and asked for the mass gainer capsules. The woman handed it over to him.

He took those capsules and started walking towards his room. By walking back to his room he kept thinking about what Janvi had done to him and what he had done to Purvi. It gave him the more courage to suicide.

He reached the room. As soon as he reached the room, he took a pen and a page to write a long suicide letter saying sorry to his parents and Purvi. He did not mention Janvi's name, not even for love. It was not like he avoided mentioning her in anger, but he wanted to save her from the consequences which might have occurred after his suicide.

After finishing that long letter with tearful eyes, he put that in his pocket so that anyone who would see him first can find that letter.

He took a water bottle to start eating those capsules. He took 5 capsules first at the same time. Putting those in his mouth he poured water in his mouth. Before he could gulp the water down to his throat, he cuffed and 5 capsules popped back in his mouth to his tongue.

He kept cuffing for a minute. He felt like choking and the water tried to come out from his mouth and nose making him suffocate more. But he was not going to stop by that. Taking more water again, he gulped those capsules in closing his eyes hard to force those capsules to go into his throat.

Then taking another 15 capsules, one by one, two by two, he swallowed them all. After swallowing 20 capsules, he started suffocating like hell. However, he did not give up. He took the 21st capsule to eat. He took another sip of water and tried to gulp that capsule too, and it went hard but he gulped it down.

The suffocation and restlessness increased as soon as he gulped that last capsule. He felt like there are thousands of worms rolling in his stomach, trying to get out of it through his throat. His chest started to pain like his intestines trying to jump up and get out of his stomach.

He could not bear that suffocation. He tried to wake up from his place and lost his balance. He could feel like the doors of hell were opening for him slowly.

Taking help of wall he started to crawl towards door. He tried to stand up again and headed towards the washbasin. But before he could reach there, he vomits at the door.

All the worms he was feeling rolling in his stomach all the pills he had swallowed were thrown out of his stomach through his mouth.

He tried to stand up again but fell down on the ground getting sudden head rush. He was getting unconscious. He started to crawl back towards his bed as his head was spinning. He wanted to die but he could not die. At least for that time.

****

He rested for long time. He could not rest in peace though. Her thoughts, her memories and her love were making him crazy. He was just reminding the time when he was everything for her and crying on the situation whether where he was now. She was not even willing to speak with him or not even hear his voice. Her thoughts and the priority list, where he was almost at the last number now, were just making him crazy.

He woke up with that dejected face. He had just one motive left in his life. And that was death. He started walking alone on the road with no sense. With the heavy steps and weak body he kept walking with countless drops falling from his eyes making their way by rolling on his cheeks to ground.

The darkness of that night was only his company. The barking dogs were running away from him in fear after looking his looks as he was walking closer to them. By walking with that beggar like look, he reached to the nearest railway track of 'Mukundwadi', about 2 km away from station all alone.

He looked at the track and stood still there for a while thinking about her. He stepped up further, and crossed the first track. He sat in between the two tracks with his head hiding in his knees. For almost an hour, he sat in that position thinking about everything. Two or three trains passed from the track until then.

He wanted her back in his life. He wanted all his happy days back. He wanted to kill that bastard. He wanted to slap her more, torture her to death as revenge. He wanted to love her. He wanted to hug her once. He was going crazy.

For that moment he felt like, only three places were suitable for him in this universe. First, her arms with her love. Second, either mental asylum or third, the hell.

The first option was not going to happen and he did not want to go for second one. So he chose the third and stood up from his place. He turned his face towards the one of the tracks. He paused himself there for couple of minutes. He wanted to die. By making a fist, he tried to inspire himself to get on the track for suicide.

He put his first leg on the track, and then second. He faced to the side from where train was going to arrive. He could hear the siren of the train which was coming from a distance and taking a short turn. He turned his face to other side.

By taking a deep breath, he tried to fix himself at that spot. He could hear the siren becoming louder. His shoulder started to bounce due to high respiration. His chest started bouncing due to increased heartbeats. His legs, his hands, his whole body started to shiver. He had never felt that much fear and nervousness before ever in his life.

To make himself quiet and fix, he started gripping the fist that his own nails started to spike his palms.

'I hate you.... I hate you... I hate you...' he started shouting.

'No, I love you .... I love you, I love her...' he changed his sentence, as the sound of siren comes closer.

He could hear the train coming closer. The siren of the train started to increase. His body shivering had increased like the door of hell was now opened for him.

'EERRGGGGHHHAAAaa.....aaaaaa......' he shouted loudly not opening his eyes, as he could feel the train and his death was just some metres away from him.

The silence of that night was spoiled by the train's sound and he was feeling like some giant evil was heading towards him while screaming like hell to take Karan with him to the hell. 'ERGHHHHAAAA, AAAA...A..AAAAAAA..' He shouted and could hear the train's wheels' sound which was passing from the other track. The train passed from other track and he fainted. He could not balance himself and fell on the track he was standing. His body was still shivering. Even though the train had passed from the other track not killing him, his heartbeat rate was trying to kill him. He felt like his body became warmer and he could feel the heat getting out from his ears. He was looking at the wheels of the train which was passing from the track beside him.

His best friend was not with him. His love had left him. His life was also not in his favour. And now, death had also refused to take his company. He was completely lost.

He tried to wake up as the train was passing from another track. He took help of his weaker hands which were still shivering in the almost visit of death. He was sobbing silently unknowingly. He had no idea when his eyes had got wet. He had become weaker than he was before standing on that track.

Slowly, slowly with those shivering legs, he stepped outside of the track. He walked towards the space beside the track with that shivering body. His lips were also shivering with no words coming out of them and had become dry. He headed towards the tree nearby and when he was away from the track, he fainted and fell down due to fear of death he had just experienced. He fell down on the ground getting giddy. Everything went black in front of his eyes and he just rested on the soil under that tree.

****

After few days with same assessment

He opened the door of his room after coming from hardware store in the night. He entered in the room, which was filled with full of dark and sound of moaning. He turned to switch the lights on. Switching on the button he threw a glance in his room with his brutal face and blood red eyes. He could see the bags, which were thrown before in anger. He could see the bed sheets were scattered, books were dispersed and pillow was in the door with that little statue of Lord Ganesha fell on the ground beside it. He ran his eyes towards the corner of room where he saw the chair, which he had left before leaving the room for going in hardware store. The chair was in the corner of room with Janvi sitting on it. Her hands tied to the chair and her legs tied to the legs of chair so that she would not run away from him to that bastard again. Her mouth was shut off by stuffing a handkerchief inside it. He had tied her mouth with her scarf after putting that handkerchief inside her mouth. She was looking pretty and happy earlier, which Karan could not bear. He didn't want that her best friend was happy when he was all alone and attempting suicides helplessly. He had tried to die many times but failed. So he had only one way to die.

He took out the saw, which he had just bought from the hardware store. He took the saw in one hand and a small blade in other hand. Looking at that saw Janvi got terrified and tried to scream, but her voice could not make its way through her mouth due to that stuffed handkerchief and scarf. Her throat started to tremble and she just tries to get rid of that chair and that room. Her eyes started to get wet and begging him for her life.

He headed towards her by closing that door. As he was going towards her, her phone beeped. Karan looked at the screen and saw the name of that bastard. Karan's anger got to its peak level and he just threw that phone in anger.

Heading towards Janvi he took chair from that corner to the middle of room. Putting her in the middle of the room he went to backside of chair. He took her face to lift. After leaning towards her, he kissed her forehead.

'I loved you so much Chiku. But look, what you've made me.' He said and ran his fingers down on her cheek removing the scarf only. Taking that blade in fingers he ran them slowly again to up from her chin to her eye leaving a long blood line on her face. As soon as he ran that blade on her face, she started to shiver due to pain and the blood started to float on her neck.

He came to the front side then. He sat in front of her. Opening the buttons of her top, he looked up into her eyes and asked her, 'Do you regret what you did to me?' He asked and pecked her lower lip followed by a bite to it. While her lip was locked with his lips, he ran the fingers with blade on her chest making a cross on her heart. As soon as he drew that cross on her heart, she gripped the chair with her fists to bear that pain. She wanted to scream and so she was, but her screaming was not making any way out of her mouth. He stuffed that handkerchief in her mouth again which she was trying to spit out. Till now the blood from cheek and the tears from her eyes had mixed up and were coming down to meet the blood coming out of her chest.

He ran his finger on her wrist. As he was touching her wrist and playing with it with a blade in his fingers, she was shaking her hand to get rid of him. The pain of first two cuts was killing her and he made a third cut on her wrist. She now had no energy to scream more and was just crying and sobbing with her tears mixing with that blood. He again got up from his place and threw that blade.

'I want to die. I want to die Chiku. But I won't die alone.' He said and took that saw in his hand. 'I will kill you first and then hang myself to death.' After saying this, he uplifted that saw to his shoulder. He raised his hand and looked at her face. Making an aim to her neck, he applied the force to that saw. He shouted loudly and raised that saw towards her forcefully. The saw in his hand was floating in the air with speed taking the path towards her neck. She was crying loudly but it was of no use, he had gone totally insane. She was crying and shaking her head to beg him to let her go and show some mercy. But it was too late now. The saw had come near to her neck and it was now ready to cut her head off her body.....

'NOOO........ CHIKUUUU....' Karan woke up from his dream with sweaty face and trembling lips with high respiration. He got up from his bed startling himself by that dream. He was breathing faster and every cell of his body was shivering. He looked around in the room gulping the saliva down to his throat in fear. He could see there was no chair in the room; books and the pillow were on their places. The statue of Ganesha was on the table as it was earlier. There was no blood on the ground and no saw in the room. Karan just got relieved that it was just a dream.

He ran his palms on his face to make himself calm. He got up from his place after controlling his breath. He felt like to go to washroom to wash his face. Splashing some water on his face, he came back and stood in front of the mirror with that wet face.

Resting his hands on the table, and letting the drops falling from his wet face on the table, he kept cuffing looking down to earth until he felt calm after sometime. By breathing for couple of minutes without moving from that place, he thought about something. Then slowly looked up in the mirror lifting his head.

His eyes looking at himself with that wild arrogance and anger. His chest and shoulder jumping due to the respiration. He had realized his motive to do. He just looked at himself and lifted his upper lip to one side to chuckle wickedly.

He opened the drawer of the table and took out the blade....

To be continued...

'Love @ lust sight'

'The frustrated Karan has done with his guilt. All he wants is to take revenge of all things they made him suffer from.

The dream he just had was a vision and a start over of his revenge. He has decided to rip their hearts off and burn them to death. But it was not going to happen that easily. He would like to enjoy every moment of their death.

In this journey, he is not alone; he gets some company who were looking for the same help. Rashmi, daughter of a rich politician cum businessman, for whom her love was the only drug that was keeping her alive. And Sagar, an innocent and happy go lucky guy who has just wasted his life's whole three years in waiting for a wrong girl.

This is going to be story of their love and their revenge. Would they get what they want? Will Karan be able to kill them? Would it really make him feel satisfied? What is the story of Rashmi? What is the story of Sagar?

Who will win? Revenge or sacrifice? Loneliness or intemacy? Hate or Love? Karan or his best friend?

'Love @ lust sight'

Coming soon'